CU01572941

Adaptations of Western Literature in Meiji Japan

Adaptations of Western Literature
in Meiji Japan

J. Scott Miller

palgrave

ADAPTATIONS OF WESTERN LITERATURE IN MEIJI JAPAN
© J. Scott Miller, 2001

First published 2001 by PALGRAVE™
175 Fifth Avenue, New York, N.Y. 10010 and
Houndmills, Basingstoke, Hampshire RG21 6XS.
Companies and representatives throughout the world

PALGRAVE is the new global publishing imprint of St. Martin's Press LLC
Scholarly and Reference Division and Palgrave Publishers Ltd (formerly
Macmillan Press Ltd).

ISBN 0-312-23995-5 hardback

Library of Congress Cataloging-in-Publication Data
Miller, J. Scott (John Scott)
    Adaptations of western literature in Meiji Japan / by J. Scott Miller
      p.   cm.
    Includes bibliographical references and index.
    ISBN 0-312-23995-5
    1. Japanese literature—Meiji period, 1868-1912—History and criticism
  2. Literature—Adaptations—History and criticism.   I. Title.

    PL726.55 M465 2001
    895.6'090042—dc21   2001021793

A catalogue record for this book is available from the British Library.

Design by Westchester Book Composition

First edition: December 2001
10 9 8 7 6 5 4 3 2 1

Printed in the United States of America.

To Judy, Michela, and Joseph

Contents

Preface and Acknowledgements

An esteemed colleague, Gary Williams, often begins an annual seminar we team-teach by discussing *Ye xian,* a Chinese version of the Cinderella tale that appeared in the late Tang Dynasty. Each year I marvel at the way fundamental elements of this ubiquitous story of misplaced inheritance and triumph, like water in a vessel, manage to remain constant while conforming to the surrounding cultural milieu. Of course, an adapted story does not transform itself into the shape of its respective cultural vessel; it is the teller who makes the cultural accommodations, trimming here, expanding there, until the borrowed tale is refit to suit its new surroundings.

The present study has emerged from my ongoing interest in the related, and equally intriguing, phenomenon of literary adaptation, which, unlike literal translation (which seeks to transport stories from other cultures in relatively correspondent shape), has as one of its fundamental prerogatives the transformation of the original to fit the particular conventions of the target culture. In my research of nineteenth- and early-twentieth-century Japanese literature I have been amazed at the variety and breadth of literary adaptations from foreign (both Chinese and Euro-American) sources. These transmutations often reflect contemporary attitudes, ideologies, and fears in concrete, if metaphoric, ways, and I have always felt that they deserved much greater attention by literary and cultural scholars for the wealth of perspectives—not to mention the strident and at times bizarre eclecticism—they contain.

Since very few formal studies of Japanese adaptations exist, either in Japanese or in English, much of what follows represents a rough pioneering foray into new territory. Accordingly, I warn the reader in advance that he or she will find neither polished theoretical sophistication nor definitive analyses in this study; the closest I come will be to attempt to place adaptations within a broader literary–historical (and occasionally social) context. Throughout this study my aim, like that of any pioneer, has been to clear a space in the wilderness so that eventually others of greater vision and means can come and build up their respective communities.

This project has, from the beginning, benefited from a great amount of support. Its first champions were Earl Miner and Janet Walker, who encouraged its nascence during my dissertation writing in 1988. From there my interest in Meiji adaptations has wandered across three continents and three universities, collecting along the way research funding and other support from the U. S. Department of Education (Fulbright-Hayes), the Japan Foundation, the Division of Humanities at Colgate University, and the College of Humanities at Brigham Young University. The late Marius Jansen of Princeton University opened my eyes to the possibilities of historical inquiry, and his remarkable narrative gifts continue to provide great inspiration. From former colleagues at Colgate University I learned how to teach, and I appreciate their warm support of my research as well. Thanks are also due to many nameless librarians and archivists who endured my pestering for all these years as I tried to track down source texts and examine original documents. I also acknowledge a great debt to my BYU colleagues, in particular George Perkins, who as a mentor taught me to enjoy classical Japanese and who as a colleague now provides me with constant encouragement; Van Gessel, who has shown me how close to perfection a translator can come; Bob Russell, Masakazu Watabe, and Paul Warnick, whose good humor and sacrifices have made this possible; and to the numerous students who have assisted in portions of this project, especially Marc Yamada, Jason Holt, Leah Hansen, and Anna Kearl. I am also very grateful for the comments of two anonymous readers and the assistance of the Palgrave editorial staff.

Finally, I thank my mother for sharing her love of literature, my father for sharing his passion for the hunt, and most of all my wife, Judy, who has made more sacrifices for this book than its humble contents warrant, and whose undying support from the beginning has made it all possible.

Introduction ↝

Translation is not mainly the work of preserving the hearth—a neces-
sary task performed by scholarship—but of letting a fire burn in it.
                                                    —Richard Eder[1]

Grushenka, Dostoyevsky's character in *The Brothers Karamazov,* tells a
story she heard as a young girl from her cook:

> Once upon a time there was a peasant woman and a very wicked woman
> she was. And she died and did not leave a single good deed behind. The dev-
> ils caught her and plunged her into the lake of fire. So her guardian angel
> stood and wondered what good deed of hers he could remember to tell to
> God; "she once pulled up an onion in her garden," said he, "and gave it to a
> beggar woman." And God answered: "You take that onion then, hold it out
> to her in the lake, and let her take hold and be pulled out. And if you can
> pull her out of the lake, let her come to Paradise, but if the onion breaks,
> then the woman must stay where she is." The angel ran to the woman and
> held out the onion to her; "Come," said he, "catch hold and I'll pull you
> out." And he began cautiously pulling her out. He had just pulled her right
> out, when the other sinners in the lake, seeing she was being drawn out,
> began catching hold of her so as to be pulled out with her. But she was a
> very wicked woman and she began kicking them. "I'm to be pulled out, not
> you. It's my onion, not yours." As soon as she said that, the onion broke. And
> the woman fell into the lake and she is burning there to this day. So the angel
> wept and went away.[2]

Within two decades of its first appearance Dostoyevsky's parable underwent a subtle, if telling, change under the creative pen of philosopher and publisher Paul Carus. In 1894 Carus transformed the Russian tale into a Buddhist legend in his illustrated volume *Karma: A Story of Buddhism*.[3] In Carus' adaptation the old woman becomes a great robber named Kandata, a spider replaces the angel, and instead of an onion the potential vehicle of salvation becomes the spider's thread. The moral of the story also contains a karmic twist: "The least act of goodness bears fruit containing new seeds of goodness, and they continue to grow, they nourish the soul *in its weary transmigrations* until it reaches the final deliverance from all evil in Nirvana."[4] Carus adapted the Russian story, transforming it into an Eastern parable, adding the trappings of Buddhism to serve his purpose of illustrating some basic tenets of Buddhist philosophy.

Although his work, printed on colored crepe by the Japanese publisher Hasegawa, was meant for American distribution, the publisher saw great potential for it in Japan as well, and so a Japanese version came out several years later. Carus' adaptation subsequently came to the attention of the writer Akutagawa Ryûnosuke, who in 1918 adapted the story once more as *Kumo no ito* (The Spider's Thread).[5] Akutagawa retains the name of the robber and most of the details, but replaces Carus' beginning and ending framing narrative—involving a dialogue between a holy man and a criminal on how to travel the path to enlightenment—with an ethereal moment in the Buddhist Paradise briefly interrupted by Kandata's aborted chance for enlightenment. So effective is Akutagawa's adaptation that, until recently, most readers assumed that the story was indeed based on an authentic Buddhist tale.

The curious metamorphosis of Dostoyevsky's story (which itself may very well have been a folk tale) into a Japanese short story illustrates an important principle of literary transmission. When a text moves from one language or culture into another it usually undergoes some kind of transformation.[6] That transformation will necessarily be influenced by the relationship between the two cultures or languages, and if, as in the case of Japan and the West in the late nineteenth century, there is both mutual fascination and fear, the transformations will offer a mirror reflecting a number of cultural misreadings and expectations. Carus' version stems from the nineteenth-century American fascination with Asian philosophy, and falls in line with a number of Western creative and adaptive literary texts ostensibly having Asian, particularly Japanese, origins.[7] These free-wheeling Western interpretations of "the Orient" (including not only literature but also, in the case of Whistler, Puccini, and *japonisme,* music and the arts as well) flourished due to their widespread and uncritical acceptance by a Western audience possessing little, if any, knowledge of Asia in general and Japan in particular.

A similar phenomenon emerged in Meiji era Japan (1868–1912) as translations and adaptations of Western literary texts found their way into the Japanese publishing mainstream. These likewise reveal both the naïveté and curiosity of Japanese readers for things Western. Some of the texts were translated quite literally, and bear the phonetic baggage of gangly English or French names and the exotic trappings of foreign settings. Not all were translated, in the strictest sense of the word, however. Many found their way into Japanese as *hon'anmono,* adapted tales of foreign origin. These adaptations were often quite creatively fleshed out even as they retained some of the central elements of the original tale, just as many of the Russian onion tale components survive in both Carus and Akutagawa.

Dostoyevsky's and Carus' variations on the same tale reveal some of the differences between Christian notions of salvation and Buddhist views of karma. In a similar manner, the difference between the Christian belief in resurrection and the Buddhist notion of reincarnation serves as an apt metaphor for the options available to Japanese translators of Western literature in the latter half of the nineteenth century. On the one hand, they could take the body of the foreign text and "resurrect" it into a correspondent version, or they could allow the textual soul to transmigrate into a more suitable reincarnation as a Japanese tale. Japanese readers of the Meiji era were thus equally served by a plethora of adaptations as well as literal translations. Beginning in the 1870s with the translation or adaptation of works as diverse as Aesop's fables, Jean Jacques Rousseau's *Social Contract,* the *Arabian Nights,* and Jules Verne, the last three decades of the nineteenth century saw hundreds of Western texts reincarnated into Japanese versions that fed an increasingly literate citizenry whose appetite for then-fashionable Western goods seemed insatiable.

Among the translator/adapters of Western literature in Meiji Japan were budding young writers, seasoned government interpreters, civil servants, and even medical students returning from studies abroad. They possessed disparate levels of skill in the source languages, and had widely varying degrees of cultural literacy. Some were simultaneously writing literal translations of Western texts (essays, legal documents, technical books) even as they completed their transmutations of Western *belles lettres.*

Many were talented men of letters, some of whom had foreign language skills well suited to literal translations. There were, of course, a number of major obstacles facing any Meiji writer who would translate a literary text literally, including a rather large difference between contemporary written and spoken language. Several rose to the challenge, making major contributions to Japanese narrative style in the process. Yet the majority chose, instead, to write *hon'an* adaptations of the Western source texts. This deference towards *hon'anmono* was not, I suggest, due to an incomplete concept of literal translation; nor was it simply a matter of linguistic incompetence. Edo period fiction is replete with examples of adapted variations of Ming narratives, rather than literal translations, despite the relative contemporary transparency of Chinese.[8] Rather, Meiji writers appear to have seen *hon'anmono* as a valid, alternative genre to literal translation (*hon'yaku*), and valued the creative liberty and critical forum *hon'an* provided.

In shaping the text to fit the expectations and needs of the Meiji reader *hon'anmono* authors eschewed correspondence. Like their contemporary Lafcadio Hearn, who recast Japanese ghost stories and legends in Orientalist fantasies for his Western readers, they found no driving need to constrain themselves with literalism, but rather exercised their freedom to elide or embroider at will. In this sense, their translations involve creation as well as interpretation. Adaptations thus inhabit the boundaries between *literature* and *criticism, art* and *interpretation,* not as flawed copies or evidences of imperfect language skills, but rather as interpretive sketches, or as creative criticism. One may even read many of these Meiji transmutations from an alternative cultural frame of reception, in which the source texts and their adaptations serve as "mobile attractors of larger cultural forces," since the works themselves demonstrate a wholesale appropriation of literature in the service of some other agenda—literary, political, social.[9] This hybrid nature makes them a particularly valuable means by which we may examine contemporary poetics as well as ideology. Likewise, they serve to illuminate some attitudes of Meiji writers about themselves, their contemporaries, and the West in general.

The adaptations I will focus on in this book span a broad segment of the *hon'anmono* genre, covering several decades. Even as one unfamiliar with the language of an original text can derive a better comprehension of the nature of the original from reading a number of different translations, so will I attempt to triangulate, to add depth to an inquiry into the issues of adaptation in translation by closely scrutinizing three examples of Meiji literary *hon'anmono*.

I compare adaptations by three different authors: comic fiction writer Kanagaki Robun (1829–1894), professional storyteller San'yûtei Enchô (1839–1900), and dramaturge Tsubouchi Shôyô (1859–1935). Each author was a well-known member of his respective literary community. Kanagaki Robun and San'yûtei Enchô represent links with the Edo period genres of comic fiction (*gesaku*) and professional storytelling, respectively. Their *hon'anmono*—a biography of Ulysses S. Grant and an oral retelling of Charles Reade's novel *Hard Cash*—reflect a blend of tradition and innovation, the former appropriating the life of a foreign war hero into the corpus of illustrated novels, the latter weaving a complex Victorian plot into a traditional oral performance. The third author, Tsubouchi Shôyô, represents a later, more reflective and critical presence in Meiji letters, and his serialized novel *Futagokoro,* the most correspondent of the three, is based upon a contemporary American dime novel by Edgar Fawcett.

I have selected these particular *hon'anmono* for their generic and chronological breadth as well as for their comparative value, since collectively they represent works of drama, narrative, biography, illustration, and oral storytelling and date from the 1870s to the mid-1890s. The fact that they were written by authors who created other, more original works, and (in the case of Shôyô) more literal translations, underscores the importance of studying these texts as willful adaptations from which we may derive a working description of the *hon'anmono* genre.

In Chapter I, I look at the literal-adaptive axis of translation and discuss how preference for one or the other varies across time and cultures. After providing some background into the different uses of these two modes in Japan I also include a short list of *hon'anmono* that reveals the variety of adaptations in the first part of the Meiji period. I then discuss the process of adaptation and consider how a study of adapted texts can benefit scholars, and I conclude with an overview of adapted biographies, suggesting that transmutation can apply to other, extra-literary, texts as well.

In Chapter II, I give some background on U. S. Grant's 1879 trip to Japan, then compare the official English-language account of the journey, John Russell Young's *Around the World with General Grant,* with Robun's three-volume *Gurando-shi den Yamato bunshô,* noting and discussing along the way some of the narrative and visual idiosyncrasies of Young's journalistic reportage and Robun's *gesaku*-like work: errors of fact, fabrications, and exaggerations. To provide counterpoint I cite passages from Grant's own diary jotted down during the trip. I conclude the chapter with a brief analysis of how Robun's text was received in America fifteen years later when it was "translated" literally by the *Century Illustrated Monthly.*

In Chapter III, I step across the street from Robun's *gesaku* workshop into the storytelling theater. During the late 1870s one of Japan's most famous professional storytellers, San'yûtei Enchô, was performing nightly in *yose* theaters all over Tokyo, and one of his popular epic oral tales was an adaptation of a Victorian novel he called *Eikoku kôshi Jôji Sumisu no den* (The Tale of George Smith, Dutiful English Son). I describe how storytellers began producing oral *hon'anmono* as part of the contemporary interest in things Western, then give some background on Enchô's adaptation, discuss its source (Charles Reade's *Hard Cash,* 1863), and suggest ways this novel might have made its way to Enchô (he could not read English). Since both works are long and complex, I offer only brief summaries, but provide a detailed comparison, touching on how Enchô reset his tale in Japan, but, by using a foreign name in the title and providing a lengthy explanatory introduction, took pains to see that his audience perceived it to be a foreign tale. I discuss Nobuhiro Shinji's comparison of the original British and altered Japanese protagonist names, and then discuss how Enchô replaced a primary motif—madness—with murder in order to bring his *hon'anmono* into line with contemporary social and political concerns. I conclude the chapter by expanding on the notion of contemporary ideology, noting that Enchô as storyteller was acutely aware of the ideologically reinforcing power of narrative, and thereby was able to turn a propagandistic Victorian novel into an oral epic that both undermined and bolstered contemporary Japanese ideology.

Just as Enchô adapted his text along ideological lines, so Tsubouchi Shôyô, a decade later, used adaptation to reinforce his poetics. In Chapter IV, I provide background on Shôyô's *Futagokoro,* including its earlier incarnation as a newspaper serial, and give a summary of Shôyô's source, Edgar Fawcett's American novel *The False Friend* (1880). I carefully examine Shôyô's preface to *Futagokoro,* citing evidence that suggests he wore the critic's—as well as the translator's—hat when he adapted *The False Friend.* As with some of his previous works (such as *Shôsetsu shinzui* and *Tôsei shosei katagi*), Shôyô offered *Futagokoro* in the spirit of didacticism and example. I summarize the differences between the source text and the final transmutation, in particular noting the changes and added bipartite nature of *Futagokoro,* and speculate on why Shôyô, who alone among the three authors had a command of English, would make such changes. I conclude the chapter by positing that Shôyô wrote his *hon'anmono* as both an experiment and as a prelude to the larger, more rigorous task ahead, his lifework of translating the complete works of Shakespeare into Japanese.

In the conclusion I suggest that the creative spirit of *hon'an* continues to exercise an influence on Japanese writers, and urge a reconsideration of adaptations as valuable resources for comparative literary and cultural studies. By examining three adaptations from the mid-Meiji period we begin to appreciate the complexities surrounding transmission of ideas and of rhetoric, and catch a glimpse of the creative dynamic that motivated three preeminent Meiji authors to eschew literal translation and create their own transmutations of Western texts.

By looking beyond equivalence, Meiji adapters exercised a type of creative license unthinkable to literal translators circumscribed by conventions of correspondence. Their transgression against our expectations for literalness in translation makes these texts both peculiar and intriguing. Their ingenuity and exuberance in reworking, converting, transmuting, and adapting across widely divergent cultural and linguistic boundaries reveals them for the creative writers and performers they were. This book seeks to introduce several of these striking works, highlighting their authors' remarkable creativity. In so doing I hope to bring into question the traditional denigration of Meiji translations, replacing it instead with a view of the possibilities of creative adaptation. I attempt throughout this study to adapt and apply several contemporary comparative methodologies simultaneously, and if my resulting *adaptation* of literary and cultural criticism does not represent a literal application of those methodologies I beg the reader's indulgence, since my aim is to initiate a comparison between these *hon'anmono* and their source materials that I hope will help enrich our present understanding of not only the Meiji period but also the process of literary adaptation in general.

Chapter I ∾

Toward a Theory of Adaptation: *Hon'an* in Meiji Japan

The pen of an original writer . . . out of a barren waste calls a bloom-
ing spring: out of that blooming spring an imitator is a transplanter of
laurels, which sometimes die on removal, always languish in a foreign
soil.

—Edward Young, *Conjectures on Original Composition,*
1759[1]

As Edward Young so charmingly demonstrates above, originality has, at times, been held in higher critical esteem than imitation. His metaphor for creative genius—a "blooming spring" called forth from a "barren waste"—is not exactly the opposite of the "transplanted laurels" he uses to represent imitation; rather, his oblique contrast suggests that the act of *transplanting* is the problem. Tacitly Young favors the *planted seed* over the *transplanted shrub,* the former epitomizing true genius, the latter falling far short, doomed always to "die on removal" or "languish in a foreign soil." The beauty of originality, he suggests, has much to do with the magical self-generative power of the seed. In contrast, the inferiority of mimicry is rooted in its extra-territorial origin, in its transfer from another place.

Young's oblique contrast between *originality* and *imitation* is mirrored in another, rather ubiquitous, conceptual opposition: that between *literal* and *adaptive* translations. Although scholars of translation theory have come up with many and varied ways of describing the different modes of translation, in general the modes tend to divide along an axis roughly defined by *literalism* (or word-for-word translation) on the one side and *license* (or adaptive translation) on the other.[2]

The modes of literal translation can be represented by the painful exercise (familiar to anyone who has suffered through elementary translation drills in a foreign language course) of lining up semantic equivalents corresponding to the original text's individual components, then employing some principle of grammatical inversion or creative leapfrogging to approach a hermeneutic recreation of the original. Its effect upon the target language is an uncomfortable contortion of familiar patterns, sometimes even complete distortion into a seemingly random scattering of words. Nevertheless, literal translation has its place, as well as its literary advocates, and has grown to possess the stamp of academic approval since there is little perceived possibility—semantically speaking, at least—of the source text's getting lost somewhere in translation.[3] Literalism in translation, like Young's notion of originality, favors the primacy of the seed (source text).

Adaptive translation, on the other hand, is more akin to imitation in that the original shrub of the source text is uprooted from its place of origin, transferred across time and space, and transplanted into new surroundings with the aim of making it appear as though *it has grown there from the beginning*. In adaptation, the translator seeks to alter the target language as little as possible, rendering the text in such a way as to minimize contortion, smoothing reception in the process to a degree that makes the work seem native to the target language. As John Dryden so memorably boasted, "I have endeavoured to make Virgil speak such English as he would himself have spoken, if he had been born in England, and in this present age."[4] Dryden, in essence, "transplanted" Virgil's Latin into the soil of the English of his day, pruning and grafting as he deemed necessary to make the shrub conform to its new British habitat.

Hence, the broad spectrum of approaches to translation can be seen to have, on the one end, a *literalist* approach that preserves the original text at the expense of the target language and, at the other, an *adaptive* approach that preserves the target language at the expense of the original. Most translations lie somewhere in between, of course, but even as there are preferential differences among cultures and eras for either originality or imitation, so, too, there are predilections for literal or adaptive modes of translation, and those preferences invite more rigorous scrutiny.

Such an investigation is particularly productive when we examine translations that emerge from the interstices of broadly divergent cultures. In the case of Meiji Japan, for example, the country, newly emerged from over two centuries of relative isolation from the West, was undergoing revolutionary social and political changes. The first two decades of the Meiji period witnessed a great deal of transplant from the West, in both literary and physical senses. Intellectual imports included writers such as Samuel Smiles, Adam Smith, Daniel Defoe, Jules Verne, and Rousseau, even as Western items such as lamps, pocket watches, and top hats became part of the urban landscape. The fact that most of the transplanted objects were divorced from their original context, often altered or incomplete, was immaterial to the contemporary (proto-postmodernist) horizon, where theme-and-variation conventions in the arts were preferred to avant-garde, solo attempts at originality. Also, in the Meiji period Japan was suddenly in immediate contact with a West that had theretofore been accessible only through the narrowest of filters. The ubiquity of exotic Western cultural artifacts and texts among widening segments of the Meiji population quickly led to their recontextualization and appropriation as (often fashionable) Japanese goods.

Against a backdrop of tremendous cultural difference, Western thought rose to the fore as one of the keys to understanding and catching up with the West, and subsequently the number of Japanese translations of Western philosophy, scientific writing, and literature increased year by year. Most literary histories of modern Japan pay homage to the early translations of Western literature, since they played an important role in the development of modern Japanese poetry, narrative, and drama. What most authors of such studies—both Japanese and non-Japanese—share in common in their discussions of the early translations is first, that they played an important role, and second, that they lack fidelity to the original text.[5]

Although from many perspectives the lack of correspondence between the original text and the Japanese translation is cause for comment, the denigration underlying most of the critics' judgments reflects a naïveté about what Japanese translators were after, and unfairly imposes preferences for literal translation upon a culture that did not share those preferences. In Meiji Japan literal and adaptive translations were not necessarily seen as superior and inferior, respectively, but rather as two different modes of translation representing two very different agendas: expediency and art.

For the first half of the Meiji period adaptation served as the primary translation standard for literary, dramatic, and lyric texts. The widespread appropriation of Western goods in Meiji Japan gave adaptive translation, which sought to bring the foreign text into line with domestic sensibilities, a distinct advantage over literal translation, which often came through the metamorphosis retaining a great deal of its strangeness, especially in the realm of literature. Over time adaptation was eclipsed by literal translation as Japanese readers became more comfortable with foreign literary styles, but for several decades literature, in keeping with traditional Japanese artistic sensibilities for variation and elaboration, found its Japanese incarnation as noncorrespondent, often broadly transformed, adaptations.

On the other hand nonliterary works, such as diplomatic and technical documents, as well as medical and scientific texts, which historically had been the focus of the Tokugawa regime's official translation bureau, the *Bansho shirabe-sho* (Institute for the Study of Barbarian Books, established ca. 1812), retained their propensity to be translated literally throughout the Meiji period. Broadly speaking, then, in early Meiji Japan literal translation prevailed in the sphere of diplomacy, law, and the sciences, while in the arts adaptive translation was the rule.

Two modern Japanese words used to describe textual translation reflect this dichotomy: *hon'yaku* and *hon'an*.[6] Although the first term, *hon'yaku*, appears in some Heian period documents, it gained a new prominence and meaning during the Tokugawa period, when it was used to distinguish correspondent translation of imported Dutch and other European-language scientific and medical texts.[7] Its meaning of literal or correspondent translation, in this context, is particularly apt. One of the founding motivations for *rangaku* (Western studies) was the realization by Tokugawa physicians that, unlike Chinese or traditional Japanese medical texts, which bore little or no correspondence to actual human internal anatomy, illustrations in Dutch medical texts showed a remarkable correspondence to that of autopsied executed criminals.[8] This fortuitous discovery led to the study and eventual translation of a number of anatomies and other scientific reference books, and thus the Tokugawa period usage of the term *hon'yaku* to denote a sense of correspondence between source text and translation contains a healthy measure of *rangaku* confidence in the Western scientific tools of dissection, observation, and identification.

The second Japanese term used to describe textual translation, *hon'an,* is analogous to the Chinese and Japanese anatomies that were eventually eclipsed by Western medical texts. Whereas the latter revealed a correspondence between observation and illustration, the former retained the exterior shape of the body while adapting the (unseen) internal organs to fit philosophical beliefs rather than anatomical truths. As works of scientific observation they fell short of the mark, yet in their power to situate the human body in a greater cosmological framework, and incarnate philosophies such as Taoist notions of yin and yang, they played an important role in contemporary Japanese culture.[9]

Now glossed as "adaptation," the term *hon'an* originally referred to translation in general. Over time, particularly since *hon'yaku* began to be used to signify literal translation, *hon'an* has come to refer to the intentional alteration or rewriting of classical or foreign literature and drama. *Hon'an* now describes what happens when a Victorian novel becomes kabuki, or a Heian tale is rewritten as a modern story. Although the two words are often used in a similar context, *hon'an* can also serve as an antonym of *hon'yaku,* shoring up the latter's sense of correspondence through its own of *transmutation.*[10] In the Meiji period the dichotomy between these two words reflected fundamentally different aims: *Hon'yaku* sought for efficiency and accuracy in the service of progress and enlightenment, while *hon'an* sought to tame and modify the foreign to fit domestic sensibilities, usually in the service of art or entertainment.

A related word, *hon'anmono,* defines an entire genre of written and performed narrative that thrived during the Meiji period and was fueled by imported Western fiction and drama. A first reading of any one of these enigmatic texts reveals a curious blend of East and West, Japanese sentiment and Western conceit, a linguist's nightmare and a postmodern critic's fantasy. Yet each *hon'anmono* (and there were hundreds) is at heart a translation in that it reflects its own author's struggle to bridge the gap between cultures, to carry over from one language to another the essence of the original. Thus *hon'anmono* texts cover a broad and richly hued spectrum of translation styles, each adding its own idiosyncratic piece to what emerges as a vibrant and fascinating genre of Meiji literature.

The coexistence of literal (*hon'yaku*) and adaptive (*hon'an*) translations in the Meiji period reveals that translation itself did not follow an ameba-to-monkey-to-man development model (incomprehensibility—rough adaptation—literal translation). Rather, by the mid-Meiji period both types of translation thrived in coexistence, sometimes being penned by the same writer.[11] From our contemporary perspective (favoring literal translation) we might speculate that such coexistence must have made *hon'an* adaptations look inferior in comparison to *hon'yaku* translations. However, the fact that both types of translations flourished simultaneously invites us to examine Meiji *hon'an* adaptations to see how they managed to thrive despite the existence of what we now consider to be the superior mode of literal (*hon'yaku*) translation. This volume's primary aim is to dispel the notion that *hon'an* translations were necessarily seen as inferior by their contemporary readers. I will accomplish this aim, in part, through an examination of several Meiji *hon'anmono* texts that invite us to reconsider our notions of translation and the degree to which we favor correspondence (or discredit adaptation) in judging translation.

The Dichotomy Between Literal Translation and Adaptation

Western literary translation practice since the late eighteenth century has generally favored literal over adaptive modes of translation. Even recent scholarship on translation theory demonstrates an assumption about translation that excludes adaptation altogether, or admits it only under certain cases. As Georges Bastin notes, "Generally speaking, historians and scholars of translation take a negative view of adaptation, dismissing the phenomenon as distortion, falsification or censorship, but it is rare to find clear definitions of the terminology used in discussing this controversial concept."[12] He suggests that one reason for the lack of clear definitions is the inherent threat adaptation poses to literal translation: "The concept of adaptation requires recognition of translation as non-adaptation, as a somehow more constrained mode of transfer."[13]

In the context of the privileged position translation enjoys over adaptation in contemporary theoretical discourse, we have generally ignored adaptation's brighter side: its freedom from the constraints demanded by correspondence to the original. Usually such freedom is the domain of what we deem "originality," and with the exception of certain performance genres our expectations for translation tend towards the literal. But what happens when there emerges within a culture a convention for translation that eschews ideals of literal translation and instead welcomes, and even revels in, free adaptation or random borrowing, in adapting or transmuting the original? Such contexts emerged, for example, in eighteenth-century France, late Qing China, and are evident even in contemporary cinematic adaptations of Shakespeare.[14] These examples of willful adaptive license beg us to reexamine the creative possibilities of adaptive translation. The constraints of literal translation usually channel creativity into a severely restricted flow; yet the freedom to modify and adjust, particularly in the realm of literature, is one of adaptation's most striking (and appealing) distinctions.

The difference in creative opportunities between translation and adaptation reveal themselves in many ways. The use of the term *interpres* (translator) by Horace—whether pejoratively or favorably is still a matter of debate—gives early evidence of the dichotomy in Western thought: *nec verbum verbo curabis reddere fidus interpres* (and you will not render word-for-word [like a] faithful translator).[15] Horace clearly sets up a distinction between those who translate literally and those who do not.

The rise of an era of free adaptations in seventeenth- and eighteenth-century France reveals another manifestation of the difference. As Myriam Salama-Carr notes,

> The free dynamic translations known as Les Belles Infidèles aimed to provide target texts which are pleasant to read, and this continued to be a dominant feature of translation into French well into the eighteenth century. Classical authors were reproduced in a form which was dictated by current French literary fashion and morality. One of the main figures to adopt this approach was Nicolas Perrot D'Ablancourt (1606–64), who adapted classical texts to current canons and genres (through omissions and "improvements") to such an extent that some of his translations are considered travesties of their originals.[16]

One of the translators to emerge from this period of French adaptive translation, Anne Marie Dacier (1647–1720), distinguished her work as *noble* (sense-for-sense) rather than *servile* (word-for-word) translation, and her *noble-servile* articulation of the literal-adaptive dichotomy illustrates the spirit of *Les Belles Infidèles:* making classical texts available for those who were unable to read them in the original.[17] Salama-Carr sees this period as a transition between classicism and the "Romantic insistence on literalism" that came to France shortly thereafter under the influence of German philosophy.[18]

At the beginning of the twentieth century, Chinese translators used adaptation for a very different purpose: to reify and modernize national culture through translating Western fiction. A major figure from this period was Lin Shu (1852–1924), who used oral versions of as many as 180 Western literary texts to create domesticated adaptations written in classical Chinese and championing family-centered Confucian ethics.[19] As Lawrence Venuti notes, these adaptations resemble "the domestication favored by translators during the French and English Enlightenment":

> The practices of late Qing translators like Lin Shu . . . demonstrate that domesticating strategies, especially when used in situations of cultural and political subordination, can still result in a powerful hybridity that initiates unanticipated changes . . . [these translators] saw themselves as reformists, not revolutionaries: they used the classical literary language to appeal to the academic and official elite, and they submitted foreign texts to revision, abridgement, and interpolated comment so that Western values and their own nationalist agenda might become acceptable to that elite.[20]

Venuti notes that subsequent Chinese writers and translators such as Lu Xun (1881–1936), whose aim was to displace traditional Chinese culture using vernacular writing, abandoned adaptation in favor of pursuing "greater stylistic resistance by closely adhering to the foreign texts," following "the foreignizing strategies favored by German theorists like Goethe and Schleiermacher, whose writings they encountered while studying in Japan."[21] Thus, early twentieth-century Chinese translation practice reveals a political undercurrent to the adaptive-literal translation axis that reflected the contemporary differences between reformists, who sought to retain (adapt) traditional culture in light of the West, and revolutionaries, who championed a more sweeping (literal) transformation along the lines of Western ideals.

As we have seen, although the political aspects were fundamentally of a different order, a similar distinction emerged in Tokugawa Japan and continued into the Meiji period and beyond, as is mirrored in the difference between the words *hon'yaku* and *hon'an*. More recently, Edward Fowler's *naturalization-estrangement* and Adrian James Pinnington's *purist-permissive* dichotomies in reference to Japanese, and, more generally, Peter Newmark's *semantic-communicative* dichotomy, as well as André Lefevere's use of the *locutionary-illocutionary* axis, underscore the universality of the dichotomy between literal and adaptive translations.[22]

But it is important to remember that, though the contrasts are most striking at the poles, both aesthetically and commercially successful translations often fall somewhere in between, since translation taken to one extreme or the other yields either painful literalness or wild license. The former is nearly unintelligible in the target language, while the latter preserves next to nothing from the source text. Even the most "faithful" and literal translation must of necessity make certain concessions in favor of the target language, especially when source and target languages are far removed temporally or culturally. Likewise, the most free-ranging adaptation must still preserve some trace of the original.

One particularly intriguing question that derives from a closer focus on the dichotomy between adaptive and literal translations is why, given the spectrum of approaches, some eras and cultures prefer the adaptive mode while others favor the literal mode. Must there be a choice between the two? Although they are often framed in mutually exclusive terms, the case of Meiji Japan clearly suggests that multiple styles can coexist, and even thrive, simultaneously. This begs the question of what cultural and literary conditions must exist in order to cause adaptation to eclipse translation, or vice versa.

In order to begin to answer these questions we must first examine a particular case—Meiji Japan—where both translation and adaptation existed simultaneously as thriving genres. We are fortunate to have sufficient examples of adapted texts to help us begin to understand what social, political, economic, and cultural factors came into play to elevate adaptations to approximate—or even surpass—the popularity of translations.

In contrast to the "blooming spring" metaphor for original genius, Japan has borrowed from China and Korea the concept of *imitation as honoring act.* As Eugene Eoyang notes,

> In East Asian literary criticism, one scarcely encounters claims of originality as a warrant of literary quality. Originality is subservient to what might be called "traditionality"—how immediate and personal is the homage to the past, how deftly past allusions figure in present discourse, how well new wine ages in old bottles. "Breaking the mold" in East Asian traditions is not likely to be encomium so much as censure. The fondness for revolution that one finds in the West is not shared by most Asians: stability rather than volatility is preferred. . . . Indeed, "breaking with tradition"—so often heard in the West as a mark of admiration—would be considered by most East Asian commentators as an impossibility, since tradition is never a thing of the past, a dead letter, but rather a living presence, where, as Eliot so presciently put it, "the past is present."[23]

Imitation can therefore serve as a form of praise, or criticism, or commentary, as well as a vehicle for the display of talent. In addition, Japan has inherited a traditionally broad definition of what constitutes originality. Rewriting, variation, and adaptation often receive deference over an original work, and so there has been a much greater tolerance for derivative elements in art. In Japanese lyric, for example, there is a strong tradition of *honkadori* (allusive variation), the overt appropriation of earlier poems (*honka*) in creating new ones.[24] Owing to this convention of allusion and variation, many of the early literary *hon'an* adaptations, rather than being condemned for their lack of fidelity, would have been seen as following traditional conventions for fiction in their use of time-honored formulae and tropes.

The plethora of *hon'an* appearing during the Meiji period attests to both the transparency of adaptive translation and also the high degree of awareness contemporary *hon'an* authors possessed concerning the expectations of their readers. What is particularly striking about these adaptations is their ubiquity: Japanese versions of Western literary works appeared in theaters, books, newspapers, even the local storytelling theaters (*yose*). And the novelty of these adaptations rewarded their creators with popularity and financial gains.

Meiji translators had at their command a remarkably varied array of foreign materials from which to craft their transmutations, including foreign novels, anthologies of poetry, and dramatic texts. The following list of selected translations, not exhaustive by any means, gives a sense of the variety and number of *hon'anmono* that appeared during the first two decades of the Meiji period (1868–1888).[25]

Chronological Sample List of Western Works Appearing in Japanese, 1868–88

Year	Title	Author
1868	*Anno 2065: een Blik in de Toekomst*	Pieter Harting
1869	*The Great Events of History*	William Francis Collier
1870	*Self Help*	Samuel Smiles
1871	*The Gospel of Matthew*	
	Peter Parley's Historical Tales	Peter Parley
	On Liberty	J. S. Mill
1872	*Napoleon* (biography)	
	George Washington (biography)	
1873	*Aesop's Fables*	
	The Gospel of Mark, The Gospel of Matthew	
1874	*Bismarck* (biography)	George Hesekiel
	Peter the Great (biography)	
1877	*Psalms*	
	Robinson Crusoe	Daniel Defoe
	Merchant of Venice	William Shakespeare
	Contrat Social	Jean Jacques Rousseau
1878	*Le Tour du Monde en 80 Jours*	Jules Verne
	Ernest Maltravers	Edward Bulwer-Lytton
1879	*Last Days of Pompeii, Paul Clifford*	Bulwer-Lytton
	King Lear, Hamlet	Shakespeare
	Noble Deeds of Women	Elizabeth Starling
	U. S. Grant (biography)	
1880	*Gulliver's Travels*	Jonathan Swift
	The Bride of Lammermoor	Sir Walter Scott
	De la terre à la lune, 2000 lieues sous les mers	Verne
	Wilhelm Tell	Friedrich Schiller

Year	Title	Author
1881	*Lady of the Lake*	Scott
	Reflections on the Revolution in France	Edmund Burke
	Le désert de glace, Voyage au centre de la terre	Verne
	Quarante-cinq	Alexandre Dumas
1882	*Utopia*	Thomas Moore
	Sketches by Boz	Charles Dickens
	Albinia: or, the Young Mother	
	Lady Audley's Secret	Mary Braddon
	The History of Lady Roland	John S. C. Abbot
	Warren Hastings (biography)	Thomas B. Macaulay
	Charge of the Light Brigade	Tennyson
	Madame Thérèse	Erckmann-Chatrian
	Decameron	Giovanni Boccaccio
1883	*Julius Caesar, As You Like It*	Shakespeare
	Discours sur les Sciences et les Arts	Rousseau
	Kapitanskaia dochka	Aleksandr Pushkin
	Arabian Nights	
1884	*Romeo and Juliet*	Shakespeare
	Coningsby	Benjamin Disraeli
	The Gentle Savage	Edward King
	Autobiography	Benjamin Franklin
	Reineke Fuchs	Goethe
1885	*Macbeth*	Shakespeare
	Antonina; or, the Fall of Rome	Wilkie Collins
	Oliver Twist	Dickens
	Hard Cash	Charles Reade
	Camille (la Dame aux Camélias)	Alexandre Dumas (fils)
1886	*Ivanhoe*	Scott
	Endymion	Disraeli
	My Lady Pokahontas, A True Relation of Virginia	John Esten Cooke
	The Pilgrim's Progress	John Bunyan
	Nibelungenlied	
	Voina i mir	Leo Tolstoy
1887	*Midsummer Night's Dream*	Shakespeare
	Murder in the Rue Morgue, The Black Cat	Edgar Allen Poe
	Love and Jealousy; or, Out of Sorrow's Depths	Lucy Randall Comfort
	Don Quixote	Miguel de Cervantes
1888	*All's Well that Ends Well, Coriolanus*	Shakespeare
	Kenilsworth	Scott

Year	Title	Author
1888	*Svidaniye, Tri Vstrechi*	Ivan Turgenev
	Various detective stories	Fortuné de Boisgobey
	Minna von Barnhelm	G. E. Lessing

As the above table shows, the number of *hon'anmono* created in Meiji Japan is not insignificant, and each text represents an author struggling to bring the West to Japan not as a literal translation but rather using the mutable lens of adaptation. As such, *hon'anmono* represent a significant and rich resource for examining Japanese perceptions of the West in both general and specific terms, and are of great value in comparative literary and cultural studies. Each work represents an opportunity to observe concrete images of the Other that carry with them particular literary-historical reference points (dates, authors, publishers) as well as source materials with which they can be compared to ascertain specific transformations. These changes can be used as a more objective means of corroborating authorial viewpoint, and help establish the image or mirage of the West (or an aspect thereof) in the eyes of the Japanese translator.[26]

Of the *hon'anmono* source texts that entered Japan in the late nineteenth and early twentieth centuries, some came through scholarly channels (hired foreign teachers at the newly founded universities, Japanese scholars returning from studying abroad), others through more circuitous routes (often beginning as travel reading on transoceanic steamers and ending up in used bookstores). What most of these primary sources share in common is that they came to Japan, and to their translators, as *printed texts,* and as concrete, physical objects fell in with kerosene lamps, top hats, and pocket watches as curious Western artifacts.

Thus objectified, printed texts took on a dimension of malleability that allowed, if not encouraged, domestication: The horizontal, foreign alphabets, photograph-based etchings, and other illustrations—even the chapbook, literary journal and hard-bound book formats—set the *hon'anmono* sources apart from Japanese textual conventions. In the case of printed sources, then, the physical strangeness of the imported text demanded localized adaptation, and Meiji writers went to varying lengths in their efforts to tone down the otherness of the originals. In a sense, *hon'an* adaptation may be seen as a method by which Japanese writers took the literary artifacts of the Other and appropriated them, reinvented them, as something Japanese.[27]

One genre of narrative that accompanied the growing number of Westerners to Meiji Japan was the biography.[28] Some of the early Meiji intelligentsia saw in the biographies of the great leaders of the West the key to Japan's modernization. Like contemporary Horatio Alger stories, which reaffirmed the archetype of the rags-to-riches hero, biography offered models of behavior and provided hope that through personal effort one could change the course of one's own and others' lives. Consequently, a host of translated and adapted biographies began to appear in early Meiji Japan that included such Western luminaries as George Washington (1872, 1873), Napoleon (1872, 1873, 1878), Peter the Great (1874), and Bismarck (subtitled in English "Mighty Defender of the Crown and Main Pillar of the State," 1874).[29]

Most of these adapted biographies clearly state their source texts, which were then adapted or translated into Japanese, often by way of an intermediary.[30] In the case of biography, however, although a single text often served as the source from which the adapting translator could elaborate and coalesce Western and Japanese cultural tropes, looming just over the horizon of that inanimate source text was a living, breathing human being, and in one particular instance the corporeality of the subject of a *hon'anmono* biography exercised a curious influence on the Japanese adaptation. I will begin my analysis of Meiji *hon'anmono* by examining the Japanese biographical adaptation of Ulysses S. Grant, who made an 1879 appearance in Japan and served as a living source for one of the more remarkable examples of early Meiji *hon'an* adaptations.

Chapter II ✑

More Romance than Reality:
Ulysses S. Grant as Japanese Warrior

One Japanese lady remarked that General Grant is treated so much like a god here that a temple to his honor should be erected immediately.

—Clara Whitney, *diary entry,* 9 July 1879[1]

My master's only intention herewith in composing this rapprochement is to quench a powerful thirst for Grant's moral influence, adding thereby another petal to our blossoming literary culture; please disregard his bold, overly wrought prose and the searing [summer] heat.

—Gurando-shi den Yamato bunshô
(A Japanese Life of Grant)[2]

I have now been six or seven weeks in Japan. The progress that has been made in this country in a few years is more like a romance than a reality.

—Ulysses S. Grant, *letter from Tôkyô,* 10 August 1879[3]

In late June of 1879, just as the rainy season was drawing to a close, Ulysses S. Grant steamed into Nagasaki Harbor aboard the *Richmond*. His arrival in Japan marked the final stage of a two-year world tour, and after several months in the tropics his entourage looked forward to spending the summer in a temperate climate.[4] Grant did not come to Japan unheralded, however. Months before his arrival the Japanese press noted the plans and preparations being made in anticipation of his visit. Never before had such a high-ranking Western dignitary graced Japan's shores, and suitable hospitality was a major concern of government and municipal leaders.

While the civil servants made their preparations for catering to Grant and his party's physical needs, others prepared diversions and entertainments. Army officers drilled their troops in preparation for official inspection by the former general, a citizens' group in Tokyo began planning a fête at Ueno Park (complete with fireworks and exotic ice cream), and the American expatriates in Tokyo made preparations for a Fourth of July reception. In addition, playwright Kawatake Mokuami began writing a kabuki drama based upon incidents from Grant's life.[5] The latter was more than just a diversion for the ex-president, however; news of Grant's pending arrival had created a commercial demand for Grant-related media that went beyond the theatre. Woodblock prints, special reports, and pamphlets all appeared to supply a commercial demand fueled by the contemporary fascination with Grant's visit. Literary adaptation can extend beyond the realm of the printed word, and Meiji period *hon'anmono* often included reports of contemporary events such as disasters, political intrigues, and scandals. Grant's visit to Japan was seen as such an important event that at least two adaptations were devoted to the subject of his life: an illustrated biography and a kabuki play. This chapter will focus on the former of these enigmatic adaptations, the illustrated Japanese biography, executed by none other than the renowned *gesaku* writer Kanagaki Robun. Robun drew from a number of printed sources for the details and facts of Grant's early years, Civil War career, and world tour, so the adaptation has its basis in textual sources. However, many curiously contorted details of the *hon'anmono* strongly suggest that Robun was appropriating Grant the man, not any one text in particular, in his unique and colorful transformation.

Mr. Grant Goes to Tokyo

Following his valorous, if somewhat controversial, military career, Grant served as president for two terms, from 1869–1877. His administration was marked by scandal, mostly resulting from his tendency to place too great a trust in those around him.[6] By the end of his tenure as president, Grant was ready to leave the sordid world of politics, and shortly embarked on a world tour. Accompanied by his wife, some friends, a reporter for the *New York Herald,* and, at intervals, by various children, Grant traveled first to Europe, where he spent the bulk of the next two years. In early 1879 he set out to circumnavigate the globe, traveling through the Suez Canal and across the Arabian Sea to India, then on via Rangoon to Siam and China. In each country he was hosted by various leaders and dignitaries, leaving behind a favorable impression nearly everywhere he went.[7] By late June his party boarded the *Richmond,* a steam ship that had played an important role in the siege of Vicksburg, and sailed for Nagasaki.[8]

A Hero's Welcome

Grant's visit to Japan, anticipated at least six months in advance, was well orchestrated by the Meiji government and civic leaders. He arrived at Nagasaki on 21 June to great fanfare (the Japanese consul in Washington, Yoshida Kiyonori, had been temporarily recalled specifically to host Grant). By this time, Grant was quite familiar with his ambassadorial role, and in his speeches at the numerous banquets held in his honor he was careful to note his opinion that Japan was destined for greatness.[9] He was also none too shy about expressing his displeasure at the blatant bigotry of other Western nations regarding Asia, and Japan in particular, and encouraged Japan in her struggle to cast off the unfair treaties enforced upon her by Western nations.[10] Naturally, Grant's attitudes were reported favorably in the press, and increased the popular anticipation of his arrival in Tokyo.

The entourage traveled along the southeastern coast of Japan, avoiding nearly all the major ports of call due to an outbreak of cholera.[11] On 4 July, General and Mrs. Grant, in their first of several Imperial audiences, shook hands with the Emperor and Empress. The group settled into lodgings carefully prepared for them at the Hama Detached Palace, and began a two-month series of official receptions, shopping sprees, and visits to cultural and industrial sites. Everywhere Grant went he was greeted by flag-waving, music, and solemn receptions. For example, Grant describes their arrival in Yokohama: "The scene was a grand one, the vessels of all nations being decked with flags all over, the stars & stripes being conspicuous in all, and a number of them firing salutes."[12]

A reporter describes another such welcome at the College of Engineering (8 July):

> In the compound there were six thousand lamps of variegated colors, the majority having the national flags of Japan and America painted on them. At the entrance to the main hall was an arch, composed entirely of lanterns, which was a magnificent spectacle. The letters "U.S.G.," in green foliage, were suspended in the centre, and the flags of Japan and America, joined together, reached from one side to the other.[13]

Another reporter describes two similar scenes:

> The citizens marched in procession past the General, beating gongs and carrying small booths, some of which were elaborately carved and ornamented. . . . For miles the General's carriage slowly moved through a multitude that might have been computed by the hundreds of thousands, the trees and houses dangling with lamps and lanterns, the road spanned with arches of light, the night clear and mild . . . [14]

Highlights of the Stay

Despite the audiences Grant had with virtually all of Japan's contemporary policymakers and rulers, his visit itself remains something of a diplomatic enigma.[15] This is largely due to the fact that he was received as a politically powerful figure (historically in Japan retired rulers had more power than those ruling) despite his recent shedding of political clout, and so was expected to be able to address a number of foreign affairs issues hotly under debate in Japan. Another source of confusion came from the fact that Grant was a retired and renowned Civil War general. Since the successful generals of Japan's own civil war (including Itô Hirobumi, Saigô Tsugumichi and Iwakura Tomomi), which culminated in the restoration of the Meiji Emperor to power, were also among the ruling elite at the time of Grant's visit, an equivalence was assumed between Grant and the Meiji oligarchy.[16] What Grant saw as a pleasure trip was, for the Meiji State and Japan in general, a major foreign policy event unprecedented since the arrival of Commodore Perry in 1854.

On several occasions during his visit Grant met with Itô, Saigô, and Iwakura, as well as others of the Meiji ruling elite, at their request. They sought his counsel on issues such as the Formosa incident, how to deal with the Ryûkyû (Okinawa) problem, and unfair treaties.[17] And, to the extent these men took away from their interviews with Grant ideas or encouragement that affected the future course of Japanese foreign policy, his visit did have some political impact. However, it appears that Grant's status, viewed from a Japanese cultural point of view, led to a situation where more was expected of his visit than an ex-president could possibly fulfill.[18]

On the whole, however, the Japan stay seems to have been a positive one for Grant.[19] During the latter half of their visit Grant's entourage took a short foray to Nikkô in mid-July and one to Hakone in mid-August. They finally departed Japan on 3 September, sailing to San Francisco and then making their way by rail to their home in Ohio.

Grant's visit to Japan is remembered for two "firsts": he was the first "ruler" from a foreign country to visit Japan (some accounts report that he was hailed as the "American Mikado").[20] And, during his audience with the Emperor, Grant became the first foreigner to shake the Emperor's hand.[21] For Japan, the visit of such a high-level leader from a Western power was an honor that added legitimacy to the Meiji government and its efforts for reform.

Multiple Narratives of Grant's Visit

In addition to the symbolic and diplomatic impact, Grant's stay in Japan offered both American and Japanese sides an occasion to read (and misread) one another. Publicity surrounding the visit focused public interest in such a way as to enhance and underscore the differences between the nations, and many of the parties involved took occasion to comment on, or describe, the events in larger-than-life terms. The numerous receptions the Grants participated in during their stay, with the foreign elite of Tokyo duly clad in their gowns and topcoats (despite the summer heat), and the Japanese elite likewise wearing either Western finery or traditional formal kimono, are emblematic of the cultural and national sizing-up and presentation that was going on between contemporary Japan and America. An excerpt from the diary of eighteen-year-old Clara Whitney suggests the symbolic overtones of dress during Grant's receptions.

> In front of these elegant apartments were congregated a large number of our Japanese friends. Mr. Kusumoto [Masataka, Governor of Tokyo]'s stately figure moved up to us and we received from His Excellency a kind greeting. Mr. Nakamura [Masanao, educator], in a swallow-tail several sizes too large for him and an unruly collar, beamed upon us from behind a door, where the crowd had forced his insignificant figure. The tall, muscular form of Mr. Fukuzawa [Yukichi, educator], arrayed in the stiffest of stiff hakama, towered above the surrounding men of shorter stature. . . . He was the only gentleman present in Japanese dress . . . he looked far more dignified and at ease in his handsome robes than did those loose-jointed, heated gentlemen in ill-fitting European dress. Mr. Fukuzawa has undergone a complete revolution in his ideas, for he has not only discarded his European house and style of living, but he no longer wears foreign clothes."[22]

In eschewing Western dress Fukuzawa was making both a political and a fashion statement: In the heat of a Japanese August evening, local tradition should prevail over imported fashions.

Grant's visit to Japan yielded a panoply of narratives, including personal diaries, letters, and memoranda as well as public speeches, press reports, and commemorative publications. The press in both countries, in particular, took advantage of the opportunity to explore each other in the public media. On both sides of the Pacific newspapers and illustrated magazines reported on Grant's visit, giving, as is often the case, each side a chance to examine the cultural idiosyncrasies of the other.

Around the World with General Grant

Grant's world tour garnered a tremendous amount of American press, and the entire trip (including the Japan tour) was officially documented in John Russell Young's *A Trip Around the World with General Grant*.[23] Young's narrative reveals much about contemporary Western views of Japan and Asia in general. It contains an interesting, bifurcated narrative, part travelogue and commentary on everyday customs of the distant and curious, part retelling of Grant's Civil War memories. Young's text, first issued serially in the *New York Herald* from telegraphed reports, was ultimately published in a leather-bound, two-volume set that included copious etchings illustrating many aspects of Japanese life, as well as important events during Grant's visit. For example, in the following scenes we see Grant and the Emperor shaking hands in Grant's quarters at the Hama Detached Palace and, in contrast, a scene of everyday life entitled "Worshiping the Mikado's Photograph."[24] These two etchings reflect the diversity of Young's narrative gaze in their own differences: one posed, formal, momentous, the other mundane, playful (note the child peeking at the viewer), yet full of symbolic overtones (the stern-faced, uniformed overseer).

As these illustrations suggest, in combining the rich textures and complex, often contradictory attitudes towards Japan and Japanese people, Young's narrative stands as an articulation, both verbal and visual, of official and subconscious contemporary American views of Japan.

Young's Illustrations

The Japan section of Young's narrative contains sixty-two separate engraved pictures, scattered across over 160 pages of text. The illustrations were drawn by a number of separate artists, some preparing etchings from photographs, others apparently drawing on site. Their efforts can be

MEETING THE EMPEROR IN THE SUMMER-HOUSE.

(FROM YOUNG'S *AROUND THE WORLD WITH GENERAL GRANT.*)

WORSHIPING THE MIKADO'S PHOTOGRAPH.

(FROM YOUNG'S *AROUND THE WORLD WITH GENERAL GRANT.*)

roughly grouped into three categories—the Japanese masses, landscape, and Grant himself—that suggest what the editors of Young's compiled report must have supposed would be of interest to his American readership.

The first category, the masses, makes up over half the illustrations— underscoring perhaps the preoccupation of American readers with the details of everyday Japanese life. In many cases the illustrations (particularly those derived from photographs) emphasize their subjects' individuality (another American preoccupation).[25] For example, in one etching (entitled "The Peddlar") we see a man who has come into the city from the country-side to sell his wares.

Note the contrasts and balance, the naïve, direct gaze, the lack of pos-turing. The subject matter—a Japanese peddler—is of course a curiosity because of the combination of exotic and familiar elements: The trade is familiar, but the costume, hairstyle, extraordinarily high backpack, the *tabi* socks, and straw sandals, all combine to underscore the sense of exoti-cism.[26] Yet the man's face is complex, individual; it is much more detailed than the stereotyped, simplified "oriental" faces that one finds elsewhere, particularly in group scenes. Young's text caters to the American curiosity about mundane Japanese life by providing both familiar and exoticized ele-ments, yet in many of the illustrations the figures retain (or perhaps gain) an individuality that suggests his readers wanted to see something more than overt contrast. Young's images often eschew the binary (us-them) gaze of the colonizer, and even seem at times to elevate the poorest classes. In the above example the subject's humanity remains somewhat intact, sug-gesting a "democratized" view of Japan.

The second category, scenery, reflects the American preoccupation with space and wilderness. One-third of the illustrations are primarily landscape or urban scenery, and in addition to mirroring contemporary artistic con-ventions the illustrations also focus on the exotic aspects of Japanese land-scapes: architectural elements, gardens, nature. Nearly all the landscape illustrations contain human elements as well (pathways, bystanders, bridges, boats), reflecting a readerly expectation for the ubiquitous presence of man in Asia as well as lending some human element to abstract scenery.

In the scene entitled "A Village on the Coast" we note that the natural elements (looming clouds on the distant horizon, the beach, the trees, the ocean) all merge with artificial (human) elements (simple boats, rustic dwellings) in a small Japanese fishing village. Humans and nature blend together in this illustration, reinforcing the American stereotype of Asians as "noble savages" at one with nature. The sketchy tone of this illustration suggests its source to be a drawing, rather than a photograph, and the

A PEDDLER.

(FROM YOUNG'S *AROUND THE WORLD WITH GENERAL GRANT.*)

A VILLAGE ON THE COAST.

(FROM YOUNG'S *AROUND THE WORLD WITH GENERAL GRANT*.)

THE HARBOR OF YOKOHAMA.

(FROM YOUNG'S *AROUND THE WORLD WITH GENERAL GRANT.*)

ground-level perspective and vanishing-point composition are well-balanced, reinforcing the sense of Japan's harmony with nature.

The contrasting illustration "The Harbor of Yokohama" comes only a few pages after the village scene in Young's text. This rather striking, view-from-above illustration of Yokohama, as with the village scene, combines both natural and artificial elements, yet here the bucolic atmosphere is replaced by the drama of urban order. Technologically advanced steam ships float in between the heavens (nature) and earth (city), a powerful (even symbolic) image underscoring the importance of trade and transportation in Japan's modernization. The various flags on foreign settlement buildings reinforce this image, and the small Japanese onlookers in the foreground suggest that Japan, too, in her struggle towards modernization, can transcend the benighted poverty of her villages by imitating the West and building well-ordered, efficient towns (upon which the rays of sunshine will certainly fall, as above, symbolizing nature's endorsement).

The illustrations in the third category, comprising only one-sixth of the total, center on Grant himself. These are the documentary scenes capturing key moments in Grant's trip, highly posed and often transmuted reimaginings of the events themselves. In particular, these illustrations are charged with symbolism, at times neatly portraying the U.S.-Japan relationship in microcosm.

One example, "Audience with the Emperor of Japan," shows such an auspicious and symbolic moment: Grant meets the Meiji Emperor. This encounter comes well before the later one ("Meeting the Emperor in the Summer-House"), and the surrounding narrative describes Grant's triumphant arrival in Tokyo. Unlike the other image of Grant and the Emperor (much more informally posed, later in the relationship, set in Grant's residence), the first contact scene documents the formal meeting of the two countries. One of the most striking aspects of this illustration is the *absence* of the handshake. Young gives his readers, instead, a view of the scene immediately preceding (or following?) that famous event.

Grant and the Emperor (with their spouses) face each other across the room. In the foreground Grant (dark on light background) and the Empress (light on shadowed background) reflect the contrasts between the United States (male, yang) and Japan (female, yin). Grant's profile partly obscures that of his wife, and his slight bow suggests respectful deference. The Emperor retains a formal, reserved posture just behind the Empress, whose open arms and slight bow suggest warmth and openness. There is a striking contrast between the entourages as well: Grant is flanked by Western male dignitaries, standing, in formal and military dress, while the Emperor is surrounded by women, kneeling, in traditional kimono. Again, the male-female contrasts prevail, reaffirming in Young's readers' minds the masculinity of the United States in contradistinction to Japan's femininity.

The documentary illustrations, especially the set pieces such as "Audience with the Emperor of Japan," are the fewest in number but carry a good deal of symbolic weight, since one of their primary functions is to confirm in the reader's mind the superiority and benevolence of the United States.

The illustrations served several important roles in Young's narrative: echoing points made in the text, providing supplementary information to the reader, and, as in the illustration above, symbolically reinforcing cultural stereotypes and underscoring assumptions about U.S.-Japan relations. The illustrations also are aimed at the broader segment of American readers, those with minimal literacy who could nevertheless "read" the illustrations, and who would depend more upon the pictures than the text.

As with the illustrations, the text of Young's narrative can also be roughly divided into three categories: descriptions of the masses, descrip-

AUDIENCE WITH THE EMPEROR OF JAPAN.

(FROM YOUNG'S *AROUND THE WORLD WITH GENERAL GRANT.*)

tions of scenery, and text focusing on Grant. In many cases the narrative surrounding the illustrations serves to expand on the illustrated images, while at times Young waxes philosophical, political, or even personal.

In his descriptions of the masses, Young reveals an eye for detail similar to that found in the illustrations. A trained journalist, he is quick to notice details that make for good press, particularly in dispatches forwarded from an exotic locale like Japan. Below, a description of their side trip to Shizuoka:

> The whole town was out, and every house displayed the Japanese flag. Schools dismissed, and the scholars formed in line, their teachers at their head, and bowed low as we passed . . . the policeman seemed quite out of place in smiling, happy, amiable Japan. The people were in the best of humor, and rumors of our coming evidently had preceded us, for all along the road we found people watching and waiting to welcome the General with a smile and a bow. . . . The streets were clean and narrow, the people in Japanese costumes. The houses were tidy, and the stores teemed with articles for sale. We saw no beggary, no misery, no poverty, only a bright contented people who loved the sunshine.[27]

Young's sublime view of the "smiling, happy, amiable" Japanese (penned during only his second week in Japan), true to the sympathetic sentiments of

Grant, maintains its fervor throughout the stay, although toward the end of the visit there are signs that the voyage is beginning to take its toll on Young's enthusiasm: "Our hosts were ever thinking of some new employment for each new day. We grew tired in time of the public institutions, which are a good deal the same the world over, and after we had recovered from our wonder at seeing in Japan schools and workshops like those we left behind us, they had no more interest than schools and workshops generally."[28]

This passage reveals that Young's expectations for the exotic could be sated, and it is significant that he notes how, after a time, ordinary Western things in an extraordinary (Japanese) context grew ordinary once more. His descriptions, likewise, grow less and less focused on the particular and curious as his narration of the stay in Japan progresses.

Young's text also contains many descriptive passages that relate to scenery and landscape. His passion for description, as well as his journalistic flair for on-the-spot coverage, are evident, for example, when he describes the party's first glimpse of Mt. Fuji, below.

> A trim orderly comes tripping up the steps with the captain's compliments and the news that Fusiyama [*sic*] is in sight. Fusiyama is one of the glories of the mountain world, with its lofty peak, wrapped in eternal snow, over fourteen thousand feet high [*sic*], occasionally sending out fire and smoke, making the earth tremble, and admonishing men of the awful and terrible glory embosomed in its rocky sides. We all go to the taffrail, and although clouds are clustered in the heavens, in time we trace the outlines of the mountain towering far into the inaccessible skies. Its beauty and its grandeur are veiled, and we dwell upon the green, dimpled hills, and the rolling plains. The sea becomes a lighter blue.[29]

Another example of Young's description of landscape casts an interesting light on the illustration of Yokohama, noted above. "There were trips to Yokohama, where our naval ships were at anchor; and Yokohama itself was well worth seeing, as an evidence of what the European had done in making a trading camp on the shores of Asia. For, after all, these Eastern . . . cities [of Europe] are but trading camps, and remind you in many ways of the shifting towns in Kansas and Nebraska during the growing, railway days."[30]

As in the illustration, Yokohama becomes a paradigm of the West in Asia. However, in Young's text the ordered streets and glorious rays of sunshine are replaced by another metaphor, that of the frontier town, as he likens Yokohama to Western railroad camps. Young's conflation of newly opened Japan with the recently pioneered American West is particularly perceptive; both were generally viewed by Americans as resources to be exploited, and Grant had been involved in both campaigns (first in the Mexican-American War, then as president in his reception of Iwakura).

Regarding Grant himself, Young's text contains much more by way of direct quotation and description than the illustrations would suggest. Page after page is filled with the General's reminiscences about the War, his terms in office, his boyhood, and other details. We are also treated to the text of many of his more important speeches. Young takes every opportunity to use Grant as the central image of his narrative, and, as with the documentary illustrations of Grant, the text also fulfills a symbolic role. Here is an excerpt from Young's narrative description of Grant's first encounter with the Emperor, illustrated above:

> His Imperial Majesty . . . advanced and shook hands with General Grant. This seems a trivial thing to write down, but such a thing was never before known in the history of Japanese majesty. Many of these details may appear small, but we are in the presence of an old and romantic civilization, slowly giving way to the fierce, feverish pressure of European ideas, and you can only note the change in those incidents which would be unnoticed in other lands. The incident of the Emperor of Japan advancing toward General Grant and shaking hands becomes a historic event of consequence, and as such I note it. The manner of the Emperor was constrained, almost awkward, the manner of a man doing a thing for the first time, and trying to do it as well as possible. After he had shaken hands with the General, he returned to his place, and stood with his hand resting on his sword, looking on at the brilliant, embroidered, gilded company as though unconscious of their presence.[31]

The most striking aspect of this passage is that Young emphasizes that it was the Emperor who advanced to Grant to shake hands, not the other way around. Young certainly contextualizes the unprecedented event, and he lingers on the description of the Emperor for a moment, but Grant is clearly at the center of the discourse, along with his "brilliant, embroidered, gilded company." Here the text complements the illustration, which, we may note, also places Grant squarely (if awkwardly) in the center.

Just prior to this passage Young describes Grant's entourage entering the audience chamber, and spends a good deal of print describing the Emperor in minute detail: "He has a striking face, with a mouth and lips that remind you something of the traditional mouth of the Hapsburg [*sic*] family. The forehead is full and narrow, the hair and the light mustache and beard intensely black."[32] That detail is also mirrored in the illustration, where the Emperor's face is distinct as opposed to the stereotypical faces of his entourage. In connecting the Emperor with the Habsburg line of hereditary European rulers Young is also, in a sense, "adapting" the Emperor for his American readers.

On the earlier trip up the coast from Nagasaki, Young makes another interesting comment: "The bay of Sumida is not open to the outside world, and we are only here because we are the guests of the Emperor . . . The Japanese would be glad to open any port in their kingdom, if the foreign powers would abate some of the hard conditions imposed upon them at the point of the bayonet. On this there will, one hopes, soon be an understanding honorable to Japan, and useful to the commercial world."[33]

Young's sympathy-filled statement of hope suggests that Americans in general should take Japan's side (as did Grant when Iwakura visited Washington in 1872) against the British and other foreign powers in rectifying the unequal treaties. More than just sympathetic discourse, the comment reflects a growing American sense of its expanded role in world affairs— both military and commercial. It also plays upon the contemporary insecurity of Americans in light of Pax Britannica: England was seen as the primary rival for global dominance, and Young's narrative contains a number of pejorative references to British behavior (including a remark on how jealous the British consulate was of the attention Grant received on his visit). One of the more interesting Britain-bashing comments comes in Young's report of Grant's advice to Iwakura and others over how to deal with the unfair trade agreements: "'If there is one thing more certain than another,' reasoned the General, 'it is that England is in no humor to make war upon Japan for a tariff. I do not believe that under any circumstances Lord Beaconsfield would consent to such an enterprise. He has had two wars, neither of which have commended themselves to the English people. An Englishman does not value the glory that comes from Afghan and Zulu campaigns.'"[34]

Young cites Grant to strengthen his case that the British Empire is in decline (as evidenced by losses in South Africa and Afghanistan), a fact that bodes well for both Japan and the United States. As with the illustrations, Young's official public discourse casts the trip in shades that reinforce contemporary stereotypes and help to establish a new modality for the U.S.-Japan relationship. In addition, addressed as it was to American readers, the text took up tangential topics and causes as well, as we see in the aspersions cast on Britain, promoting American autonomy and championing a growing United States world presence.

Young's Appropriation of Grant

Young's text, presenting as it does a public narrative of the journey, represents a type of translation that, in many regards, parallels Japanese *hon'anmono*. Young effectively translates Grant's experiences into illustrated journalistic prose, appropriating elements of Grant's trip in constructing his own adapted version of Grant and his life. His reporter's point of view often tends towards the hyperbolic or the polemic, and if we were historians seeking accurate reportage this would certainly diminish his narrative. But Young's readers fully recognized and accepted the contemporary conventions for press coverage. His narrative was a resounding commercial success, and through it we can see how skillfully and creatively Young was able to use his narrative to entertain, inform, and influence the perceptions of his readers on a broad spectrum of topics, including lionizing a scandal-plagued Grant and shoring up and defining a theretofore ambiguous U.S.-Japan relationship.

Grant's Visit: The Private Narrative

In contrast to the public narratives of Grant's trip to Japan is the small pocket diary Grant kept with him through much of his trip from Paris to Japan, in which he penciled brief impressions from the trip.[35] This succinct account contrasts sharply with Young's lengthy, detailed narrative; it is a traveler's sketch pad, filled with brief impressions jotted down during moments of leisure on the trip, and a survey of some of Grant's reactions provides a striking, personal glimpse that stands in strong contrast to the public transmutations of his voyage.

Grant notes in his diary things that are new to him, exotic, or curious, particularly those that fell within his own range of experience. For example, in India and Burma Grant—an expert rider—was impressed with the use of elephants as beasts of burden:

> Distance from Judaipur to the quarry about 12 miles. First ten was made in carriages; the last two on elephants—my first experience in this mode of conveyance. Was much pleased with the intelligence of these animals (Vol. I: 19 February entry).

> I visited the saw mills to see the elephants at work. Intelligent strong-bodied beasts looks like reason rather than instinct. Their strength too is

wonderful. I've seen them place one foot against the end of a log 16–20 feet long and 15 inches square in the cross section and walk across the ground pushing the log (Vol. II: 23 March entry).

On several occasions during the trip Grant comments on a scene and then offers some of his own insights, at times philosophical and at others clearly reiterating common attitudes. For example, in the Gulf of Aden, Grant wrote about boys swimming out to the steamer to dive for coins: "The natives are of a low-order of savages; hair dirty—or colored from some process—red, curled with small cord and screw tufts. It is fortunate that enlightened nations take possession of such people and make them, and their soil, produce something for the advancement of civilization of the human race" (Vol. I: 6 February entry).

Although the condescending attitude of this passage clearly reflects the sentiments of the day, Grant's particular focus on production is a recurring theme in his diary. Over and over again he notes details of crop yields, wages, costs of commodities, and other economic indicators, revealing a man with profound interests in technology and commerce.

Another, related, leitmotif that fills Grant's diary is a recurring reference to immigrant Chinese. For example, in Singapore he first notes the ubiquity of Chinese workers:

The business of a large nature is conducted principally by Europeans, but the . . . Chinese and Malayans and some other nations of the east are not inconsiderable competitors. The mechanics and small traders are almost exclusively Chinese. There is not that objection here to Chinese immigration that exists in Australia and the United States, but the reason is that the European cannot or would not if he could settle here to do the drudgery of cultivating the soil. . . . All who come wish to . . . and are willing to take labor where they can get it . . . which makes the Chinaman an objectional [*sic*] class in both Australia and the United States. (Vol. II: 1 April entry)

Later on, in Saigon, his attitude is somewhat less favorable:

The people of Saigon, the natives, seem to be prosperous and happy. They would not probably change their conditions if they could. But here, like every place in the east, the Chinese are the leading people. They monopolize all the small trade, steal all the mechanical work, and the house servants and market gardeners. (Vol. II: 26 April entry)

By the time Grant has traveled to Hong Kong and Canton, however, he has found a new sympathy for Chinese workers:

> The population is very dense and must far exceed a million of [*sic*] people. The Chinese appear to be a most industrious and frugal people. It is from here a majority of the immigrants to the United States go. It might be said that Malay, Burma and the Strait settlements are populated from here. I am satisfied that the Chinese are badly treated at home by Europeans as well as when they immigrate . . . I should not blame them if they were to drive out all Europeans, Americans included and make new treaties in which they would claim equal rights (Vol. II: 6 May entry).

As we have seen above, this sympathetic attitude towards the Chinese also extended to the Japanese, and was a crucial part in Grant's intermediary advice to Iwakura and others in resolving the Ryûkyû problem.

The diary is not without its comic moments. In Bombay, a speech-weary Grant notes the following: "In the evening had a dinner party of 48 persons invited to meet my party. The guests includes [*sic*] most of the American colony, the judiciary of Bombay, and a few military and naval officers. Party broken up early and there was but little speaking, the abomination of such gatherings. I do not mean the little speaking is an abomination but that there should be any." (Vol. I: 15 February entry)

Likewise, after visiting Macao and seeing its relative squalor under the hands of the Portuguese, he ends his appraisal as follows: "Now it is in a languishing condition and derives a large part, possibly the largest part of its income from . . . gambling. It is to be hoped that the Chinese will retake this port" (Vol. II: 9 May entry).

Grant in Japan

One of the attitudes that characterizes the Japan section of Grant's diary is surprise. We are constantly treated to favorable comparisons and remarks that suggest Grant was, on a regular basis, pleasantly surprised by what he saw. In Shizuoka, for example:

> We went ashore and through two of the villages but saw nothing to interest except the general [neatness] of the simple homes of the people, the perfection of the cultivation of their patches of ground, and the great & simple curiosity of the people, of all ages and both sexes, to see so many foreigners. This not being a port open to trade cannot be visited by foreign-

ers except by permission of central authority, hence it is probably that our party was the first White people ever seen by the majority of these people. All day our steamer was surrounded by native boats filled with men, women and children exhibiting a great curiosity. (Vol. III: 1 July entry)

Neatness surprised Grant (compare his reaction in Japan to that in the Gulf of Aden, above), as did the "perfection" of agriculture and their open curiosity. On several other occasions Grant commented on the "cultivation," and on the masses who came out to receive him. He also made recurring references to displays of fireworks, the finely crafted gardens, and the natural beauty of the countryside. "At [Shizuoka] we were first entertained at an old temple in the edge of the City, surrounded by magnificent grounds where nature and art have competed to see which could do most to beautify. Nature got the best of it, but art has no reason to be ashamed" (Vol. III: 2 July entry).

As the tour progressed, Grant saw Japan in the throes of internal political reform, industrialization, and change. His constant surprise suggests that his preconception of Japan, combined with his tour to other Asian countries, had bred rather mediocre expectations for Japan, expectations that were shattered everywhere he went. This is apparent in his entry describing his first audience with the Emperor:

On the 4th my party, with quite a delegation of our naval officers, were presented to the Emperor and Empress. I believe this is the first occasion when the Empress has ever given a formal reception to foreigners. But Japan is striving to become both liberal and enlightened . . . her efforts are honest and in the interest of the whole people . . . .On the 5 [*sic*] Mrs. Grant & myself, with party, were received by the Emperor and Empress with no more ceremony than is observed at the smaller and less ostentatious Courts of Europe. Both the Emperor & Empress came forward and shook hands with Mrs. Grant & myself. (Vol. III: 5 July entry)

It is interesting to note that Grant mentions that both the Emperor and Empress shook hands with both Grant and his wife, Julia. Young, whose narrative and illustrations had other aims, makes no mention of this, while Grant, usually rather matter-of-fact about the pomp and ceremony of meeting royalty, takes pains to note that "this is the first occasion" for the Empress to greet foreigners.[36]

Clearly, Grant sensed that his visit to Japan was of a different nature from his visits to other countries, and his enthusiasm for the country can be found in his relatively effusive descriptions of Japanese landscape and customs.[37] Note, for example, his description of his various receptions and watching the fireworks in Tokyo:

> Evening was a dinner party except Sundays and two evenings given up to receptions by the Citizens—native—of Tokio and Yokohama. These were gorgious [sic] affairs consisting of brilliant alluminations [sic] of the two cities, extensive fireworks, theatrical and musical performances, banquets &c. We also visited an annual ceremony still observed in Tokio, of opening the river, with fireworks &c. On this occasion all the population of Tokio that could be was out. The river was filled for a long distance, up and down, brilliantly illuminated and each boat filled to its utmost capacity with people. Every available place on shore was also filled. The fireworks which followed were in the best Japanese style. (Vol. III: 17 July entry)

Likewise, when his party spent two weeks at Nikkô, Grant commented on the landscape, using familiar American scenery in the process:

> The scenery through this section of Japan is much like that of the White Mountains in our own country. The streams are very beautiful and constant waterfalls & rapids are encountered. . . . On the 25th visited Lake Sachi-no-Midzumi, six or seven miles from Nikko, & 2400 feet above it, and a smaller lake beyond and some 800 feet higher. These lakes are in the midst of mountains of great beauty. . . . The outlet of the second to the first is through a deep canion [sic] with numerous waterfalls & rapids present much such scenery as some parts of Clear Creek Canion in Colorado. (Vol. III: 27 July entry)

Grant's diary, as an autobiographical sketch, is of a different order altogether from Young's public discourse. Grant's diary represents a first-person commentary, while, as we have seen, Young's text is a "translation" of Grant's experiences. Since the topic of both is the same—Grant's experiences in Japan—we may consider Grant's personal diary to be the original and Young's account the adaptation, a biographical sketch "as told to" a journalist: in essence, it is a *hon'anmono*. Despite the derivative nature of Young's narrative, however, the two cover similar ground, with Young's text providing much more detail and emendation in contrast to Grant's cryptic comments. A third—Japanese—public narrative of Grant's visit markedly deviates from these two, and upon it we shall now focus our attention.

Grant's Visit: Another Public Narrative (Japanese)

Prior to and during Grant's stay in Japan a bounty of Grant-related souvenirs appeared for sale in bookstores and on the streets. Young invokes Harvard naturalist (and Tokyo resident) Edward S. Morse in describing this phenomenon:

> The military side of General Grant's career has taken hold of [the popular Japanese] imagination, and the street literature of the day is devoted to the achievements of the General and the Northern armies. You find these written in pamphlets, in broadsides, in penny tracts. You find rude engravings of the General in the shop-windows. Sometimes these pictures are in a heroic stage of color, and although I am not familiar with the Japanese text, I am sure, from looking over the illustrations in the pictorial lives of the General, that he has achieved tremendous feats in war. Most of these engravings depict the General as a military athlete doing marvelous things with his sword. This, however, is how history becomes mythology; and in looking over these rude designs you see the operation of the doctrine of evolution, how fact is gradually blended into romance and poetry . . . it shows the hold that General Grant had taken upon the imagination of the people, down to the lowest and most ignorant classes.[38]

One of the texts "in a heroic stage of color" that Morse may have been alluding to was a special adaptation of Grant's life by Kanagaki Robun, one of the last authors of traditional Japanese comic fiction (*gesaku*).[39] Robun began issuing his three-volume "biography" of Grant while Grant was still in Japan, and there are several interesting aspects of this work that make it stand out among the other Grant commemorabilia: It was a serialized work of some length (three volumes in nine fascicles); it went into much greater detail than any Japanese Grant biography published before; and it took pains to adapt Grant's life to the conventions of Japanese heroic illustrated tales ("a military athlete doing marvelous things with his sword"). We will now examine Kanagaki's *hon'an* of Grant in more detail.

Kanagaki Robun (1829–1894) entered the Meiji period as one of the last practitioners of *gesaku*.[40] Although he came from a family of fishmongers, he was apprenticed to a family of means and developed a love for *gesaku* classics written by the likes of Santô Kyôden (1761–1816), Jippensha Ikku (1765–1831), and Shikitei Samba (1776–1822). As a young writer Robun focused on works that capitalized on contemporary events, such as the Ansei earthquake (1855) and the repeal of the age-old prohibition of women climbing Mt. Fuji (1860), and his most famous works include Western themes. He is best known for two pieces that may themselves be seen as *hon'anmono* of Edo period *gesaku*—*Seiyôdôchû hizakurige* (A Journey through the West by Shank's Mare, 1870) and *Aguranabe* (Cross-legged around the Stew Pot, 1871)—as well as for founding a popular illustrated newspaper, the *Kanayomi Shimbun* (1875), in which he lampooned leading political figures and celebrities.

Seiyôdôchû hizakurige is an adaptation of Jippensha Ikku's *Tôkaidôchû hizakurige* (Along the Eastern Seaboard by Shank's Mare, 1802; sequels through 1822), a tale of two feckless travelers, Kitahachi and Yajirôbei, who make their way from Edo to Kyoto. Robun's imitation took two bumbling Tokyoites (the grandchildren of Kita and Yaji) on a journey from Yokohama to an international exposition in London. The highly illustrated work contains many visual allusions to Ikku's earlier story, playing on similar themes of cultural naïveté and regional difference, but in a new, wide-ranging global context.[41] *Aguranabe,* on the other hand, takes its lead from the *Ukiyoburo* (Floating Bathhouse) and *Ukiyodoko* (Floating Barbershop) narrative strategies of Shikitei Samba. In these works, the setting remains fixed while the characters come and go, allowing the author to portray and parody an ever-changing flow of subjects. *Aguranabe* is not, however, set in a traditional Edo locale but rather a newly fashionable "beef bowl" restaurant in Tokyo. These works reveal Robun's fusion of traditional and novel elements, a characteristic that suited him well for the production of *hon'anmono.*

Robun was renowned for his ability to work in short, furious bursts of creative energy. One of his pupils, Saitô Ryokuu (1867–1904), noted that "If Robun sat long at the desk pondering, nothing good would come of it. He was an improvisator. In his long novels and other lengthy works he was simply a clever writer; when he wrote short pieces, however, he was truly unparalleled."[42]

Robun was also very sensitive to public opinion, and he no doubt saw great opportunity in the contemporary publicity surrounding Grant's visit to Japan. Many of his earlier works—*Aguranabe, Seiyodôchû hizakurige,* an adaptation of *Hamlet*[43]—capitalized upon the early Meiji enchantment with the West and he saw in the growing popular fascination with Grant an opportunity to improvise on a grand scale.

Robun cobbled together his biography of Grant using materials close at hand. He gleaned some of his basic biographical information from several short Grant biographies published on the eve of the General's arrival in Japan, and also borrowed from his own earlier work and reportage of kabuki performances.[44] The final product, issued serially in three volumes, weaves this material into a brightly colored adaptation whose text is part life story and part geography primer.[45]

Robun's biography is both textual and pictorial, with illustrations complementing (and at times upstaging) the written text. The vivid colors and traditional illustrated (*ezôshi*) format (and the fact that all difficult words are glossed to show readings) leave little question as to the nature of his intended audience: the marginally literate masses (for whom many of Robun's earlier works had been tailored). Yet Robun's biographical adaptation of Grant had a more serious literary side to it as well. In *Takahashi Oden yasha monogatari,* a work published several months earlier, Robun had revealed his desire to write a novel based on real life, and Grant's arrival gave him the subject he was looking for.[46] Robun had earlier completed a biography of Napoleon, but this work was written in an archaic style and was described as nonsense, with elements of the fantastic blended in.[47] Robun's biography of Grant, in contrast, was written in a modern style, went into great detail on specific events in Grant's life, and, though somewhat hagiographic, nevertheless purported to its readers to be a factual (if romanticized) narrative of Grant's life.

The work began serialized publication while Grant was in Japan, actually only a few short weeks after his arrival. While it is difficult, if not impossible, to reconstruct actual sales figures, the ubiquity of Robun's *Gurando-shi den* in book stores is hinted at by Morse's oblique reference to it, as well as by the fact that, one year later, a concerted effort to locate a copy in Tokyo failed, proving that all the stock had been sold.[48]

A Closer Look at Gurando-shi den Yamato bunshô

Let us now turn our attention to *Gurando-shi*[49] *den Yamato bunshô* (Grant's Life, in Japanese or, more literally, The Life of Grant: A Japanese Ap-prose-al).[50] The cover of Volume I contains a central portrait of Grant in an oval frame beneath a garland of flowers from which hang six flags, three American on the right, three Japanese on the left.[51]

Robun's introduction, in typically ebullient rhetoric, sings the praises of the United States and its heroes, Washington and Grant. The text opens with flag-waving illustrations depicting Grant's arrival in Japan, as well as scenes of domestic bliss in Washington, D.C. and Grant's boyhood home.

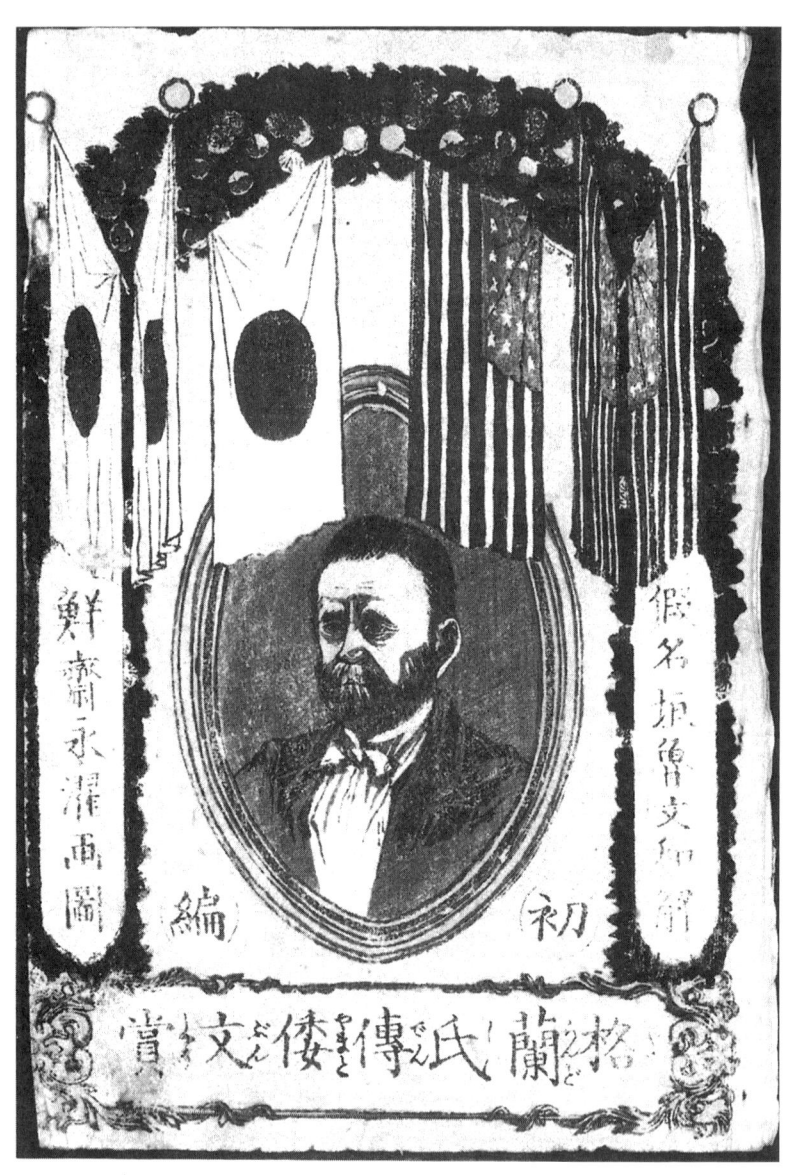

COVER, VOLUME I OF KANAGAKI ROBUN'S GURANDO-SHI DEN YAMATO
BUNSHÔ (1879) (COURTESY OF L. TOM PERRY SPECIAL COLLECTIONS,
HAROLD B. LEE LIBRARY, BRIGHAM YOUNG UNIVERSITY).

The narrative, on the other hand, begins with an extract from Robun's earlier work, *Sekai miyakoji* (Great Cities of the World, 1872), a school primer on geography. For the sake of summary, I paraphrase below.[52]

> In "ancient times" there were only three known continents: Asia, Africa and Europe. Then the German astronomer Yobernicus[53] sent out ships that saw a new land from afar, which Columbyus confirmed. This new land, divided into north and south, was explored by Admiral Amerikyus, who put forth great effort in opening the land for development, hence the name America.
>
> Thirteen states, led by Washington, fought for freedom and autonomy, leaving England broken and powerless ninety-seven years ago. America, now an independent country, set up a people's government where whoever received the most votes ruled for a four-year term. The new capital was named after Washington. Washington's fifteenth successor, Ulysses S. Grant, was born fifty-eight years ago in Ohio. Exceptional even at birth, he was an eleven-pound baby. When he was a toddler some neighborhood boys fired a pistol near his head, and he was not shocked, but pleased with the sound. He also demonstrated skill at horsemanship while yet a toddler when a show rider came to town and Grant insisted that he be allowed to ride. As a youth he was playing ball and broke a neighbor's window. With preternatural self-possession he went inside, apologized to the owner and sought forgiveness, offering to have his father make restitution. This set him apart as a remarkable child.
>
> Grant's father was an impoverished tanner, and Grant helped him in his trade. From age four Grant entered the local school, but because funds were scarce he withdrew until age eleven, when he went for a few months and then was forced to quit to help his father again. At age seventeen Grant confronted his father, saying that he planned to be on his own in four years. Grant's father asked what he would do instead of tanning, and Grant replied that he wished to serve his country on the battlefield, like his ancestors.
>
> At twenty, through the intervention of a local attorney, Grant entered West Point, the Army Military Academy, graduating in four years. He fought in the Mexican-American War, under General Lincoln, demonstrating courage and valor when trapped by the enemy at Monterrey. He stayed in the army for eleven years, and at age thirty-three returned home to farm. He married Julia Dent, from St. Louis, and together they farmed, faring poorly and losing nearly everything. They moved to Galena, Illinois, where Grant was forced to make a living as a tanner. He was rescued from this dour fate, however, in 1861, when the United States divided into civil war between the

North and the South. Grant gathered a group of local men into a regiment and trained them in the art of war. They went south to Missouri and defeated the Southern troops, driving them like fish before killer whales. Grant was put in charge of larger troops, and in other battles the tide turned against Grant, but he rallied his men and overcame.

A similar scenario is repeated with larger proportions as Robun describes some of the details of several battles, including figures of numbers killed, wounded, and taken prisoner on both sides. Grant emerges as a remarkable strategist and leader. Robun narrates other battles in detail, one in particular showing Grant in a moment of valor when, as it looks as though the Northern troops will be routed, Grant turns back toward the enemy on his horse, light blazing from his eyes, sword in hand, letting out a shout like thunder, and leads his troops to victory. The first volume ends with a description of Grant approaching Vicksburg as Confederate Generals Pemberton and Johnston consolidate their forces.

The battle narrative continues in Volume II. Grant, after several more

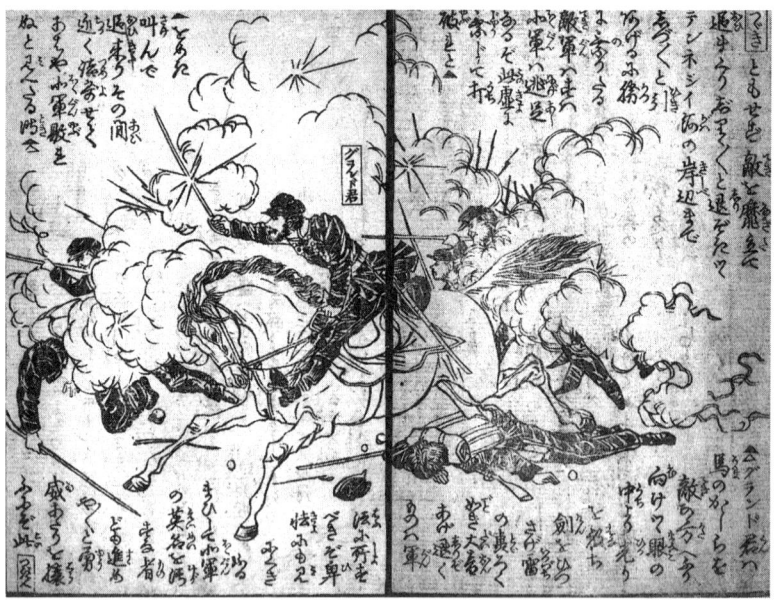

GRANT ON HORSEBACK LEADS A RALLY (COURTESY OF L. TOM PERRY SPECIAL COLLECTIONS, HAROLD B. LEE LIBRARY, BRIGHAM YOUNG UNIVERSITY).

battles, is elevated to supreme commander in 1864. Resolved to win the war, he goes out in full force against Confederate supreme commander Lee. Robun describes some of the battles and strategies, then the final negotiations between Lee and Grant as Union forces invade North Carolina. Lee surrenders at Appomattox, and the war is over.

Robun describes Abraham Lincoln's assassination, incorrectly stating that villains stabbed him to death while he was attending the theater. Again, a paraphrase of Robun's text:

> Johnson, the Vice President, took over, and Grant, appointed the first supreme commander of the United States military forces since Washington, fought diligently to reunite a divided nation. Although Johnson had great enmity for Lee and the Confederate leaders, Grant interceded for mercy on Lee's behalf. When Johnson revealed his ill will towards the South, Grant ran for his office and was elected president in 1868. He ruled with great humanity and benevolence. Since England had lent arms to the South during the war, Grant appealed to European governments to extract financial compensation from England. In 1872 Grant was re-elected by an overwhelming majority and completed his second term of four years with prudence and justice.
>
> In July 1876 he retired from office to the quietude of Point Pleasant, Ohio. In order to dispel fatigue from his great labors, Grant departed with his wife and son on a world-wide voyage. As they left the station by train bound for Europe, the people shed tears, declaring the great fortune of other countries to receive one possessed of such rare nobility and virtue. With the autumn breeze Grant's entourage left their homeland and crossed the Atlantic for England, where they were met by British officials and the American ambassador, taken to their quarters in London, and then warmly received by Queen Victoria and were given a tour of the city.

At this point Robun's narrative takes on the style of an almanac, listing the number of public and private schools, hospitals, armories, theaters, markets, trains, and subways in London, and commenting on the division of the city into three sections. Grant marveled at the parks, the glass lanterns hanging from eaves that make the town unaware of darkness, and the size and grandeur of St. Paul's dome. Robun elaborates on London Bridge and the Tower, and a tunnel that allows one to pass underneath the Thames. Their sightseeing done, Grant's entourage crossed over to France.

Robun then lists statistics for Paris: its population (largest in Europe), area (a third of London), famous neighborhoods, topography (straddles the

Seine), numerous bridges, and some of the more famous sights. After Grant met with the president of France, he paid honor at the grave of Napoleon I and visited the French Parliament building, the Place Vendôme, with its statue of Napoleon, as well as the Pont Neuf with its equestrian statue of Henri IV. Robun notes that Paris is filled with open, planted parks with stone statues and fountains. He remarks that Paris is the capital of a hundred amusements, her citizens vying with one another for gaily colored clothing. From Paris fashions flow throughout Europe, with Paris Mode defining new styles in clothing, hairstyles and hats. Grant, charmed by Paris, felt quite at home.

The first chapter of the third volume opens with a scene showing an apprentice for the publisher (Kinshôdô) apologizing to the reader for his master's absence on a Sunday, a lighthearted *gesaku* touch. The first page of the text is decorated with a scene of a huge colorless elephant flanked by two black "Indian natives," the woman bare-breasted and the man wearing only a loincloth. The visual dissonance is mirrored by narrative dissonance: The previous chapter left Grant enjoying Paris, but now Robun treats us to a further series of geographical facts about India (location, size, division, British colonization), Annam (ties with China, rubber manufacture, customs of native women to wear a single piece of cloth or go topless, the gaudiness of temple architecture), and Siam (area, population, capital city, ties with Annam and India, topless natives who, in place of tobacco, chew betel, leaving their gums stained crimson and dirty black). To paraphrase further:

> Siamese temples are richly decorated with huge Buddhist statues, and everywhere they use elephants to haul loads and fight battles. Siam has many natural resources including silver, lead, tin, incense, wood, ivory, rhino horn and rattan. The present king loves Western fashions and can speak and read English. Even the general populace demonstrates Western manners, and by means of steamships seek not only European but other Western trade; the people are approaching true civilization.

Robun's narrative then switches back to Grant and his entourage. They departed England and France and made a pilgrimage to India, Siam, Burma, and Annam. Following this (according to Robun) they set sail from India to visit Egypt, "the premier port of Africa."[54] Robun treats the reader to a few more facts about Egypt: neighboring countries, area, population, geography, etc., and notes that the country was once ruled by Turkey but is now semi-independent, paying homage to Turkey and beholden to Turkish military intervention in times of crisis. Egypt is the oldest civilization, with a rapidly multiplying population rivaling China and India. Paraphrasing Robun again:

> Grant, who made his way from India to Asia and China, finally arrived in our country in early July. He was met with great fanfare at Yokohama and, after a short train journey, at Shimbashi Station by Japanese diplomats. The thoroughfares along his route were lined with flags and lanterns bearing the emblems of both countries. He lodged in the detached palace at Shiba, and visited government offices, factories, museums, and parks. He was impressed with Japan's rapid modernization, and met the Emperor and Empress, listening attentively to imperial advice.

> He was invited to attend the theater at the Shintomiza, and the event was attended by the great and noble as well as the common folk, sponsored as it was by both government and municipal leaders. On 16 July Grant, along with his wife and son, came to the theater in the early evening and joined a crowd of top dignitaries including the British Governor of Hong Kong, the American Ambassador, German royalty, Japanese nobility, company chiefs, and editors from the press, all seated by rank. The night's program was a specially prepared adaptation (*hon'an*) of battle scenes designed to pay tribute to the valor of Grant by equating him with the ancient hero Minamoto Yoshiie.[55] The greatest kabuki actors appeared in various roles in this four-part performance.

> The evening began with actors invoking the gods of poetry. The second part depicted the birth and boyhood of Grant. Grant's (Japanese) father was a maker of taiko drums living in the provinces, a widower whose (adopted) son was of noble Minamoto parentage but, at an early age, contracted an illness that turned him into an imbecile. The father lamented this fate and beat his son, who subsequently snapped out of his daze and recognized his true birthright.

> In the next part, Yoshiie and his uncle joined forces to quash a rebellion. Yoshiie had become a great general who, in victory, showed mercy to the defeated general, with whom he corresponded. Together they worked out a face-saving surrender, Yoshiie's noble acts attributed to his "true Minamoto blood." The final part of the entertainment included over seventy of Tokyo's finest geisha lining up in front of the Shintomiza curtain to dance and sing. They had lanterns and fans decorated with American flag designs, their kimono dyed in similar flag motifs. The performance ended, and Grant was extraordinarily pleased, thanking the organizers profusely and presenting to the theater a curtain in honor of the event.

After the performance Grant visited parks, suburbs, historical sites, and had more evening receptions. On 3 September he left Yokohama, seen off by our finest dignitaries. Grant crossed the Pacific on the *City of Tokyo*, arriving in San Francisco 20 September. The city celebrated, and all the homes were decorated with flags. The whole town met Grant at the pier, and cannons roared greetings. His launch set him ashore at the Market Street pier, where he was greeted by the Governor of California and other dignitaries, and went by horse carriage to the Palace Hotel. A noble and humane hero returns home, at fifty-eight years possessing the strength of a youth!

A close reading of the text reveals many features of the *hon'anmono* genre, and demonstrates how these adaptations could range far beyond the narrow scope of printed texts for subject matter. I will divide my analysis into four major areas of focus: the work's *spontaneity,* its *illustrations,* its *blend of traditional and realistic elements,* and its *adaptive idiosyncrasies.*

Spontaneity

Robun's biography, coming as it did in response to Grant's visit, was composed on the spur of the moment, each fascicle completed, as with other illustrated works of *gesaku,* in a matter of days. Although Japanese officials may have learned of Grant's possible visit a year or more in advance, Grant's own correspondence suggests that he only finalized the idea of traveling to Japan in late 1878.[56] This gives a maximum lead time of six months for Japan to have prepared for his arrival.

Although little is known about the publication details of Robun's biography, the text itself suggests that Robun borrowed many of his facts from contemporary Grant books issued in May and June prior to Grant's July arrival in Tokyo. Thus we may speculate that Robun, seeing a growing interest in Grant biographies, decided to put one together as well. As we have seen earlier, one of Robun's fortes was quick response to current events and this work demonstrates once more his ability to quickly rise to the occasion.

From a broader perspective, adaptations of Western literature were, like Robun's biography, often spontaneous works executed in response to the serendipitous arrival of a novel or other Western text in Japan. Rarely, if ever, did *hon'anmono* authors make systematic, concerted efforts to obtain the best and most highly regarded Western texts for their adaptations. Rather, they used whatever texts came into their hands.[57] Some were available at specialty bookstores like Maruzen or through the private libraries of returning expatriate Japanese. Others came to Japan with foreign travelers or workers. To a certain extent the reading tastes of foreign visitors in Meiji Japan helped determine the repertoire of potential source texts for transmutation. Arbitrariness of selection is thus one characteristic of adaptations, as is spontaneous or occasional creation: *Hon'anmono* were often impromptu variations on a theme from an original Western text. In Robun's case, however, the "text" that found its way to Japan and into his creative focus was not paper and ink, but rather flesh and bone.

Illustrations

Illustration plays an even more important role in Robun's work than in Young's narrative. The *gesaku* tradition that flourished during the Edo period included a very visual component. Since the texts were printed using woodblock printing techniques, rather than moveable type, the process of printing lent itself to merging illustrations with text, and skillful *gesaku* writers, sometimes employing a studio of artists, took full advantage of the visual elements to complement (and at times to undermine) their written words. A Meiji addition to the illustrator's palette was the importation of aniline dyes from Germany, which initially gave a vivid impression of bright color but did not fade into subdued colors as earlier works did.[58]

Robun employed two artists for *Gurando-shi den*. The first two volumes were illustrated by Sensai Eitaku (1843–90), an artist of some reputation who had studied under the traditional masters of the Kanô as well as the *nanba* schools before developing his own, realistic style.[59] Eitaku began his career as the official painter for the Ii clan of Hikone. After his master, Ii Naosuke, was assassinated in 1860, Eitaku wandered the country, eventually settling in Tokyo and specializing in historical subjects and figures. He also was an illustrator for a Yokohama newspaper, so his familiarity with the foreign made him a very logical choice to prepare the illustrations for Robun's biography.

The third volume was illustrated by Baidô Kunisada (1848–1920), who had originally appeared as a "guest artist" at the beginning of Volume II, where a brightly colored two-page illustration of geisha in American flag kimono bears his name.[60] Baidô was a much less renowned artist than Eitaku, having focused primarily on fashion plates and illustrations.[61] The bulk of his illustrations center on Grant's Asian trip and the kabuki *hon'an* of Grant's life.[62]

The most immediate and striking visual aspect of *Gurando-shi den* is the dramatic imagery of the illustrations. Upon unwrapping the first volume, the reader is treated to a barrage of flags, ornaments, and a none-too-flattering (but in the context faithful) portrait of Grant. The ornamentation is typical for *gesaku,* a visual genre that is sometimes seen as the antecedent of modern Japanese comic books (*manga*). The portrait stands in strong contrast to one of Commodore Perry done twenty-five years earlier, and, unlike the demonization of Perry's face, Grant's realistic visage may be read as positively flattering.[63]

The contrast serves to underscore the overtly celebratory nature of Robun's text, as do the mirror images of Japanese and American flags hanging above the portrait.[64] But this is not the last we see of flags in Robun's banner-filled text. Of the next nine pages alone (each one comprised of or containing an illustration), seven contain flags or flag elements. Of these seven, five are the American Stars and Stripes.

While the profusion of national flags may seem somewhat overdone, we must remember that historically Japan has placed great emphasis on flags, banners, and crests in identification, particularly during battles. *Gesaku* and other visual narrative arts also employed a great deal of signifying through the use of patterns on clothing. National flags, at a time when Japan was becoming increasingly aware of the importance of "nation," take on increased significance as emblems of nationhood, and can serve as metaphors for not just nations, but also East and West or tradition and modernization. For example, on the cover of the first volume of *Gurando-shi den* the Japanese "Rising Sun" flag hangs in contrast to (but parallel with) "Old Glory," not only framing Grant's portrait but also suggesting the cultural battle underway in 1879, when traditionalists vied with modernizers over the path Japan should take, and the watch cry of the Japanese State was "Catch up with, and surpass, the West!"[65] Another similarly charged illustration is found several pages into the first volume. The scene, "Grant's Arrival in Greater Japan," depicts the prow of the *Richmond* sailing into Nagasaki harbor as the rising sun appears on the horizon. Flying from the ship's rigging, in the foreground, is a brightly hued American flag. In contrast to this, the sun, in the background, rises a bright aniline red above the tree-covered hills and blue water. The flag images here, more subtle than on the cover, nevertheless suggest a parity or balance between nations: The United States is represented by large warships, rigging, the crew of the *Richmond* in Western dress, while Japan is represented by nature, both serene (flocks of birds, Japanese vessels sailing on a tranquil bay) and powerful (the highlighted rays of a blood-red sun).

Robun's text is full of visual tension that comes from combining West-

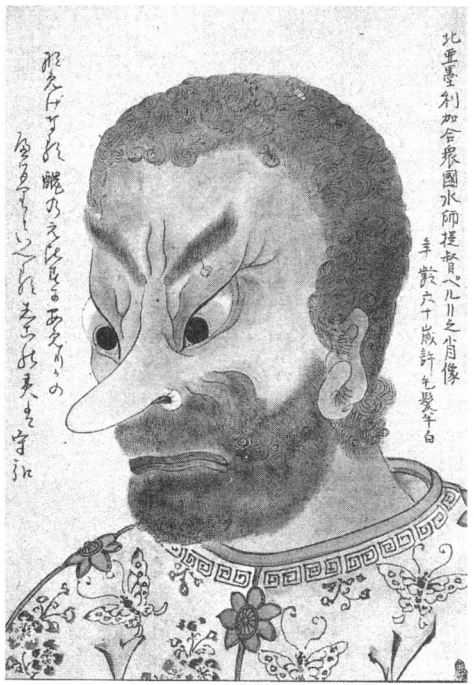

PORTRAITS OF GRANT (1879) AND PERRY (1854) (COURTESY OF L. TOM
PERRY SPECIAL COLLECTIONS, HAROLD B. LEE LIBRARY, BRIGHAM
YOUNG UNIVERSITY AND THE KANAGAWA KENRITSU REKISHI
HAKUBUTSUKAN).

"GRANT'S ARRIVAL IN GREATER JAPAN" (COURTESY OF L. TOM PERRY SPECIAL COLLECTIONS, HAROLD B. LEE LIBRARY, BRIGHAM YOUNG UNIVERSITY).

ern and Japanese motifs. Some of the more striking examples of such tension are the illustrations by Baidô of geisha row dancing across the stage dressed in American flag-dyed kimono. One triptych in particular highlights the intercultural tension in a remarkable way.

Juxtaposed in vivid reds, greens, blues, and purples are Grant (in a blue-eyed portrait) and a geisha. The strong physiological contrast between male and female, Westerner and Japanese, is undermined, however, by the Rising Sun motif on the *uchiwa* (summer fan) Grant holds before him and, in contrast, the American flag pattern of the geisha's kimono. Each half of this intercultural duo is signifying the emblem (flag) of the other, suggesting that political (Grant) and commercial/cultural (geisha) exchange can reconcile the tension between East and West, Japan and the United States.[66]

A Blend of Opposites

Just as his images fuse East and West, Robun's text includes elements of traditional *gesaku* narrative combined with the more concrete details of Grant's life. During the latter half of the Edo period there arose a fashion for illustrated scrolls and screens that portrayed foreigners.[67] The scrolls were often commissioned on the occasion of visits from foreign delegates (Korean, Chinese, Ryûkyûan, and Dutch) to the capital. One function of the scrolls was to highlight and underscore the exotic differences of the outsiders, emphasizing the spectacle of their presence in Japan. A more subtle role for the scrolls, and more particularly illustrated maps, was to reinforce the notion of Japan as center (the envoys were travelling *to* Japan, and the maps showed Japan squarely in the center of the world). Robun's narrative combines both elements—spectacle and self-congratulation—but adds a new dimension (biographical detail) as well as a new focus: Grant's reactions to Japan. The biographical detail adds a sense of realism, complementing Grant's physical presence in Japan at the time the work is published. Grant's favorable reaction to Japan—and his praise as recorded in Robun's narrative—adds even greater magnitude to the event of his visit. Robun's illustration of the graciousness with which Grant is hosted may also be seen as another form of national self-congratulation.

Once we enter into the text we begin to see more evidences of Robun's appropriation of Western elements for domestic effect. In a foreword Robun notes that he has transformed Grant's life into a Japanese text expressly for the edification of Japanese—especially women and children—so that all might learn from Grant's example. Historically, Japanese and Chinese leaders served as role models in didactic forms of Japanese

FIRST SECTION OF TRIPTYCH FOR VOLUME III (COURTESY OF L. TOM PERRY SPECIAL COLLECTIONS, HAROLD B. LEE LIBRARY, BRIGHAM YOUNG UNIVERSITY).

narrative, owing to the Confucian view of ruler as father figure; now Grant, the American, serves as an equally worthy model.

Robun uses a broad brush in portraying the heroic qualities of his main character. Grant is shown to have been destined for greatness from his birth: Robun mentions incidents from Grant's childhood (his great size as an infant, his uncanny lack of fear of loud noises) to underscore his remarkable character and fitness for leadership. The reader is then treated to highly detailed depictions of key battles and events from Grant's Mexican-American War and Civil War service. These scenes highlight Grant's heroic qualities: his courage, cunning, brilliance as a military strategist, and, in negotiating the surrender with Lee, his kindly noblesse oblige in regard to Confederate troops. Grant's kindness is mentioned in particular, and this unexpected attitude towards an enemy epitomizes Robun's portrayal of Grant, the hero.

Up to this point in the very visual text Grant is portrayed as an American hero, his life inseparably linked with the expansion and growth of the American republic. However, from the depiction of President Abraham Lincoln's assassination onward, the images and narrative take on a curious change towards the Japanese end of the spectrum.

The illustration of Lincoln's assassination represents one of Robun's more significant transmutations of reality. The text notes that Lincoln was "stabbed to death" (*sashikorosu*), and the accompanying illustration portrays a group of men with long daggers overpowering a valiantly struggling (and youthful) Lincoln in an open setting.[68] Gone is the private theatre box, the lone assassin, the small pistol; even John Wilkes Booth's name is elided.

Why the change? Perhaps, to contemporary Meiji readers, a man of Lincoln's stature deserved more than an ignominious death by one shot from a lunatic's pistol. Where, they might ask, were his bodyguards? And what, they might also wonder, was a president doing at a public theatre in the first place?[69] Robun has deftly avoided the disorienting strangeness that direct translation of the facts of Lincoln's assassination might produce in his readers by transmuting them to conform to Japanese expectations. Lincoln, a great leader, was overpowered in public by a large force of armed men and stabbed to death. This is a much more believable assassination and falls in line with how the great leaders of Japan might possibly meet their deaths.[70]

To Japanese readers in 1879 there was a relatively recent event that added a new parallel to Robun's text: Five years prior to Lincoln's death Ii Naosuke, reigning regent and a prime mover in Japan's modernization efforts, was assassinated by a group of sword-wielding samurai at the Saku-

THE ASSASSINATION OF ABRAHAM LINCOLN (VOLUME II) (COURTESY OF
L. TOM PERRY SPECIAL COLLECTIONS, HAROLD B. LEE LIBRARY, BRIGHAM
YOUNG UNIVERSITY).

rada Gate of the Imperial Palace.[71] The image of Lincoln in Robun's text
would very likely have led its readers to conflate the two events, replacing
Lincoln with Ii, and thereby invited them to draw further parallels between
American and Japanese history. Here we see Robun's creative talent, and
one of adaptation's greatest strengths. In changing the details to match
Japanese cultural conventions Robun not only removes a potential obsta-
cle to smooth readerly understanding, but in the process substitutes a Japanese motif that increases the dramatic tension even as it alludes to parallel
events in Japanese history, enriching the text rather than making it strange.

Once Lincoln is assassinated in a proper Japanese manner, the remaining chapters of Robun's narrative become more and more Japanese. The
world tour section reads like a combination of Edo period illustrated scrolls
and contemporary geography texts (*bankoku zusetsu*), the images showing
caricatures of foreigners while the text highlights the economic and cultural differences between countries. As with the picture scrolls, Robun uses
his illustrations to reinforce contemporary racial stereotypes about foreigners. First we see images of Americans, British, and French (tall, white, elab-

orately dressed, in dignified poses) and read about the greatness of their urban spaces (London, Paris). Robun's depiction of other ethnic groups and races stands in sharp contrast. The Indians, Malays, Thai, and Chinese (portrayed in varying shades of brown or black and usually half-dressed) demonstrate Robun's not-so-subtle hierarchy of color, and his textual description of their countries is restricted primarily to curiosities, religious monuments, and export goods.

At times the images also call to mind earlier models of *gesaku* in their playfulness. One example of this playfulness substitutes the Grant family for a pair of buffoons straight out of Edo period comic fiction. As noted above, shortly after Japan's opening to the West, Robun wrote *Seiyôdôchû hizakurige* in imitation of Ikku's earlier tale of two humorous travelers, Kita and Yaji. An allusion to both works appears in Robun's biography of Grant, only now the travelers are General and Mrs. Grant, who circumnavigate the globe and allow Robun to visually and verbally comment on the peculiarities and exotic aspects of foreign people and places. There are striking parallels between Ikku's original 1802 images, those of Robun's Westernized version, and those found in *Gurando-shi den,* including basic format, placement of mountains and vegetation, the pose of the guide, and even the inclusion of an umbrella (or umbrella-like hat in Ikku's original).

Despite the straightforward "diplomats on tour" scenario, the Meiji reader familiar with either or both of the earlier works would be subtly invited (through visual repetition) to see the Grants as fellow travelers of Kita and Yaji, a Japanese illustrative technique known as *mitate* (visual parody) often used in *gesaku* illustrations.[72] Its use in Robun's text is another example of Robun's transmutation of the facts to accommodate his Japanese readers. By using traditional *gesaku* formats and techniques to illustrate and describe the foreign, Robun again minimizes the alienating effects exposure to the Other might generate in his readers, even as he uses stereotype to transpose Grant from Other to familiar. In his adept use of *mitate* Robun again reveals a creative aspect of *hon'anmono:* the possibility for making the strange familiar through subtle allusion rather than direct metaphor.

Five of the images of the Grants in Japan—the arrival of the *Richmond* in Yokohama, the Grants riding to the theater in a carriage, the interior of the newly built modern theater, the Grants riding to the pier in a train, and the departure of their ship home—depict a modern (Western) world (steam ships, gas lighting, trains), and each is patterned after earlier European scenes. This use of internal *mitate* invites Robun's readers to compare Japan favorably with the Western, elite countries of the world. Here we see

JIPPENSHA IKKU'S *TÔKAIDÔCHÛ HIZAKURIGE* (1802); ROBUN'S *SEIYÔDÔCHÛ HIZAKURIGE* (1870); THE GRANTS IN SIAM (1879) (COURTESY OF NATIONAL DIET LIBRARY, DÔSHISHA DAIGAKU GAKUJUTSU JÔHÔ SENTÂ, AND L. TOM PERRY SPECIAL COLLECTIONS, HAROLD B. LEE LIBRARY, BRIGHAM YOUNG UNIVERSITY, RESPECTIVELY).

Robun's use of *hon'anmono* as self-congratulation: In choosing to focus visually on the technological elements of Grant's visit, and ignore images of Grant at Nikkô or in traditional villages, Robun transforms the real Japan into a textual version that suggests European, modern countries rather than Asian, backward nations (or, as Grant so aptly notes, "more a romance than a reality"). While his readers were certainly familiar with the real Japan, Robun's transmutation of their reality into an idealized version was not a new experience but rather an expected convention of *gesaku* fiction.[73]

Grant as Meiji Hero

Once the textual Grants reach Japan, the illustrations—aside from those reinforcing the Japan-West parallel—change dramatically. Much of the remaining images portray scenes from the kabuki performance at the Shintomiza Theater. In the theatre world of Robun's day kabuki was a vibrant, flexible genre of drama that quickly incorporated new elements and contemporary themes while maintaining a strong traditional flavor: It was avant-garde and conservative at the same time. The idea of *hon'an* was very much at the center of the kabuki playwright's creative strategy. There existed a number of fixed settings or dramatic horizons (*sekai*) to which innovative elements such as plot changes or new characterizations (*shukô*) would be grafted to form new permutations.[74] In the case of the play Grant's entourage witnessed, playwright Mokuami chose the *sekai* of the historical hero Yoshiie and grafted onto that a *shukô* that mirrored some of the events of Grant's life. In the contemporary world of kabuki, Mokuami's *hon'anmono* of Grant's life was well within a traditional playwright's domain, and such adaptation kept kabuki vibrant and innovative, allowing as it did the incorporation of new elements into familiar scenarios.

Robun's visual and verbal description of Mokuami's play, which takes up the bulk of parts two and three of Volume III, contains illustrations of the more dramatic scenes as well as a detailed retelling of the unfolding drama. To the extent that Robun's work transmutes three-dimensional performance into two-dimensional retelling, his narrative becomes an adaptation of a *hon'an* performance appearing within the broader context of a *hon'anmono* of Grant's life. This rare situation is complicated even more by the fact that the subject of both Robun's and Mokuami's respective adaptations, Grant, was in the audience at the time of the performance *and* in Japan when Robun's work began its serial publication.[75] Grant was thus both transmuted subject and audience for a transmutation, not once but twice!

Mokuami's play and Robun's textual report recast Grant's life in a way that fits traditional Japanese archetypes, and the retelling often uses familiar Japanese narrative topoi. One particularly intriguing detail in the dramatization is casting the Japanese hero's (adoptive) father as a *taiko* drum maker from the provinces. Both the provincial setting, and more especially the low-caste occupation (drum makers worked with leather, putting them on the very bottom of the Japanese social hierarchy), mirror Grant's actual beginnings (born on the Western frontier, his father a tanner). Yet a hero's rise from such inglorious beginnings to greatness is, in a Meiji world enamored of Horatio Alger stories, the quintessential Western success story. Again, in Robun's *hon'anmono* of the play, *mitate* plays a crucial role in underscoring the ties between American and Japanese heroes. Note the resemblance between the illustration of Grant's boyhood tanning days and Yoshiie's own youth, in particular the detail of green hides hanging above the scene. Robun invites his readers once again to *see* Yoshiie as a transmutation of Grant (and Grant as Yoshiie's reincarnation?).

Adaptive Idiosyncrasies: Hon'anmono as Reconciliation

Robun's biography of Grant contains many elements typical of contemporary *hon'anmono,* with several twists made necessary due to the mortal nature of his subject/text. While he borrows freely from some of the Japanese biographies of Grant, he also applies creative license to Grant's itinerary (for example, having the Grants travel from India *back* to Egypt and then to Japan). The disparity between Grant as man and Grant as textual creation lends a tension to the work that, from the beginning, Robun acknowledges and uses to his advantage. Along the way, we learn something about Robun's own theory of *hon'an.*

Returning once more to the cover of *Gurando-shi den,* we see an example of Robun's wit that reveals his view of translation as appropriation. Above and to the right of the title of the text, next to Grant's portrait, is Robun's own name. Although he usually used the phrase *gicho,* "playful author," after his name to designate his authorial role on works of *hon'an,* in the case of *Gurando-shi den* Robun uses a phrase that has two possible readings, with two different meanings: Kanagaki Robun, 和解. At first glance, the meaning seems simple enough; the most common gloss in this context is *wage,* an early word for "Japanese redaction (from a Western source)."[76] However, the two Chinese characters that make up the word are not glossed, so another potential reading also exists: *wakai,* meaning "reconciliation" or "rapprochement."[77] From the beginning Robun employs a pun (like many of his *gesaku* peers, Robun was a master of the pun), perhaps to deflate the self-congratulatory tone of the title.[78]

Thus we may read into Robun's use of the unglossed phrase a desire, perhaps, to introduce his readers to his role in this *hon'an* biography as *both* adapter and mediator, since his narrative brings together two very disparate entities: Grant's life and Japanese language. From the first page Robun invites his readers to see his "translation" of Grant's life into a Japanese text as a kind of battle or conflict, one that can only be resolved through the intervention of a skillful textual arbitrator. Robun's view of translation as reconciliation underscores the traditional *hon'an* view of the translator's prerogative—adaptation—and takes it a step further, into the realm of mediation.

Prior to the Meiji period, during over two centuries of official national isolation, the Other as embodied in foreign cultures and languages was seen

YOSHIIE (GRANT) AS ADOPTED SON OF A DRUM MAKER (VOLUME III) AND YOUNG GRANT (VOLUME I) (COURTESY OF L. TOM PERRY SPECIAL COLLECTIONS, HAROLD B. LEE LIBRARY, BRIGHAM YOUNG UNIVERSITY).

primarily as a distant, if threatening, curiosity. With the dramatic events that opened Japan to the West, and with the remarkable changes taking place within Japan by 1879 largely motivated by a new sense of national inferiority, it was both witty and accurate for Robun to define his role as more than simply transporting the details of Grant's life into Japanese. Grant himself had arrived in Japan, the West was now present, rather than distant, and the potential imbalance created thereby needed some kind of rectification. We are, Robun seems to be saying to his readers, engaged in a de facto cultural war, and a visit from a top rival warrants a reconciliation between the culturally polarized world of Meiji Japan and a progressive, democratic America.

Robun accomplishes this reconciliation using a number of techniques. His lengthy, iconically rich text contains a host of complex elements. As with any biography, what is ignored is as important as what is included, and although divining Robun's sources can be difficult, his detailed retelling of Grant's boyhood suggests that he could have had access to extant contemporary accounts written in great detail. Also, since the standard reading of *wage* suggests his work is an adaptation of a target text rather than one created *ex nihilo,* what Robun chooses to include—and in many cases magnify or change—gives us insight into what elements of Grant's life required "reconciliation" with Japanese readerly expectations.

Robun puts a great deal of textual and visual emphasis on Grant's father's occupation: Jesse Grant was a tanner, in the American context a suitable occupation for a frontier settler. In the Japanese context, however, Grant's family occupation represents a trade reserved for the pariah class— the *eta* or *burakumin.* Although within the American context the "model" of Grant's success may be attributed to his pluck and hard work, Robun's extra emphasis on Grant's background may be seen as underscoring the remarkable upward mobility Grant's life demonstrates: From outcaste leather worker to military commander to "American Mikado," Grant has broken through the status barriers at every turn.

Underlying this reading is the possibility that, to Japanese readers toying with nascent democratic ideals as embodied in the contemporary Freedom and People's Rights Movement, the American model posed the happy possibility—or dreadful specter, depending on one's politics—of equal opportunity for all.[79] It certainly underscored Grant's self-made success, a trait also lionized in other contemporary Japanese translations of Western writings, most notably Samuel Smiles' *Self-Help* (translated 1871). On the other hand, from a more parodic (even jingoist) perspective, Robun's alliance of Grant with leather-working may also have been read as a pejorative association that invited readers to expand the personal to the national: America as a land of pariahs.[80]

Another element that Robun "reconciles" in his narrative is Grant's military career. The Mexican-American War and the Civil War occupy over a quarter of the entire narrative. It is also revealing that, when Grant visits the theater in Tokyo, Robun emphasizes the point that the performances highlight great military moments in Japanese drama—and that Robun's Grant is captivated by the military display. There are several possible reasons for the military emphasis in Robun's text: Japan's own civil war overlapped the American Civil War, so war was a relatively recent memory to Robun's readers. Also, conventional narrative treatment of heroes in Japan tended to underscore military prowess and tales of valor on the battlefield. From the perspective of appropriation, a detailed description of Grant's military adventures brought the biography of Grant into line with familiar Japanese archetypes. And if we read Robun's text as rapprochement, each anecdote from Grant's military career adds to the collective Japanese body of tales of valor, softening the foreign element and bringing the Otherness of Grant into more familiar territory.

Finally, although Robun only touches briefly on Grant's presidency, most of the third and final volume is devoted to his world travels. Certain segments of Grant's journey are described in great detail, as though Robun wishes to use Grant's tour as an opportunity to teach geography. Grant receives honors and accolades and takes in famous sights in country after country. Visually, the illustrations are heavily weighted towards "civilized" Western nations (England and France in particular), while lesser countries such as India, China, and Siam receive only brief attention. In contrast, Grant's arrival in Japan, and especially his visits to the theater, are covered in exhaustive detail. This strategy may be seen as a subtle inference that Japan, by hosting Grant so well, ranks as one of the premier countries of the world.

Grant's tour is itself a novelty for Japanese readers—no historical Japanese Emperor had ever traveled abroad—and is one potential source of tension for Robun's readers: Why would an Emperor-equivalent travel outside his realm, except to claim newly annexed territory?[81] This tension is reconciled, in part, by Robun's portrayal of Grant's visit as paying tribute to the Meiji ruler. Grant's visit to Japan could then be seen as a parallel to the Iwakura Mission of 1872–73, when an official delegation of Japanese leaders traveled to America (and was hosted by then-President Grant in Washington, D.C.) and Europe on a fact-finding tour in order to help Japan catch up with the West. From this perspective, Grant's visit to Japan was flattering indeed, since his "mission" there would be to examine, evaluate, and where possible to appropriate uniquely Japanese systems, just as Iwakura had scoured the West several years earlier. Further evidence of this may be found in Robun's description of the audience between the Emperor and Grant: Although the meeting is not depicted visually, Robun notes that Grant "listened attentively to imperial advice."[82] Once again, Japan's status is elevated through appropriating Grant's visit as proof of Japan's global significance.

Biography as National Narrative

Benedict Anderson addresses an interesting parallel between individuals and nations in his discussion of memory: "All profound changes in consciousness, by their very nature, bring with them characteristic amnesias. Out of such oblivions, in specific historical circumstances, spring narratives. . . . As with modern persons, so it is with nations. Awareness of being imbedded in secular, serial time, with all its implications of continuity, yet of 'forgetting' the experience of this continuity . . . engenders the need for a narrative of 'identity.'"[83]

In contrasting the personal with the national, Anderson invites us to consider the impact of rupture—adolescence in the former; civil war, revolution, origination in the latter—on historical memory. Ruptures—such as birth—cannot be remembered, hence the need for narrative, for a structured retelling of the unremembered event. And this retelling, mandated in the case of individuals as well as communities and nations, is a crucial part of identity.

Considering, then, the need for narrative to transcend national rupture, I propose that Robun uses this need as he finds (or creates) a natural affinity between Grant the person and Japan the nation. Grant, clearly portrayed as one of the founding fathers (or midwives) of America, brings with him to Japan's shores a kind of sympathetic magic, the power of fathering, of fostering the birth of a new, post-rupture Japan. Robun begins with birth—both that of Grant and of the United States—in his biographical narrative, retelling (and mythologizing) the life of both. As Robun's narrative reveals and shapes Grant's life the events Robun chooses to include bring Grant inexorably closer to his (narratological) fate of visiting Japan. Robun then uses his narrative to underscore the identity of Grant and the Emperor/Japan, weaving the two almost seamlessly together, an odd mixture unless one considers the contemporary need, in the Japanese national consciousness, for an identity that was at once both traditional and revolutionary. And, to the younger generations (and vast majority of newly literate masses) for whom the bloody details of the Meiji Restoration could not be memory, this need for narrated identity was even greater.

In satisfying this need, then, Robun took the opportunity to narrate the "history" of Japan under the pretext of retelling Grant's life. Though much of the detail is Grant, both the title (*Yamato bunshô*) and Robun's self-proclaimed mediator status (*wakai*) invite readers to see parallels between the two. The ruptures of civil and cultural wars, and their concomitant forgetting, is narrated anew, the retelling effecting a kind of healing and regeneration for subject, reader, and nation. Robun intensifies the sense of national identity through underscoring the parallels between Grant and the Meiji oligarchy, between a post-bellum ("U. S.") Grant and a post-isolation Japan.

Robun's narrative contrasts strongly with that of Young, since both have very different motivations for adapting Grant's story.[84] Yet there are similarities. Both Young and Robun seek to bolster their respective country's postwar self-image through narratives of identity, Young portraying Grant as America's *Jedermann,* ambassador to the world, while Robun turns Grant into a Japanese hero. Both also use a combination of text and image to underscore their appropriation and expand their audiences. Yet, in the final analysis, Robun's narrative bridges the wider chasm. *Gurando-shi den Yamato bunshô* is, generically speaking, both realistic biography and playful *gesaku*. This discrepancy may be seen as representative of the many conflicting elements brought together in this work of rapprochement. From the traditional Japanese perspective Robun's "reconciliation" of Grant and the Emperor, American life and Japanese text, West and East stands as a remarkable and noteworthy achievement, a *hon'anmono* that provides both humor and high-minded parallelism, even as it demonstrates the art of adaptation as reconciliation.

A Curious Echo

After Grant left Japan, and the flags, lanterns, and garlands were set aside, Robun's *hon'anmono* made its own curious journey abroad, and in the process, as epilogue, sounded an exotic, transposed echo across the Pacific.

One year after Grant's trip to Japan an American in Tokyo, fascinated by a copy of Robun's text on display at a bookstand, purchased the work and brought it back to New York. Through a mutual friend, he eventually lent it to Grant for review (it was returned a week later without comment).[85] Following this, the owner apparently commissioned several translations into English, which were rejected because they "were made by Japanese who deemed it their duty to make the translation sound as American as possible, paraphrasing all Oriental expressions in such a way as to destroy their characteristic force."[86] Ironically, the Japanese who "paraphrased all Oriental expressions" were, in fact, *adapting* the work for an American audience: They were creating a seamless *hon'an,* rather than an exotic *hon'yaku.* And for this their efforts at reconciliation were rejected outright, since they lacked the eccentricity of style that would mark them as faithful translations.

An Orientalist Translation

Fourteen years later, in 1895, when the Robun text came to the attention of editors for the popular magazine the *Century Illustrated Monthly,* published in New York, they found a native Japanese, the Reverend (later Bishop) Joseph Sakunoshin Motoda, who was then "residing at the Episcopal Divinity School in West Philadelphia," to translate "the more interesting parts of the work" into English.[87] Motoda completed the task, and selected chapters and illustrations were published in the July edition of the magazine. What is most striking about the Motoda translation is that, while full of footnotes and captions under the illustrations suggesting correspondent translation and scholarly integrity, the translation itself is not correspondent so much as overtly literal. In its wildly idiomatic language the translation reinforces contemporary American stereotypes of Japan. Note the Orientalist style of the following two passages:

> From the time of his birth he was different from an ordinary baby. His body was large. He weighed 1 kwan, 292 me. As he grew, his thought became deeper accordingly. It was seen by the eye of every man. He showed no color of fear, however great the sound that came into his ear. . . . The people at large are commanded by the government to show their thick will.★ (★Kind feeling) To receive Gurando Kuen [they] hung lanterns at each door, with the flags of Nippon and America on both sides of the street. The bridges of great roads fluttered with the flags of both countries as if it were the feast-day of Ubusuna★ (★A local god, supposed to govern one or more streets).[88]

The text has been translated quite literally, with apparently little or no editorial intervention on the part of *Century Illustrated Monthly.* Grammar is intentionally primitivized, proper nouns are left in syllabic Japanese style ("Gurando" for Grant), commonplace Japanese idioms are translated verbatim for the sake of exoticism ("thick feeling"), and some Japanese words are left intact (*kwan, me, Kuen*). One reading of this curious editorial neglect is that the magazine desired to give the work an exotic flavor and so chose to leave the translation in its rough, more literal form. In so doing, however, the eccentricity of the style caters to other readerly prejudices. Although this overtly literal style of translation does, indeed, approach a correspondent literality, it is correspondence as parody.

Thus we see yet another aspect of adaptation that enters into a contemplation of the uses of *hon'anmono:* the idea of intentionally distorted language. In certain narrative or performance contexts language can be deliberately contorted for a particular effect (for example, Hollywood cinematic portrayals of stereotypical Nazis or Native Americans with thick accents to accentuate their Otherness). In the case of a retranslation of Robun's text, however, the return to its "original" idiom (English) should have been a fairly straightforward process. The fact that the *Century Illustrated Monthly* was not satisfied by that, and settled instead on a "literal" translation by someone who could very likely have come up with a much less exoticized version, suggests much about the goals of the magazine's editors. It also parallels, in a rather curious way, the dynamics of Meiji translation, with Japanese translators struggling between the poles of seamless transparency (*hon'an*) and exotic literalness (*hon'yaku*).

The echo of Robun's text that appeared in the *Century Illustrated Monthly* suggests that one virtue of *hon'anmono* specifically—and adaptation in general—is its diminished sense of Otherness, leading to more open reception of the transmuted text (and, obliquely, the original after which it was modeled). This counter-intuitive benefit accrues when there exists the possibility that an overtly literal approach to translation leading to deliberately contorted language may evoke stereotypes ("Kraut," "Injun," "Jap") that can only promote further polarization, not reconciliation.[89]

Robun's distorted English-language echo, *Gurando's Life, Yamato Bunsho,* is itself a kind of American *hon'anmono,* with a curious twist. The source text is not seen as Grant, but rather a *Japanese reading* of Grant. And, in a manner that parallels the way Japanese writers (often using summaries prepared by native speakers) appropriated Western texts in their *hon'anmono,* the *Century Illustrated Monthly* has used its own summary by a native Japanese to distort and reinforce stereotypes about Japan. Thus, as with the Japanese appropriation of Grant, the source text ceases to be the message; that role is filled by the transmutation. Robun's text is not transposed for the sake of its hermeneutic value, but is rather parodied to reiterate cultural assumptions.

It is ironic that the English version of Robun's text has itself been appropriated, this time in the service of American stereotypes of the Orient in general and Japan in particular. Ulysses S. Grant, originally transmuted into a rather curious text that seeks to reconcile the differences between Japan and the West, has in turn been reshaped into an American *hon'anmono* that seeks to underscore those differences. In the latter case the adaptation of an adaptation loses its diplomatic function and becomes, rather, a lens projecting the transmuted vision of a backwards, exoticized Japan for its jingoist American readers.

Chapter III ✐

From Madness To Murder:
Victorian Novel As *Ninjôbanashi*

The [storyteller] is one of the institutions of Japan. Sometimes by read-
ing a low native novel, or by extemporising some story of vulgar fun,
he gathers a little audience around him in the public street, or exhibits
for a pecuniary reward his mimic powers among the inmates of a pri-
vate dwelling.

—George Smith, Bishop of Hong Kong 1861[1]

[Enchô], a . . . story-teller of Tokio, also composes in the colloquial
style. Indeed his novels are first delivered in a spoken form, and are
taken down in writing. . . . Some of his plots are said to be taken
from the French.

—W. G. Aston, 1899[2]

The ordinary novel, which deals . . . with shadows only, is one kind
of property, a story that cuts deep into realities . . . and has already set
hundreds discussing it as history and law, is a different thing; it finds
buyers as well as readers, and that amongst a class that does not buy
novels as a rule.

—Charles Reade[3]

When General Grant was visiting Japan in 1879, Ichikawa Danjûrô, one of the foremost kabuki actors of the day, portrayed
the ex-president as a twelfth-century samurai hero. Six years
later the legendary Danjûrô performed a very different role, that of a contemporary ex-samurai forced, through social changes brought about by the
Meiji Restoration, to eke out a meager living as an innkeeper. The play

itself, *Seiyôbanashi Nihon utsushie* (A Western Tale as Japanese Magic Lantern Show, 1885), was a dramatization of an oral epic tale narrated by one of the premier professional storytellers of the day, San'yûtei Enchô (1839–1900). Enchô's story was, in turn, an adaptation of a Victorian novel, Charles Reade's *Hard Cash*. This chapter will focus on the vibrant Meiji world of professional storytelling, in particular the important role oral storytellers played as entertainers of the masses, and examine how oral adaptations of Western novels mirrored the contemporary world. In the process I will show how Enchô's *hon'anmono* of a propagandistic British novel was tailored to the concerns of his diverse and changing audience.

During much of the nineteenth century a vibrant storytelling tradition had coexisted with written literary culture in Japan, but there had been only minimal interaction between the two. In 1884, with the invention of Japanese shorthand and the appearance of oral stories in print, these two distinct worlds began to merge. One of the key figures in this fascinating story of oral transposition was raconteur San'yûtei Enchô. At the time of Grant's visit to Japan, Enchô was already an established professional story-teller, renowned for his ghost tales and romances. But he was also beginning to experiment with adapting stories from Western sources, as were his fellow raconteurs, and, as their transposition into kabuki drama attests, these *hon'an* tales rapidly became very popular fare among the audiences of the *yose* storytelling theaters. These adaptations offer yet another example of the remarkable flexibility of *hon'anmono* as a translation genre, in particular the seminal role it played in the Meiji oral tradition.

The Meiji World of Professional Storytelling

Professional oral storytelling was enjoying a period of great popularity in urban Japan during the latter half of the nineteenth century.[4] Nearly every neighborhood had its storytelling theater, where daily matinee and evening performances included serialized romances, classical war tales, intrigues, and ghost stories punctuated by musical acts and brief humorous monologues (*rakugo*). Many of the more popular tales went on for a fortnight, with audiences returning day after day to hear the continuing story. At times the more famous raconteurs even went on tour, reciting their tales at theaters in the countryside. In their peregrinations *yose*-based storytellers were actually retracing the footsteps of the original wandering balladeers who established storytelling as a profession centuries earlier.

Japanese literary expression has consistently demonstrated a strong oral component. Even after the introduction of Chinese writing and the creation of the *kana* syllabaries, Japanese literary works maintained strong ties with the oral tradition throughout the Heian (749–1192) and medieval (1192–1600) periods; many classical Japanese literary masterpieces, including *Genji monogatari* (The Tale of Genji, ca. 1006), contain a great deal of residual orality.[5] Between the tenth and fourteenth centuries itinerant Buddhist preachers often used oral fables (*setsuwa*) in their efforts to enlighten both the illiterate masses and the literate elite. Some of these parables found their way into written collections and are preserved today in works such as the *Konjaku monogatari* (Tales of Times Now Past, 1108). More secular, *märchen*-like narratives called *otogi-zôshi* were transcribed into written collections during the medieval period.[6]

Medieval Storytelling

Widespread civil war led to chaotic conditions in Japan during the fourteenth, fifteenth, and sixteenth centuries, which gave rise to a more secularized oral narrative. Battle survivors, eye-witnesses, and masterless samurai (*rônin*) wandered the countryside telling war stories in exchange for food and lodging. For some this was only a temporary means of survival, but for others it turned into a profession. By the beginning of the seventeenth century, when political control in Japan was consolidated by the Tokugawa family, some of these itinerant storytellers began to settle down, affiliating themselves with popular temples or plying their trade at the intersections of major thoroughfares in the growing cities.

During the seventeenth and eighteenth centuries, storytelling became established as one of the popular arts, and references to the *yose* (storytelling stage) began to appear in literary texts. In 1623, for example, Anrakuan Sakuden (1554–1642), a priest and master of tea, compiled a collection of humorous stories derived from the *yose*. Likewise, in polymath Hiraga Gennai's (1728–1779) social satire *Fûryû Shidôken den* (The Dashing Life of Shidôken, 1763) the protagonist is modeled on a famous contemporary storyteller.[7]

Nineteenth-century Storytelling

By the beginning of the nineteenth century, the urban centers of Osaka and Edo witnessed the establishment of professional storytelling theaters where epic oral narratives would unfold nightly to a diverse audience of samurai, merchants, tradesmen, and their families. As Japan opened its doors to the West in the mid-1860s the previously immobile masses began to converge upon the urban centers, and professional storytelling underwent unprecedented growth. *Yose* multiplied in number, springing up in nearly every neighborhood, and a continuous flow of storytellers, musicians, impersonators, and magicians entertained an ever more diverse audience.[8] The importance of *yose* halls in Meiji life was noted by Inoue Jukichi in 1895:

> Artisans and small-tradesmen, with their families, and students seek at the hall a relaxation from the hard day's work; and as they are after all no unimportant sections of the city population, the influence of these halls on Tokyo life cannot be overlooked. Newspapers are, it is true, now leavening the whole society; but it is still from the halls that the artisan to-day gets all his knowledge, meager as it is, and to the same source may be traced his familiarity with the notable events and heroes in the history of his country. In its educating influence, then, the story-teller's profession is an important one . . . taken even at their own valuation, story-tellers are among the most influential of the multitude who live to please.[9]

The world of late nineteenth-century professional storytelling was divided into schools, or clans, that included both apprentice and veteran performers.[10] A typical evening at the *yose* began with several apprentice storytellers performing brief tales interspersed with vaudeville-type variety acts. As the evening progressed, the more experienced storytellers would appear in succession, and the final story would usually be an installment of an ongoing epic recited by a *shin'uchi,* or master raconteur.

Repertoires varied, and a well-trained storyteller was capable of reciting anything from a ten-minute comic monologue to an episodic work of thirty-plus installments.[11] Thematically, the tales included both traditional fare (war stories, didactic tales, ghost stories, and romances) as well as the avant-garde (biographies, current intrigues, and adaptations of Western tales). Over time, storytelling divided into two distinct styles of narrative, one clearly grounded in the oral world and the other based upon written texts. The former (referred to generically as *ninjôbanashi* or *rakugo*), whose performers were called *hanashika,* consisted of oral narratives performed from memory by storytellers who faced their audiences directly and employed minimalist props (such as a hand towel and a fan) to serve as visual additions to the story. The latter (*kôdan*), whose performers were called *kôdanshi,* consisted of written texts (usually drawn from the Japanese classics or military annals) that were placed upon a lectern, quoted or paraphrased, and then explicated by the storyteller. These *kôdan* offered a mixture of chanted rhythmical reading, punctuating beats on the lectern, and personal commentary. Both types of storytelling involved mimetic dramatization of dialogue and a certain amount of acting on the part of the storyteller, although *ninjôbanashi* sometimes included theatrical elements as well.[12]

Changes to Storytelling in the Meiji Period

Professional storytelling, unlike written narrative, was enjoying something of a renaissance at the end of the Tokugawa period, and after the Meiji Restoration it reached unprecedented levels of popularity. Within a decade, *yose* theaters became a ubiquitous part of the new urban landscapes of Tokyo and Osaka.[13] The growth of storytelling during the Meiji period, which facilitated the further adaptation of Western literary works, can be attributed to several factors: changing urban demographics, the invention of Japanese shorthand, and the adaptability of storytellers to their audiences' changing narrative appetites.

Changing Urban Demographics and the Yose

One factor that influenced changes to professional storytelling during the early Meiji period was a shift in urban demographics. With the new government's push towards modernization, the urban centers, Tokyo in particular, became frenetic areas of development and opportunity. People flocked to the cities to fill a growing demand for factory and service workers as well as to enjoy city life. Improved roads and the establishment of railroad lines increased the flow of people from the countryside into the cities.

Once there, the urban immigrants learned to enjoy new entertainments, including the widely accessible and affordable *yose* theaters. Their addition to the traditional *yose* audience brought new challenges to the storytellers, whose tales had focused primarily on the narrow topos of Edo inner-city culture. The arrivals offered new material for storytellers to incorporate into their repertoires, and the growing diversity of urban Japan allowed storytellers to create new stock characters reflecting the broader differences of their audiences. Audiences, likewise, shared more than just laughter and tears in the *yose;* as storytellers' audiences became more diverse and their interests and concerns changed to reflect the shift from Tokugawa proto-bourgeois contentment to Meiji upward mobility, the repertoires of the storytellers expanded to include not only traditional stories about class differences in the local milieu but also tales describing successful entrepreneurs from the countryside.[14]

As Tokyo's population continued to swell, so did *yose* audiences. Storytellers themselves rose in popularity, and their oral delivery and function as social commentators, as well as the availability of *yose* and accommodating performance times, made them a very popular form of entertainment, eclipsing even kabuki in attendance figures.[15] Their popularity did not go unnoticed by the Meiji government, which quickly sought to rein in their potentially subverting rhetoric by appointing storytellers as "moral educators."[16] Despite the formal title, however, by and large storytellers continued to serve as a sounding board for social issues throughout the first three decades of the Meiji period.

The Invention of Japanese Shorthand and the Rise of Sokkibon

A second development that influenced the spread of storytelling's popularity among the urban masses, and the Meiji population in general, was the invention of Japanese shorthand (*sokki*) in 1883.[17] Prior to *sokki* there had been no effective means of simultaneously transcribing Japanese speech, and, given the broad divide that separated written from spoken Japanese at the time, a great deal of editorial license could undermine the integrity of newspaper reportage of contemporary political debates. Takusari Kôki (1854–1938), a young man of samurai heritage from the provinces, spent four years experimenting with various forms of Western shorthand until he finally came up with a system suitable for Japanese. He trained several students as stenographers, who were first employed to record political assemblies, court proceedings, and college lectures.

Within a short time, the new Japanese stenographers found themselves employed at the *yose,* transcribing some of the longer oral tales for publishers of fiction. The first tale to be stenographed and published was a popular oral ghost story, *Kaidan botandôrô* (The Ghost Tale of the Peony Lantern, 1884) that Enchô was performing in the *yose* at the time. The printed version of this oral tale was so well-received by an increasingly literate public that, within twelve months five more Enchô tales, as well as an increasing number of stories by other professional raconteurs, appeared in printed form thanks to *sokki* stenographers.[18]

After the advent of *sokki,* then, storytellers had two avenues of public expression: live performance in the *yose,* and written transcription in newspapers, magazines, and books. The latter appeared as a pecuniary windfall at first, but over time pirated versions and imitations led to widespread devaluation, to the point that, by the end of the Meiji period, the *yose* was in decline and storytellers were abandoning the lengthy serialized *ninjôbanashi* in favor of short, one-sitting humorous monologues (*rakugo*).[19] The emergence of *sokkibon,* however, gave nationwide celebrity to storytellers such as Enchô and spread their tales, and concomitant observations about contemporary social issues, to the far corners of the Japanese archipelago.

Experiments in Adaptation: Hon'an as Oral Tale

A third aspect of early Meiji storytelling that led to its rapid growth was the ability of storytellers to meet their audience's changing narrative appetites. Between 1850 and 1885 *yose* audiences underwent a number of transformations, in terms of both their makeup and their collective interests. As Edo became Tokyo, large numbers of immigrants from the countryside added a greater diversity to the audience. What had previously been a group of local merchant and tradesman families (and the occasional samurai) swelled to include a broad spectrum of provincials, including families from impoverished villages seeking their fortunes, wealthy scions of moneyed country estates studying at some of Japan's first modern universities, single women working in new factories, and former samurai attempting to make new lives for themselves after being cut loose from their regular stipends.[20] Storytellers, naturally attuned to their audience's tastes, recognized the varied interests of this diverse group and added new stories accordingly.

Likewise, as Japan entered into a stage of frenetic industrial growth, the occupations and preoccupations of *yose* audiences shifted from relatively domestic concerns (ghost stories, romances, vendettas) to broader issues, such as the threat of Western imperialism, economic and political systems in flux, the prospect of social revolution, and the changing urban landscape in the wake of technological progress. Storytellers altered their repertoires to accommodate these changes as well. For example, their tales become increasingly political during the 1870s and '80s, when a grassroots movement for democracy was on the rise.[21] Moreover, storytellers were quick to exoticize some of their tales by describing Western clothing, food, and manners.

During the 1870s, the *yose* audience's yearning for exotica was met, in part, when a young Englishman named Henry Black (1858–1923), living in Japan with his journalist father, took to the *yose* stage offering his own Japanese-language renditions of Victorian novels and Western legends.[22] As Black rose in prominence as a storyteller, his use of Western tales as source material caught on among other storytellers, who relied upon Black or Western language-speaking Japanese for plot summaries of Western novels. These *hon'an* were very popular in the *yose,* and corresponded to

TWO MEIJI STORYTELLERS, FROM JULES ADAM, *AU JAPON: LES RACONTEURS PUBLICS,*1899 (COURTESY NATIONAL DIET LIBRARY).

the exotic written adaptations and translations of Western novels popular during the first decades of Meiji.

Both *kôdanshi* and *hanashika* created tales patterned after Western novels. *Hanashika* Enchô performed at least four full-length *hon'an* of Western stories between 1878 and 1895, in addition to numerous short adaptations.[23] Likewise, *kôdanshi* Shôrin Hakuen (1832–1905) incorporated Western materials in some of his *kôdan*.[24] Oral adaptations of written Western literature were not presented as "faithful" translations, since the transposition from written text to oral performance obviated the assumption that the viewer would be observing something that was identical to the source text. Rather, the tales were usually reset in Japan, with protagonists renamed and reidentified as Japanese (in order to avoid unwieldy foreign proper nouns). These adaptations were very popular for several reasons. They appealed to the contemporary fashion for things Western by incorporating modish Western buzzwords and customs. The stories also, unlike Tokugawa–period tales that were required to be set in the past, often addressed contemporary issues and evoked the present-day world. This sense of currency made them very appealing, and Enchô in particular capitalized upon his audience's interest in adapted Western stories.

The First Printed Version of an Oral Adaptation:
George Smith, Dutiful English Son

The appearance and rapid popularization of the new oral *hon'anmono* circa 1880 can be attributed to several causes. Most obvious, of course, was its novelty; a growing number of Western artifacts made their way into everyday life in Meiji Japan, and the unfamiliarity of these items—Western cloth umbrellas, various types of clothing (top hats, pants, shoes, gowns), telescopes, woolen blankets, fountain pens, and more—created a popular interest in things Western that led, naturally, to audience interest in stories from the West as well. To the extent that the adapted stories maintained a degree of correspondence to the originals, *hon'an* oral narratives presented Western literature to a broad segment of the Japanese population in a form that required no knowledge of a Western language. The fact that they were performed in the *yose* also meant that they transcended the barrier of literacy, since, although an increasing number of translations and adaptations were appearing in print, mass literacy was far from a realized goal in the 1880s.

The first oral adaptation of a Western work to be transcribed (through *sokki*) and published was San'yûtei Enchô's version of Charles Reade's novel *Hard Cash*.[25] Enchô's adaptation, *Seiyô ninjôbanashi Eikoku kôshi Jôji Sumisu no den* (A Western Romance: The Tale of George Smith, Dutiful English Son), was published in 1885, the third of Enchô's *sokkibon*. A closer look at this enigmatic adaptation, including its means of transmission and comparison with the source text, reveals Enchô's keen awareness of his audience, his talent as a storyteller, and the degree to which the Japanese oral tradition in the Meiji period can serve as a mirror reflecting the concerns and issues of the times.

The first question we might ask in examining Enchô's earliest published *hon'anmono* is how, and in what form, he received his "original" text. In terms of how, there are several possibilities: Henry Black would seem to be a natural candidate, since Black was a *yose* performer and had access to English and literary texts. However, Enchô never mentions Black as the source for any of his *hon'anmono*. Rather, in his introduction to *Eikoku kôshi* Enchô describes his source, albeit rather elliptically: "As I am certain those who have read it will agree, my use of Japanese names in the tale, which was relayed to me (*kuchi-utsushi*) by a certain scholar of Western studies, makes it much less stuffy." His use of the term *scholar of Western studies* rather than *Westerner* nearly excludes Black as a candidate, since Enchô would certainly have used Black's ethnic origin for both its exotic and corroborative effects. Moreover, Black, an entertainer, would not have been considered a scholar, since entertainers inhabited a much lower class than scholars during the Meiji period.[26]

The fact that Enchô uses the term *gakusha* (scholar) narrows the possibilities to Japanese scholars who had a healthy command of English in the early 1880s. Although a number of Enchô's contemporaries may fit this description, the source provider would have run in the same circles as Enchô, reducing the possibilities even further. Nobuhiro Shinji, a scholar of the Japanese oral tradition, suggests that the most likely candidate was Fukuchi Ochi (1841–1906).[27] Fukuchi, who trained as a Tokugawa interpreter and later was a patron of the theater, had provided summaries for other Enchô adaptations, so he is very likely the intermediary. He traveled to the West four times between 1860 and 1872, became editor of the *Tokyo Nichi-nichi* newspaper in 1874 and held positions of influence in the stock exchange, local government, and the Tokyo Chamber of Commerce (in which capacity he spearheaded the "people's reception" held at Ueno Park for Ulysses S. Grant in 1879). He also served as a member of a theater improvement society, working to Westernize the stage, and helped build the Kabuki-za. Both his language skills and his interest in theater and writing strongly suggest that Fukuchi could have easily read and redacted the details of a lengthy Victorian novel such as *Hard Cash*.[28]

How the novel made it to the attention of Fukuchi is another question. Fukuchi may have picked up *Hard Cash* during one of his trips abroad, or perhaps he acquired it from someone living in the foreign quarter at Yokohama, or from one of the early diplomats. However, there is no question, from the detailed correspondence of Enchô's version, that his intermediary had access to the work in its entirety.

Assuming, then, that Fukuchi passed the summary to Enchô, we must consider the form his summary took. A comparison of the two texts reveals that a certain amount of detail must have been available to Enchô, since he carries some of the parallels to great lengths in ways that demonstrate a fairly clear awareness of the original textual elements.[29] In his introduction, Enchô specifically uses the term *kuchi-utsushi* (oral summary) to describe the form of his source. The fact that complex details from *Hard Cash* are preserved in *Eikoku kôshi* suggests that either Enchô was an extremely astute listener with a prodigious memory (not beyond the realm of possibility for a professional storyteller of his stature) or he had access to a detailed written summary of the story. Perhaps we shall never know, but for the purposes of our analysis we may surmise that Enchô did begin with a fairly detailed summary of *Hard Cash* as he worked his rhetorical magic to adapt the work into Japanese.

Source text: Charles Reade's Hard Cash

Let us now turn our attention to the source text of Enchô's *hon'anmono*, which itself remained a mystery for nearly a century.[30] Meiji adaptations and translations in general came from a corpus of Victorian novels by writers such as Edward Bulwer-Lytton, M. E. Braddon, and Sir Walter Scott, so Charles Reade's *Hard Cash* does not seem out of place by any means.

Charles Reade (1814–1884) was a Victorian writer of no little reputation. At the height of his career he was seen by his contemporaries as a literary giant; William Dean Howells and Henry James had both, as younger critics, included Reade among the likes of Dickens, Thackeray, and George Eliot.[31] An Oxford don, Reade started out writing drama, then expanded into novels in midlife, quickly making a name for himself through his prodigious use of newspaper clippings and excruciatingly detailed descriptions of arcana. He was the quintessential Victorian, filling the space of his novels to overflowing with a potpourri of information about locations, processes, and curios. This surfeit of miscellanea was delivered to the reader by means of sentimental, melodramatic plots bolstered by the Victorian "tendency to rejoice in one's own righteousness while condemning the wickedness of others."[32] George Orwell notes that the attraction of Charles Reade was "the charm of useless knowledge. Reade . . . possessed vast stocks of disconnected information which a lively narrative gift allowed him to cram into books."[33]

He is perhaps best known for his work *The Cloister and the Hearth* (1861), a historical novel based on the star-crossed fate of the parents of the scholar Erasmus (1469?–1536). Reade also wrote a number of plays and nearly two dozen novels and tales, among the latter of which *Christie Johnstone* (1853), *It Is Never Too Late To Mend* (1856), *Hard Cash* (1863), and *Griffith Gaunt* (1866) are seen as his best writing. Reade's novels primarily focus on either romance or social issues, the latter covering a wide spectrum of causes including standards of medical care, banking, labor disputes, mining and prison conditions, lunatic asylums, and clerical celibacy. He championed a great number of social causes, and his enthusiasm gave his novels a propagandistic flare approaching that of religious tracts, particularly in *It Is Never Too Late To Mend* and *Hard Cash.*

Reade's reputation and critical reception waned following his death, owing to changes in literary conventions as well as the rise of realism. At the apex of his career his novels' realistic detailing appeared revolutionary, but as realism matured his works, which were long on detail and short on plausibility, suffered in comparison. For example, Howells changed his early favorable opinion several decades later: "[Reade] was a man who stood at a parting of the ways between realism and romanticism, and if he had been somewhat more of a man he might have been the master of a great school of English realism; but, as it was, he remained content to use the materials of realism and produce the effect of romanticism."[34]

This tendency is everywhere apparent in *Hard Cash,* the source of Enchô's *hon'anmono.* Reade, purportedly in response to an article in *The Times* on private asylums, hunted far and wide for "materials of realism," gathering notes, consulting sources, and collecting anecdotes from former inmates, friends, and even family as he prepared his lengthy and melodramatic text.[35] As Reade states in the opening lines of his preface, "[*Hard Cash*] is a matter-of-fact romance; that is, a fiction built on truths; and these truths have been gathered by long, severe, systematic labor from a multitude of volumes, pamphlets, journals, reports, blue-books, manuscript narratives, letters, and living people, whom I have sought out, examined, and cross-examined, to get at the truth on each main topic I have striven to handle."

The plot of the novel divides into two threads, one a love story, the other a tale of theft and restitution. While the former keeps Reade (and his readers) squarely on familiar ground, the latter allows him to expose at great length the terrible conditions of Britain's contemporary private insane asylums, as well as the inequities of lunatic laws. For the sake of comparing *Hard Cash* with Enchô's adaptation, I present a brief summary of the story below.[36]

> Captain David Dodd survives storms, attacks by pirates on the China Sea, a shipwreck on the coast of France, and an ambush by desperate highwaymen to deliver his savings (£14,000 in "hard cash") safely home to his family in England. As soon as he steps ashore he entrusts his money to banker Richard Hardie, who, unbeknownst to Dodd, is on the verge of bankruptcy. He demands and receives a receipt, then heads off to be reunited with his family when he meets an old acquaintance who tells him of the bank's impending closure. Dodd returns to the bank and confronts Hardie and his clerk, Noah Skinner, but the two defer, reluctant to let go of potentially redeeming assets. The delay throws Dodd into an apoplectic rage; he collapses and, upon awakening, is found to be insane—thus leaving his loving family ignorant as to the money's whereabouts, and Richard Hardie in possession of the cash.
>
> In the meantime, however, Dodd's son Edward takes a liking to Jane Hardie (Richard Hardie's daughter), and Alfred Hardie (Richard Hardie's

son) has fallen in love with Julia, David Dodd's daughter. Alfred suspects his father's theft, and threatens to expose his father; whereupon Hardie, Sr., secretly arranges to have Alfred incarcerated in a private madhouse (something relatives could do under contemporary British lunacy laws), and, as a consequence of his mysterious disappearance (just before he is to be married) everyone but Julia comes to believe that he has deserted her to run off with some other woman.

Richard Hardie, his son safely incarcerated and his bank flush with Dodd's money, rebuilds his fortune, but under a cloud of doubt raised by his inability to locate and destroy Dodd's (mysteriously vanished) receipt. He is visited one day by Skinner, who, threatening to reveal Hardie's theft, blackmails the banker for £1,000, then disappears to London.

While Alfred Hardie is confined behind asylum walls, Edward Dodd (Julia's brother) becomes Julia's provider in the outside world. The Dodd family, increasingly impoverished, moves to a London flat and takes on odd jobs to survive. Edward casts aside all foolish notions of gentility to become a fireman—and in this capacity rescues his father and Alfred Hardie from the burning asylum in which they have been confined. Following their rescue both Alfred Hardie and David Dodd escape to the coast, where Dodd, still insane, ships as a common sailor.

Meanwhile Alfred returns to London, finds Julia, fights off thugs hired to recapture him, and, with the aid of an eccentric doctor, brings suit for illegal confinement. During this time he also completes his studies at Oxford, taking a first-class degree in time to rush back to London and into court, where, pitted against the best legal minds present, he will defend his sanity and his honor.

On the eve of the trial Skinner resurfaces and tries to blackmail Hardie, Sr., once again, and Hardie learns to his horror that Skinner is in possession of the receipt. Before Skinner and Hardie meet again to exchange cash for the receipt Skinner, touched by Julia Dodd's Christian charity to him in the past, wills his estate to her and, one cold evening, expires of carbon monoxide poisoning in his meager lodgings.

Captain Dodd, cured of madness by a coma induced at sea (while saving a drowning sailor), returns to England, claims the receipt when Skinner's smoke-mummified corpse is discovered, and his family is reunited. The verdict is in Alfred's favor; Alfred and Julia marry, and Hardie, Sr., through a fortuitous windfall on the stock market, returns the £14,000 and amasses another small fortune. However, he eventually goes insane worrying over the possibility of losing his wealth again, and finishes his days under the watchful care of his son and daughter-in-law.

Of all his novels, *Hard Cash* appeared to be Reade's favorite. He labored for years collecting notes on insane asylums and lunacy laws, and even publicly defended a man wrongfully accused of lunacy. Wayne Burns, one of Reade's biographers, suggests that one reason Reade found the topic so compelling was his own less-than-stable mental state, and accusations of eccentricity and madness that had haunted him from his school days.[37] Yet the novel contains much more than simply a call to arms against unfair policies; Reade also takes aim at contemporary doctors (who bleed patients at every opportunity and take kickbacks from private asylums for inmate referrals), lawyers (who hinder Alfred's attempts at self-vindication), and a host of smaller topics ranging from evangelical religionists to speculation fever.

Since its appearance *Hard Cash* has seen both praise and scorn. Swinburne, for example, praised both Reade's characterization of Captain Dodd (comparing it favorably with that of George Eliot's Caleb Garth) and his epic structure and purpose, remarking on Reade's genius that "if it should not live as long as the language, so much the worse for all students of the language who shall overlook so noble an example of its powers."[38] Orwell, on the other hand, sees in *Hard Cash* the epitome of the Victorian dream of wealthy idleness: "Alfred Hardie . . . is the typical [hero who] at the age of twenty-five . . . inherits a fortune, marries his Julia Dodd and settles down in the suburbs . . . in the same house as his parents-in-law . . . the Victorian happy ending—a vision of a huge, loving family . . . all crammed together in the same house and constantly multiplying, like a bed of oysters."[39] More recent critics see *Hard Cash* as a novel "better plotted, and written with more literary tact and skill" than his previous works, yet unremarkable.[40] Elton Smith also damns with faint praise: "For vigor, the book can have few rivals; but the total effect is marred by Reade's bad logic in assuming that, if an episode works well once, it works better twice or even thrice in the same volume."[41]

Despite its flaws, *Hard Cash* stands as a remarkable example of the thoroughness of Reade's narrative prolixity even as it serves to underscore the melodramatic style of Victorian fiction. Suspense is a prime narrative mover; we, as readers, are constantly kept on the verge of disaster or redemption as the plot shifts back and forth between its two threads of romance and restitution. It contains many typical conventions for Victorian fiction: sudden turns of fortune, emotional hyperbole, plenty of violence and blood, dramatic encounters, and sudden changes of heart.

Hard Cash is a novel that underscores several fundamental Victorian values as well: Besides Orwell's vision of domestic, bourgeois bliss, these also include faith in the scientific method (in matters material and medical), a fragile trust in the processes and systems that sustain fiscal and political stability, the resilience and power of true love, and an abiding belief that good will triumph over evil. These values are often tested by sudden shifts in the story's winding plot, and this in turn heightens the all-important element of suspense that is necessary to keep the reader going through over four hundred pages of encyclopedic detail. Yet by the end the reader has experienced a reaffirmation of the equity and merit of Victorian legal, fiscal, romantic, and moral systems: The innocent Alfred Hardie is vindicated, the £14,000 is restored to its rightful owners, Alfred and Julia are married, and the good David Dodd is cured of insanity while the evil Richard Hardie goes mad.

Thus, the end of the novel *Hard Cash* validates several Victorian notions of justice, although it is justice that has been a long time in coming. Reade's use of suspense, of having evil prevail and the good suffer throughout most of the novel, is also a convention of Victorian melodrama. And the novelty of delayed justice is one aspect of *Hard Cash* that Enchô found particularly attractive when he set about adapting Reade's novel as a Japanese oral story.

Hard Cash as Ninjôbanashi: Enchô's Eikoku kôshi

Enchô's adaptation of *Hard Cash,* entitled *Seiyô ninjôbanashi Eikoku kôshi Jôji Sumisu no den* (A Western Romance: The Tale of George Smith, Dutiful English Son), was performed originally as a serialized oral narrative of eight installments, and was first published as eight corresponding printed fascicles. I offer, for the sake of comparison, a summary of the tale, which takes place a few years after the Meiji Restoration.

> Shimizu Sukêmon, a former supplier of goods to the (now defunct) Maebashi daimyô, must find another market for his wares, so he mortgages his property for ¥3,000 and travels to Tokyo to procure an inventory of Western products. Knowing no one in the big city, he stops at an inn run by a former Maebashi samurai Harumi Jôsuke, who in like manner has been forced to find a new occupation. Unbeknownst to Shimizu, Harumi is nearly bankrupt and, at the moment of Shimizu's visit, is fending off his former underling, Ibumori Matasaku, who is pressing him to return money Harumi borrowed in the past.
>
> Shimizu, worried about carrying a large sum of cash in dangerously foreign Yokohama, offers to entrust his money to Harumi for safekeeping. Ibumori, fearing that the lack of servants and shabbiness of the inn might make Shimizu change his mind, plays the role of Harumi's "clerk" and issues

Shimizu a receipt on Harumi's behalf. Shimizu heads off to the public bath, while Harumi uses some of the money to pay off his debt to Ibumori and the two celebrate the influx of such a large amount of capital.

On the way to the bath Shimizu glances into a barbershop and notices an old friend, Bunkichi, working as a barber. When Bunkichi hears where Shimizu is staying, he warns him about Harumi's dubious reputation and Shimizu immediately heads back and demands his money from Harumi and Ibumori. Harumi defers, which makes Shimizu even more suspicious and upset. Finally Harumi turns to get the money from the storehouse, but realizes the money will return him to prosperity, so he grabs a heavy ruler and cracks open Shimizu's head. Ibumori, looking on, reaches out and surreptitiously pockets the receipt.

Harumi pays off Ibumori to dispose of the body in the provinces, then repays his other debts and begins to prosper once more. Shimizu's wife, hearing nothing from her husband, sends son Jûjirô to Tokyo, where he visits Harumi, who feigns ignorance of Shimizu's whereabouts. Jûjirô, after a fruitless search, returns to Maebashi.

Over the course of the following seven years Harumi's fortunes soar (even as he worries that Ibumori may have the damning receipt), while Shimizu's wife, son Jûjirô, and daughter Maki lose their property and Mrs. Shimizu contracts an eye ailment. Eventually they move into a row house in Tokyo and work at odd jobs to survive. Jûjirô, now a rickshaw man, still cannot make enough to provide for his mother and sister so, appealing to pre-Restoration ties, he asks Harumi for a job. Harumi rebuffs him (fearing that if the Shimizu family prospers his secret might out) but Harumi's daughter, Isa (who overheard the scuffle and murder seven years earlier and feels sorry for Jûjirô), gives him three yen to help relieve their poverty.

Moments after Jûjirô departs, Ibumori, now reduced through dissipation to selling noodles from a stand, suddenly reappears and blackmails Harumi for more money, threatening to reveal the murder. Harumi agrees to meet him with the cash a few nights later near a certain bridge.

Jûjirô returns home with three yen only to have debtors arrive demanding repayment in full. A calculating elderly neighbor, Tora, intervenes on their behalf, then pushes Maki, Jûjirô's sister, to become a mistress of her patron in return. Maki refuses, and Jûjirô's sick mother offers instead a solid gold Buddhist amulet as collateral. Tora takes the amulet and returns home, to be visited shortly thereafter by Edoya Seijirô, a solid, resourceful man and a roofer by trade. Seijirô confesses that he is fond of Maki; eventually Tora brings the two together (for a price) but returns the amulet to Maki. When Seijirô sees the amulet he recognizes the Shimizu family from a visit to Maebashi years before, gives them money to pay their debts, and agrees to help them out of their poverty.

On his way home from visiting the Shimizu family one night Seijirô stops near a bridge to repair his broken clog and overhears the conversation between Ibumori and Harumi. The latter, short on cash, promises to bring the balance to Ibumori's home a few days later, and Ibumori, piqued, reminds Harumi of his nefarious deeds. Seijirô hears enough to grow suspicious and follows the two home, learning that Ibumori lives only a few flats down from the Shimizu family.

Jûjirô, on one of his regular trips to a nearby temple to pray for his mother's recovery, is met by Harumi's daughter Isa, who confesses her love for him and, following the exotic Western custom, exchanges rings with him as a token of her affection. Jûjirô also has feelings for Isa, but keeps them secret from his family.

On the night Harumi visits Ibumori with the money, Seijirô hides in the vacant flat next door and, through a crack in the plaster wall, watches as Harumi sends Ibumori out for saké, unsuccessfully searches the flat for the receipt, gets Ibumori drunk, strangles him and then lights the flat on fire in order to destroy the evidence and any possibility of a well-hidden receipt. Seijirô rushes next door, salvages the receipt (he saw Ibumori hide it before Harumi arrived), and extinguishes the fire before it engulfs the neighboring flats.

A few days later Isa meets Jûjirô once again, and Jûjirô gives back the ring, saying they can only marry when his status in the world has risen to her level. She promises to remain true despite his deferral, but, heartsick, grows ill, causing Harumi great concern. As he is worrying about her, he receives a visit from Seijirô and Jûjirô. Seijirô produces the receipt and Harumi, wishing to keep it quiet, agrees to pay back the ¥3,000.

Seijirô then asks Harumi to return the remains of Sukêmon. Harumi, realizing that the murder has been found out, invites Seijirô and Jûjirô to the storehouse where he will explain everything. The two follow the former samurai warily, then watch in shock as Harumi plunges his short sword into his abdomen, apologizing for his crimes by committing ritual suicide. As he is dying, Harumi confesses to the murder and reveals that Isa is not his real daughter but the illegitimate daughter of his former lord. Feeling an obligation to marry her off well, he had sought to amass a fortune that would elevate her status, and that aim had led to Shimizu's murder.

Harumi then admits his own wish that his fortune go to Jûjirô, who should then, as a wealthy man, marry Isa. Harumi writes a fake loan agreement to facilitate the posthumous transfer of assets, oversees the betrothal of

Isa to Jûjirô (with wine substituting for saké), and expires. The loan agreement satisfies the investigating authorities, the estate is transferred, Jûjirô marries Isa, Seijirô marries Maki, Mrs. Shimizu's eyesight is restored, and all live near one another happily ever after.

As we can see from the summary, *Eikoku kôshi* is a curious, amalgamated tale filled with star-crossed lovers, shifting fortunes, colorful characters, and exotic Western customs (an exchange of rings, wine). Like *Hard Cash,* it is both a romance and a story of restitution, the latter combining a traditional samurai vendetta motif with a more "civilized" concern for bureaucratic propriety.[42]

Throughout *Eikoku kôshi* Enchô continually reminds his audience that his story is, at heart, a Western tale. He makes it clear at the very beginning that the work is not a translation but rather an adaptation:

The story I shall relate is a Western romance (*ninjôbanashi*) called "The Tale of George Smith, Dutiful English Son," and will be told in successive installments. Since it is impossible for me to render one of these foreign stories as is, and also difficult for my esteemed audience to understand in its original form, I'll substitute Japanese place and character names as I tell the story. The English city of Liverpool is located about three hours' return journey from London;[43] it is a very prosperous port like Yokohama, and quite similar to the Tokyo neighborhoods of Reiganjima and Teppôzu, where my story will take place. Smile Smith was captain of a steam ship over there; in this story I will recast him as Shimizu Sukêmon, a former government supplier living in the Tatsumachi area of Maebashi. His son George Smith becomes Shimizu Jûjirô, and George's older sister Marie I will call Maki. Edward Seville, the resourceful hero, is Edoya Seijirô, the master roofer who saves the day in my story. In addition, John Hamilton (in that country's tongue) and his associate Nathan Bull murder Smile Smith and steal his enormous fortune.[44] Nathan Bull is now Ibumori Matasaku, and John Hamilton is Harumi Jôsuke, a former high-ranking samurai from Maebashi.[45] These local adaptations are the only changes I have made to the story. As I am certain those who have read it will agree, my use of Japanese names in the tale, which was relayed to me (kuchi-utsushi) by a certain scholar of Western studies, makes it much less stuffy. With that in mind, I will now begin.

After the fall of the Tokugawa house, around the fourth or fifth year of Meiji,[46] many new inns, including a number of very large establishments, appeared in the neighborhoods of outer Kanda, around Matsuei-chô and Sakuma-chô. One of these, the Harumiya, was founded by Harumi Jôsuke.

Its façade was broad and tall, and it also had an inner storehouse and many servants. Jôsuke led a very sumptuous existence. He had only one daughter, whose name was Isa; in England, her name was Eliza, you see. (479–80)[47]

As the opening lines demonstrate, Enchô made it explicitly clear to his audience that his tale was Western in origin and Japanese in execution. Several aspects of his introduction (his assertion that "local adaptations" are the only changes he has made, for example) are intended to reassure his audience that they are, indeed, listening to a foreign tale. In point of fact, even as there is close correspondence in some areas of Enchô's adaptation, there are also some significant differences, two of which emerge during the introduction: Enchô has devised new names for Reade's characters, and his Captain Dodd equivalent suffers no apoplectic fit leading to insanity, but rather is murdered in cold blood. In his groundbreaking article on *Eikoku kôshi,* Nobuhiro Shinji not only identifies the source of the adaptation but also points out these two differences and elaborates on their significance.[48]

The first difference Nobuhiro notes is the fact that the intricate oral dramatis personae Enchô uses to open his adaptation contains a curious double-transformation. Note how Enchô took the liberty to modify or change the original English names in *Hard Cash,* then altered the new English names to make similar-sounding Japanese names[49]:

Hard Cash	New name	Eikoku kôshi
David Dodd	Smile Smith	Sukêmon Shimizu[50]
Alfred Hardie	George Smith	Jûjirô Shimizu
Richard Hardie	John Hamilton	Jôsuke Harumi
Edward Dodd	Edward Seville	Edoya Seijirô
Jane Hardie	Eliza	Isa
Julia Dodd	Mary	Maki

Why did Enchô take such pains? Nobuhiro speculates that first, Enchô selected new names that could be easily mirrored in Japanese (*Edward Seville* becomes *Edoya Seijirô*) and second, that Enchô was attempting to conceal his source text.[51] As far as the first reason is concerned, we can speculate that, considering the exoticism of Western names in 1880s Japan, Enchô felt that one way to make his tale "less stuffy" than the original was to target foreign names that were familiar to his audience. Samuel Smiles' *Self Help* (Japanese translation 1871), John Stuart Mill's *On Liberty* (Japanese translation 1872), and Adam Smith's *Wealth of Nations* (Japanese translation 1885) were among the first English-language books translated into

Japanese, and the concepts contained in these tomes made their own significant contribution to the Japan of the late nineteenth century.[52] Enchô's rendering of David Dodd into the equally alliterative Smile Smith may be seen as an attempt to give his audience English names they were familiar with.[53] This underscores Enchô's perspective on adaptation: Although he sought correspondence, he was not striving for onomastic verisimilitude as much as names his audience were familiar with and would remember as foreign counterparts.

As for the second reason for Enchô's double transformation—that he was trying to hide his source—Nobuhiro suggests that in the contemporary Japanese oral tradition storytellers were particularly careful to disguise their *hon'anmono* sources, especially in the printed *sokkibon* versions.[54] He speculates that this was both to diminish the possibilities of plagiarism and to avoid the appearance of competition with Henry Black, whose signature style included retelling Western novels in Japanese without a great deal of adaptation.[55]

Another major difference between Reade's source and Enchô's adaptation that is obvious from the introduction is Harumi's murder of Shimizu. In Reade's story Dodd returns to the bank, produces the receipt, and demands his money back. His rage over the delay, combined with his exhaustion and unhealed wounds from traveling home, suddenly render him senseless and he falls to the floor, with Hardie and Skinner standing helplessly by until their greed overcomes their scruples.

In Enchô's revision Shimizu is also piqued by Harumi's delay in returning his money, but Enchô plays out the interaction in a very different manner. First Shimizu uses honorific language as he addresses Harumi (mirroring the pre-Meiji class distinction that put samurai above merchants). As Harumi continues to put Shimizu off, however, and patronizingly suggests that he only use small amounts of the deposited money as necessary, Enchô reveals Shimizu's interior thoughts ("It's just as Bunkichi said—there's something fishy about a huge inn without a single servant." [491]), which are very direct and filled with indignation. As Harumi continues to defer, Shimizu's language changes: He begins using the more immediate Maebashi dialect, and his tone changes from deference to anxious pleading. Finally, as Harumi turns to retrieve the money from the storehouse, Shimizu, fearing he is trying to escape, grabs hold of Harumi's sleeve and begs him to return the cash, then adds "If I do well in my business I promise to give you three-hundred yen, just like old times" (493).

This allusion to the pre-Meiji world, where Shimizu was a government supplier and Harumi a kickback-receiving samurai, underscores Enchô's clever use of the complex dichotomy between Tokugawa and Meiji social systems that was part of his audience's experience. And, in fact as in fiction, people in dire straits would often revert to pre-Meiji modes of interaction. Harumi, no longer a samurai, nevertheless reacts as one when he feels a subordinate insolently grabbing his sleeve and interfering with his progress: He reaches out for a sword-like wooden rod and dispatches Shimizu with one bloody blow.

Regarding this more violent difference, Nobuhiro notes that in Meiji Japan treatment of the mentally ill was still not a major social issue (although a contemporary scandal involving insanity may have led Fukuchi to Reade in the first place).[56] Instead, a more pressing issue was the shift from a system of retributive justice embodied in the samurai code to one of statutory justice. Nobuhiro focuses on the role of the receipt in *Eikoku kôshi* and sees in it the key to understanding some of Enchô's motivations for the shift from madness to murder.

Madness plays an important narrative role in *Hard Cash:* Insanity appears to be a threat to everyone in the Victorian tale. Julia nearly goes mad when she is left standing at the altar; Alfred fears he will lose his mind while unjustly incarcerated in an asylum. Dodd loses (then regains) his sanity, Hardie eventually goes mad worrying about his fortune, and a host of other minor characters all slip from their secure social positions once their reputation is tarnished by the suspicion of madness. In a society caught up in the worship of rational argument, Darwinism, and the miracles of science-backed medical discoveries, insanity stands as a barbaric infidel at the gate, to be feared and avoided at all costs.

Madness may also be seen as the hand of God, meting out punishment to those who become obsessed with the "hard cash" of the title. Yet within *Hard Cash* there is little difference between the madness brought on by preoccupation with lucre and by fixation on a lover, and the similarity suggests the Victorian obsession with control of passion as well as property. Reade's novel is successful, if in no other way, in touching a raw nerve, revealing in his screed against lunacy laws a deeper insecurity that permeates a society obsessed with order and control. Sanity represents order and responsibility; the loss of sanity introduces a dangerous element of chaos into society, hence the justification for isolating the insane in asylums.

There are, however, neither lunatics nor asylums in *Eikoku kôshi*.[57] Enchô has replaced these, in a nearly correspondent manner, with theft and murder, particularly of the violent type, social problems that threatened the order of a society now acutely conscious of the need for "civilization" and political stability based on law.

This disorder was doubly malignant when initiated by disgruntled ex-samurai (exemplified by Harumi) whose government stipends had recently been commuted and who were struggling to redefine their position in the new society.[58] The often arbitrary outbursts by disenfranchised samurai had led to open rebellions during the 1870s, and fear of the more belligerent samurai was universal at the grassroots level. Enchô, ever sensitive to his audience's concerns and fears, eschewed the theme of lunacy in *Hard Cash,* substituting instead violent murders to underscore the potential for disorder lurking in contemporary Japanese society. In an indirect way, however, Enchô uses insanity to underscore his point. First, *greed* led to Harumi's temporary "insanity" and its consequent unleashing of traditional samurai arbitrary violence. Also, at the end of the tale, *insecurity* over his ability to pay back the debt serves as Harumi's pretext for the (insane) act of *seppuku.*

Nobuhiro speculates that, had Enchô adapted *Hard Cash* before the Meiji Restoration, he would most likely have transformed it into a tale of vengeance, a ghost story, or both.[59] A major genre of oral story still popular at the beginning of the Meiji period was the *adauchi,* or vendetta. Enchô could very easily have reworked the theme of *Hard Cash* into an *adauchi* tale, complete with ghosts, as follows: Shimizu is murdered, and the receipt burned with his body. Years later, Shimizu's ghost comes back to haunt Harumi and Ibumori, eventually terrorizing one or both into making a confession to the Shimizu family, whose son Jûjirô would then avenge his father's death by executing the two scoundrels. In fact, Enchô's audiences (like all good storytelling audiences) would likely have anticipated this type of an ending as soon as Enchô described Shimizu's murder, if they had not already guessed such an outcome based upon the title of the work ("dutiful son" suggests avenging a father's death). Enchô, who was renowned for his ghost stories, was fully capable of turning the murder-revenge motif of *Hard Cash* into a chilling ghost story of haunting and vengeance, but instead makes the significant choice to leave the ghosts out of the story and substitute, instead, a flimsy paper receipt as the vehicle of justice.

Nobuhiro sees this step as marking a swing away from the traditional Edo world of custom and family vis-à-vis criminal justice, and towards the modern Meiji world of statutory justice.[60] *Eikoku kôshi* contains no revenge initiated by family members out of a sense of loyalty; rather, the familial prerogative for vengeance is minimized: It is Seijirô—who is unrelated to the Shimizu family—not Jûjirô who risks life and limb to save the receipt and who ultimately confronts Harumi. Shimizu's ghost is strangely silent for seven long years, yet justice triumphs nonetheless through the vehicle of documentary evidence to convict the guilty and redeem the innocent.

Enchô's focus on the receipt can be seen, then, as a revolutionary departure in terms of his own style of storytelling as well as in its emphasis on the power of documents in protecting property rights. By altering the theme of lunacy and focusing instead on murder Enchô was adapting his tale to fit his audience's concerns; in shifting the emphasis away from vendetta and onto the receipt he was educating them about the statutory legal system that was simultaneously being created under counsel from Western legal experts.

Enchô educates his audience about other innovations of Meiji modernization as well. For example, when Seijirô confronts Harumi with the receipt and demands repayment on behalf of the Shimizu family, and Harumi agrees, Seijirô amends his demand: "Now, sir, it wouldn't do to return the money without paying interest, would it? Why, a man like you with money in the bank and shares of stock certainly knows something about loans and deposits. So much money borrowed for seven years . . . even at a minimal seven percent, that would yield ¥1,470. Please add the interest as well" (579).

Many in Enchô's audiences were newcomers to Tokyo seeking their fortunes, or at least a better life, in the opportunities urban growth presented. Seijirô's demand for the extra money, complete with calculations, suggests that Enchô recognized his audience's "interest" in the topic of investment and building wealth.[61] A similarly practical aside comes earlier in the tale, when Harumi encourages Ibumori to be frugal. The noodle vendor then goes into a very detailed description of how he procures the ingredients for his noodles at a discount, where he buys his pots secondhand, how he waters things down to save money, and even describes how he saved on hiring a calligrapher by making his sign himself. Enchô not only uses his stereotype of the parsimonious vendor to comic effect, but gives his audience advice on where in Tokyo things can be purchased cheaply.[62]

Difference and Correspondence

In commenting on Enchô's *hon'anmono* Japanese scholars Koike Shôtarô and Fujii Shûtetsu have noted that "Enchô's adaptations are not simply equivalent Japanese editions of Western literary works; they possess the special quality of being particularly Enchôesque elaborations on sections of the original story that caught his fancy and upon which he focused his creative energies. In this respect, there is no question that Enchô's Western stories pioneered theretofore nonexistent literary paths."[63]

The notion that Enchô chose key sections of the original and elaborated thereon certainly holds true in his rendition of *Hard Cash.* The Japanese adapted version is roughly one-tenth the size of the English original, so assuming Enchô only had access to a summary of *Hard Cash,* the length of *Eikoku kôshi,* his expansions included, seems to fit the pattern described above, and suggests again that the summary he received from Fukuchi, although detailed, would have been relatively brief.[64]

The differences between *Hard Cash* and *Eikoku kôshi* are many, of course, but revealing. The resourceful hero, for example, is Dodd's son in *Hard Cash,* but Enchô takes pains to see that Shimizu's son Jûjirô is a dutiful, suffering victim who tries his best but is *not* the hero. That honor is reserved for Seijirô, a relative stranger who saves the day and *then* is "given" Maki as his wife in order to strengthen his bonds with the family.[65] The circumstance under which the two meet (a virtue-thwarted act of prostitution facilitated by Tora) varies considerably from the chaste Bible discussions in *Hard Cash* that bring Edward and Jane (Hardie's ill-fated daughter) together before her tragic death. Enchô's introduction of the theme of prostitution—underscoring the desperation of Tokyo's poor who are forced to sell themselves to survive—signals a difference between how openly Victorian and Meiji authors chose to treat such issues. Other narrative differences likewise reveal social, cultural, and ideological disparities, but it is where the works correspond that we see the genius of Enchô's transposition.

In comparing the two stories one can see, despite the license Enchô exercised in resetting his adaptation in Japan, certain clusters of correspondence that indicate which elements of the original story Enchô's "creative energies" found particularly alluring. These clusters of correspondence between the two include: (a) the protagonist entrusting a huge amount of money to a near-bankrupt acquaintance; (b) his subsequent incapacitation upon learning of the danger; (c) a family thrown into dire circumstances as a result; (d) a blackmailing henchman; (e) offspring of thief and victim falling in love (and their eventual marriage as a form of restitution); (f) a fire as a central plot device; (g) the death of the henchman leading to the implication of the thief; and, most importantly, (h) a receipt as the narrative vehicle of (suspensefully delayed) justice.

Skinner and Ibumori

Two of these clusters stand out in ways that underscore Enchô's masterful appropriation of Reade's original: the role of the henchmen and a receipt as the catalyst for justice. The striking parallels between the two henchmen—Noah Skinner and Ibumori Matasaku—bear fruitful comparison. Both emerge in their respective narratives as idiosyncratic flunkeys duty bound to the main antagonist. Skinner's father served Hardie's bank, and though he resents his treatment and position he (like Dickens' Bob Cratchit) is loyal nonetheless. But he notes Hardie's plunge into dishonesty and decides to use it to his own advantage even before Dodd's £14,000 enters into the equation. Ibumori is likewise bound to Harumi in an inferior position (from their samurai past), but, like Skinner, has gained some leverage through Harumi's indebtedness to him (and is about to use that power just as Shimizu arrives with his ¥3,000). Their oppression makes them more complex characters, and both authors have portrayed them in ways that elicit the reader's sympathy.

In *Hard Cash*, Skinner's initial dissipation results in his impoverishment, a condition that eventually leads to his discovery of Christian charity through Dodd's daughter Julia, who works with the destitute in the slums of London. His heart softened, Skinner wills the receipt and his property to Julia when he learns her true identity. Ibumori, likewise, first makes a descent into crime (to destroy evidence he kills the rickshaw man hired to transport Shimizu's body) and then dissipation. Later, desperately poor, he joins the host of new Tokyo immigrants peddling his wares on the street. Unlike Skinner, however, Ibumori does not discover redemption through religion, although karmic retribution does bring about his grisly demise. In both stories the henchman's death involves smoke and fire (Skinner plugs up the air inlets to his small flat and, hungry and drowsy, lights a foot warmer that burns up the remaining oxygen; Harumi douses Ibumori's body in kerosene and throws a lamp on him), and in both cases their deaths propel the receipt into the proper hands.

As blackmailers, both turn up at strategic moments and move the respective narratives forward by agitating the antagonists and suggesting to the reader that evil will not always triumph. Like ghosts, Skinner and Ibumori haunt their former superiors and add suspense to the stories; we are aware of their presence but are oblivious as to their whereabouts. They remain offstage, but we remember them well and are curious as to when they will make another entrance.

The clear and detailed correspondences between Skinner and Ibumori reveal that Enchô recognized an effective narrative foil in the figure of Noah Skinner. The fact that there are so many parallels between the two henchmen, and that Ibumori is used to effect similar ends in *Eikoku kôshi,* suggests that Enchô's source text was detailed enough to allow him to craft an effective elaboration on Reade's oppressed blackmailer.

The Receipt and Bureaucratic Protocol

We have already seen how the receipt functioned in *Eikoku kôshi* as a symbol of statutory justice. In Reade, as well, the absence of the receipt makes justice impossible, owing to the scheming and intervention of shrewd but evil men and women. It is only when the receipt emerges that claims for restitution—which have been made, but without the proof so necessary in Reade's contemporary legal system—can be validated by the ruling authorities. There is a clear correspondence of function for the receipt in both stories; Enchô's tale, however, evades the need for the receipt to be certified and processed by the legal system (Harumi simply hands over the money once he is shown the document). This underscores two important aspects of contemporary Japan. First, there was still a great residual regard for reputation and word of honor. Harumi, despite his being a thief and a murderer, was also a former samurai, and Seijirô can (and does) appeal to that ethic without undue concern over Harumi's refusal to comply: "You used to carry two swords, sir, and even though we're 'civilized' now, a samurai is always a samurai. Think of how your great name would be tarnished if you keep insisting you never received the money" (577).

Seijirô's appeal, then, is not to the courts but rather to Harumi's sense of honor. And, at the end of *Hard Cash,* the restoration of Hardie's fortune— if not some of his former reputation—just before he goes mad is mirrored in *Eikoku kôshi's* ending, where Harumi's samurai heritage finally holds sway over the greed and selfishness that have characterized him throughout the story. Seijirô's appeal to Harumi's nobler motives leads the latter to go decisively to the storehouse, where he changes into formal crested clothing and performs the atoning ritual suicide (*seppuku*) that will expurgate his evil deeds. This behavior is not what the audience nor Seijirô expect (Enchô notes that the latter takes a small pot of coals into the storehouse, hidden behind his back, as a possible defense in case Harumi tries to cut him down; audiences would have taken Enchô's detail as foreshadowing that just such a thing was about to happen), and the surprise underscores Harumi's sudden change of heart.

As Harumi undergoes a protracted, painful death, he ties together sev-

SEPPUKU SCENE IN FINAL INSTALLMENT OF *EIKOKU KÔSHI NO DEN*
(COURTESY OF DÔSHISHA DAIGAKU GAKUJUTSU JÔHÔ SENTÂ).

eral loose narrative ends: First, he atones for the murder of Shimizu before
his victim's son's eyes; second, he reveals that Isa is *not* his daughter, so Jûjirô
need not be reluctant to marry her; and third, he deeds all his property to
Jûjirô, as an apology for murdering Shimizu and also as a way to ensure that
Isa, daughter of his former lord, retains her wealth and status.[66] Insisting
that the betrothal ceremony take place immediately, he ensures the marriage, but deeding his property, particularly in the early Meiji period, is not
so easily vouchsafed. Enchô uses this occasion to teach his audience about
the importance of bureaucratic protocol.

> SEIJIRÔ: But how can Jûjirô inherit your property?
> JÛJIRÔ: And won't there be complications getting authorization for the
> inheritance, since you are dying an unnatural death?[67]
> HARUMI: You need not worry about that. You can avoid all difficulties if you
> simply file a report stating that seven years ago your father, feeling sorry for
> me, lent me ¥100,000, due this year. The deed of lending includes a clause
> stating that, should I ask for an extension of the deadline, all my real prop-

erty, including my daughter, would go to you. Report that your imminent claim drove me insane and I committed *seppuku*; that should forestall any complications. (588–89)

Harumi takes an ink stone, rubs ink (made, in the best melodramatic tradition, with Isa's tears), and writes the deed of lending. He then attaches the proper stamp and affixes his seal. All of these actions, in particular the creation of a false deed of lending, were necessary not only for the happy ending to follow but also in light of contemporary regulations regarding inheritance, death, and document notarization.[68] Enchô's earlier reliance upon the receipt as a narrative fulcrum prepared his audience for the dramatically unusual ending of *Eikoku kôshi* as well as for the realities of a world increasingly filled with statutory regulations. In essence, Enchô emphasizes the use of documents, loopholes, and bureaucratic propriety in his text to heighten the sense of relief that comes when proper attention to bureaucratic detail precludes potential tragedy.

Lobbying the Masses: Oral Literature and Adaptation

Unlike literal translation, adaptation allows for selective appropriation with particular ends in mind. Enchô, for example, eschews the compulsion to create a story that equals Reade's in length (even legendary storytellers had limits to their stamina), and avoids the theme of lunatic asylums that Reade found so compelling. Yet he chooses to make close correspondence between Skinner and Ibumori, and highlights the role of the receipt. These correspondences reveal Enchô's keen sensitivity to his audience; professional Japanese storytellers were very aware of their audiences, in particular their attitudes and backgrounds, likes and dislikes. The nature of live performance put them in tune as well with subtle changes that took place, say, when a new law came into being or when some current event made the rounds of gossip.[69] To this extent, they were not dissimilar to their Victorian author contemporaries, who also, through close ties with the news media and a widely targeted readership, kept abreast of the latest trends and social issues.

When, in 1885, *Eikoku kôshi* was transcribed and published, it grew even closer in form to its Victorian counterpart and broke new ground as one of the earliest examples of contemporary mass *written* literature. Considering, then, that Reade's primary narrative purpose was propagandist in nature, we may speculate that something about that purpose also made its way into Enchô's adaptation. Whether this was purely circumstantial or intended is beyond knowing without access to Enchô's source summary, but we can infer that Enchô's skill as a highly regarded veteran storyteller may have helped him see the propaganda value of *Hard Cash*.[70]

Meiji storytellers were not unfamiliar with the influence their positions gave them over their audiences. Throughout the early nineteenth century the Tokugawa shogunate had made regular attempts to censor storytellers, since their performances were much harder to police than printed texts and left no evidence. During the early Meiji years storytellers were designated as "moral instructors" of the people in a governmental attempt to coopt (and thus disarm) their potential for inciting the masses. Enchô, then, was certainly aware of the power he held to lobby his audience, and it is clear that in *Eikoku kôshi* he was both educating them about the new Meiji world and promoting a number of social, ideological, and literary innovations.

In considering *Eikoku kôshi* from a comparative perspective we might speculate that Enchô, recognizing Reade's propagandistic intent, saw ways in which that same intent might be used within a Meiji context. It was certainly not useful in the sphere of asylum reform, but could be used to rally the cry for modern forms of justice, embodied in legal measures abolishing the ambiguous, often overreactive customary revenge prerogative that marked ex-samurai discontent, replacing it with a system grounded in statutes and procedures.

Enchô's oral delivery made him accessible to a much wider audience, and his colloquial narrative style made his message even more immediate. The effect of his adaptation is difficult to gauge accurately, but a comparison between Reade's original and Enchô's version underscores the fact that both authors were targeting a sweeping audience with issues that addressed far-reaching concerns. They are both obscured by the century that has passed; yet a reevaluation of the similarities and differences of a work they have shared in common reveals two masters of narrative skill seeking to promote reform among the widest possible audience. Reade sought to highlight the dismal conditions of asylums and the injustice of lunacy laws in Victorian Britain. Enchô opted to give his version a similar social function, but altered the plot in a way that changed madness into murder, then substituted a simple paper receipt for the ghosts hovering on his audience's horizon of expectations. A new legal system was in the making, and Enchô used his rhetorical talents to simultaneously retell a Western story and promote legal reform along statutory lines.

But Enchô was preparing his audience for more reforms as well. As we have seen, he inserts comments and scenes that teach them about investment in banks and stocks, suggests alternative, "modern" ways to channel vengeance instincts, and offers suggestions about negotiating the general upheavals of early Meiji social and economic transformations. In the literary realm, Enchô's adaptation proves the efficacy of using a contemporary setting, experiments with new archetypes and structures, and, perhaps most significantly, provides an alternative to the moribund *kanzen chôaku* (reward virtue and punish vice) didacticism that had dominated Tokugawa literary narrative.[71]

In the beginning of the final two sections of *Eikoku kôshi* Enchô addresses his audience directly (a typical storytelling device used to summarize what has happened to date and whet the audience's appetite for the next installment). However, he waxes somewhat philosophical in these particular cases, moralizing about how this "Confucian" story resembles that of a Western tale. At the beginning of section seven, for example, he opens as follows: "The plot of this Western *ninjôbanashi* is very complex; though the antagonist tries to burn up the proof-containing receipt, precisely because of that attempt the important receipt comes to light" (570).

Here we see Enchô helping his audience come to grips with the irony found in his adaptation. In a similar manner, at the beginning of section eight Enchô offers more assistance to his audience.

> My serialized Western ninjôbanashi ends with this installment, in which I omit the tedious parts and the virtuous prevail, the evil are destroyed, tender lovers marry and a lost fortune is restored. These are, of course, didactic (*kanzen chôaku*) contrivances, found as well in the theater and in popular fiction (*kusazôshi*). Normally, in the theater and such, one can soon figure everything out: Some treasure goes missing in the morning, is searched for all day long, and by evening, without fail, all is restored and everyone rejoices. The audience departs with peace of mind.
>
> But applied to this very different type of tale, where there is neither scenery nor actors, the term *kanzen chôaku* seems a bit strange, since the good people suffer throughout and the evil are safe all the way to the end; no peace of mind in that! (580–81)

In his narrative aside Enchô builds up his audience's expectations for the finale even as he reveals to us a typical audience reaction to *Eikoku kôshi*. Apparently the suspense that prevails in his adaptation of *Hard Cash* challenges his audience's patience as well as their expectations for a quick and definitive triumph of good over evil. The didactic propensity that had dominated literature and drama for the past century contributed in part to the relative stagnation of both at the end of the Tokugawa period, and there is little doubt that the forestalled justice of *Eikoku kôshi* was one of its most refreshingly challenging aspects.

In this light, Enchô's statement "no peace of mind in that!" turns the Confucian didactic structure on its head by underscoring the excitement his audiences must have felt listening to such an unpredictable tale. Enchô's aside not only helps his audience make sense of their thwarted expectations conditioned by previous *kanzen chôaku* works, but also suggests to them a new narrative structure, even a new morality, that could be borrowed from the West.

The printed version of *Eikoku kôshi* actually has three titles. The first— *Eikoku kôshi Jôji Sumisu no den*—is on the cover, with the superscription *Seiyô ninjôbanashi* (A Western Romance) clearly added to attract potential readers with its double promise of Western exotica and a love story. The second, at the end of the work, drops the superscription but maintains the name *Jôji Sumisu* (George Smith), again an appeal to exoticism. The third, used within the text, drops the name and reads simply *Eikoku kôshi no den* (Story of a Dutiful English Son). This common denominator—*Eikoku kôshi* (dutiful English son)—blends exoticism (*Eikoku,* 'England') and tradition (*kôshi,* 'dutiful son'), the latter phrase carrying strong Confucian overtones which might suggest to the new reader that the tale will demonstrate Confucian virtues at the global level.[72]

However, it is curious to note that the "dutiful son" of Enchô's tale, Jûjirô, is not the obedient son overflowing with filial piety who avenges his father's death. True, he searches for his father, cares for his mother, and takes on the menial job of rickshaw man to support his family, but the prime mover in this tale of restitution is the roofer Seijirô.[73] Seijirô's resourcefulness, pluck, and courage save the day. Enchô gives his audience a clue, in the form of an appended moral, about how to read the Confucianism in his tale: "And they lived in continual prosperity from then on, all because Jûjirô the son possessed the virtue of filial piety, which caused Heaven (*Ten*) to lead a chivalrous soul like Seijirô to him, and in the end evil men were punished and good men prospered" (590).

While Jûjirô may not fit the self-sufficient hero archetype common in Meiji success stories, Enchô's use of the term chivalrous (*giki aru*) to describe Seijirô suggests overtones of the "knight errant" who comes to the Confucian gentleman-hero's assistance in the Chinese narrative tradition.[74] To some extent, then, even though the "son" in *Eikoku kôshi* does not effect the tale's denouement, his Confucian virtue of filial piety earns him the reward of Heaven: a knight errant whose talents finally bring about justice.

The ending of Enchô's *hon'anmono* contains one final correspondence with Reade's *Hard Cash,* what biographer Elton Smith calls "the essence of sensational melodrama."

> All the spate of facts . . . had to be fitted into a very simple ethical pattern. Good had to triumph: evil had to be defeated. . . . The essence of the sensational melodrama . . . always resided in the same situation: evil may appear to triumph and good to fail, but one need not fear. Although the plot winds its convoluted way and turns back upon itself, at the moment when all hope is lost, the kaleidoscope is shaken by a Celestial Hand, and all the pieces fall at last into their rightful places and relationships.[75]

Smith's use of the term "Celestial Hand" underscores the Judeo-Christian, messianic structure of Victorian melodrama: Good will triumph in the end, despite evil's current success. Enchô's adaptation of Reade also contains a "Celestial Hand" that shakes the pieces into their rightful place, but it is the Heaven (*Ten*) of Confucianism rather than that of Christianity that intervenes.

Enchô does not translate the messianic hope for salvation in his adaptation of *Hard Cash,* but preserves the suspenseful tension nonetheless. The fact that justice has been postponed until the very last moment, and that, until the final installment, his readers' expectations for a typical ending have been thwarted, demonstrates not only Enchô's skill as a raconteur but also the effectiveness of his adaptation of the Victorian novelistic technique of sensational melodrama for an audience whose expectations for a moral were conditioned by Confucian ideology.

Western fiction represented a new mother lode of stories for Meiji raconteurs, a vein they did not hesitate to mine, and Enchô overtly suggests that the morality of Western literature was of a different order from that which had been championed during the Edo period. He cites the plot difference (evil goes unpunished until the end) to suggest a new, "enlightened" *kanzen chôaku* worthy of a more civilized Japan. But in a way Enchô is also prophesying the end of *kanzen chôaku:* His use of contemporary settings and his elaborations on practical matters foreshadow the decline of didacticism and the emergence of realistic literature over the next two decades.[76]

In like manner, Enchô's *hon'anmono* also foreshadows the sweeping changes that will continue to take place in the Meiji social, economic, and political worlds. Harumi, the ex-samurai who profits from theft and murder, is nevertheless more than just the stereotypical villain; by the end of

Enchô's tale he is even somewhat redeemed by his generosity, his penance, his *seppuku,* and his heroic efforts to make restitution, including the bureaucrat-satisfying deed written with his last ounces of strength. In the new Meiji society, which can itself be seen as an adaptation of the West, documents and bureaucrats replace swords and samurai, and storytelling will never be the same again.

Chapter IV ∾

A Visible Poetics:
American Dime Novel as
Paradigm for Theater Reform

*On the Japanese stage of today historical plays (jidaimono) retain
nothing of their former glory, and the newer domestic dramas (sewamono) are even more insipid; perhaps the style of this translation may
serve to edify and inspire those who would seek to reform our native
drama.*

— Tsubouchi Shôyô, *Preface to Futagokoro*, 1896[1]

*The drama is almost an impossibility for the artist, just now. But let
him go on writing. If he be a real dramatic artist he must. . . . The
novelists are having it all their own way, just now; but never mind
that. Rome wasn't built in a day, and the big, absurd, giddy crowd
can't be coerced in one. They don't know what they really want or why
they want it.*

— Edgar Fawcett, 1888[2]

*It is much more difficult to make a foreign text Japanese than to turn
one's own impressions into text.*

— Tsubouchi Shôyô, 1895[3]

A decade after Grant's visit to Japan, and three years following the
appearance of *Eikoku kôshi* as a written text, a young Japanese
scholar of Western theater, Tsubouchi Shôyô (1859–1935) began
to translate an American melodramatic novel entitled *The False Friend*.
Over the next four years Tsubouchi reworked his literal translation into the
serialized newspaper novel *Daisagishi* (The Swindler, 1892), which was then

reissued as the single-volume novel *Futagokoro* (Two Hearts, 1897). The original English text opens with the following dramatic introduction: "When, at the awful battle of Fort Donelson, Grant's storming columns, with Smith and Wallace at their heads, tore away the abatis and seized the key-point of the fort itself, one man on the Confederate side fought with such tigerish fury, mingled with an icy coolness, that it roused the comment of both friend and foe. The name of this man was Lucian Gleyre."[4]

Shôyô's adaptation opens with a similarly dramatic, if somewhat different, passage that underscores how great a mythic force Grant's visit to Japan had become in the years following it.

> The so-called American Civil War has now receded some forty years into the past. The ex-president, General Grant, who himself once visited our shores, led the Federal, or Northern, forces, and his frequent displays of military prowess should be familiar to all. Among the General's many great exploits was his capture of Fort Donelson, one of the most violent battles of the War.[5]

Shôyô then introduces the protagonist of his adapted novel, expanding the original:

> In that same battle, on the side of the Southern, or Rebel, forces, there appeared a young champion who, though in his early twenties and exhibiting a gentle demeanor and a graceful elegance, possessed keen, deeply set eyes that revealed a type of unspeakable menace and a stern, unwavering dignity. In rank he appeared lower than a general but higher than a corporal, and when General Grant swept through the front ranks of the Southern forces, from the midst of a confused and indecisive body of troops came a solitary mounted soldier who, unflinching as granite, stood his ground. Paying no heed to the bullets and shells that fell around him like hail, he pressed forward into battle with the wildness of a wounded tiger, defending on his right, attacking on his left until all save he alone had retreated. He sent a chill down the spines of the triumphant Northern troops, who, though he was an enemy, praised the noteworthy deeds of this splendid, strapping figure. When the mêlée was ended they watched, muttering "Who is that man?" in dumbfounded respect, as he disappeared into the ranks of the enemy, parting the bloody, retreating horde as though riding down an empty track. That redoubtable soul, who goes by the adapted name of Kogure Rishirô and of whom we shall learn more, is the main character of this novel.[6]

Comparing Shôyô's adaptation with the original, one sees how Shôyô has adjusted the emphasis of his text to themes and characters familiar to his readers: He contextualizes Grant by mentioning his prior visit to Japan and his presidential status; he also focuses attention on Grant by eliding the names of Smith and Wallace. While retaining descriptive elements of the original ("tigerish fury," "icy coolness," and "roused the comment of . . . foe") Shôyô expands his description of Gleyre/Kogure twofold, using traditional rhetorical flourishes that echo Robun's earlier descriptions of Grant.

Shôyô's transformation of an American dime novel into a Japanese serialized narrative again demonstrates the flexibility of Meiji adaptations. However, since Shôyô completed *Futagokoro* at a time when adaptations of Western literature had become a ubiquitous part of the literary landscape, his *hon'an* comes closer to the sense of literal translation than the earlier adaptations I have studied above. *Futagokoro* does, of course, contain several "adjustments" that are worth examining, despite its close correspondence to the original. Also, unlike the earlier adaptations, its creator did not rely upon a mediating translation, but rather was one of the foremost contemporary scholars of English literature, and combined his correspondent translation with a desire to produce a literary work that demonstrated his ideas for the reform of the Japanese theater. This chapter will examine how Shôyô, as translator and critic, used his adaptation of an American dime novel to encourage a new poetics of Japanese drama.

Meiji poetics and Tsubouchi Shôyô

During the 1870s and 1880s, Japanese writers, artists, educators, and other intellectuals were engaged in an ongoing debate about the nature of the Japanese language.[7] The debate arose from the discrepancy that existed between written and spoken Japanese, and may be seen to have been triggered, in part, by the perceived "inferiority" of Japanese art, literature, and drama in comparison to Western examples being brought into Japan. The discussions of form led frequently to proposals for reform, and dialogue regarding the poetics of mid-Meiji narrative, lyric, and drama was fueled in part by the contemporary popularity of imported foreign literature. The situation in Tokyo was not unlike the contemporary climate in Paris, where *japonisme* was all the rage and led to a poetics of art and design derived from the polemics sparked by the challenges presented by very different Asian, particularly Japanese, art forms.

In Japan, Western examples of literature often led contemporary intellectuals to disparage the traditional Japanese narrative arts and press for new, "enlightened" forms of narrative. Tsubouchi Shôyô, a student of traditional Japanese narrative as well as English drama, emerges from this context as an outspoken proponent of reform, and his life can be seen as a continual dialogue between traditional Japanese arts and those of the West, in particular drama.

Shôyô was one of a host of Meiji intellectuals concerned over the future of Japanese literary expression. Their opinions covered a broad spectrum, including very conservative positions that advocated resistance to all change, moderate approaches that called for adaptation and assimilation of foreign models, and those who recommended the wholesale abandonment of traditional genres and styles (and even Japanese language altogether!) in favor of the adoption of Western poetics *en masse*.[8] In translation as well there were several camps of opinion regarding how "literal" translated texts should be, and, as we have seen in earlier chapters, adaptation, grounded on a tradition of *hon'an* variations, emerged as a natural arbitrator between the strangeness of the foreign text and the background of traditional language.

More often than not these curious adaptations, blending Japanese settings with dramatic Western images and sensibilities, catered to readers whose Japanese version of Orientalism—or Occidentalism—sought reinforcement for their exoticized views of the West in imported cultural artifacts. Both of the examples of *hon'an* I have examined in the two preceding chapters demonstrate how adaptations underscored their readers' preexisting notions of the West. Beyond a certain point, however, even anticipated strangeness and exoticism produce the contrary effect of alienating the reader. We have also seen in the earlier texts how some of the more exotic elements have been toned down; in effect, *correspondence* has been compromised in favor of smooth reception. Many early Meiji *hon'an* tamed the strangeness of the original by resetting the tales in Japan and giving the characters Japanese names. Only the bare bones of the plot remained from the original stories. In later decades, however, as foreign geography became a commonplace in Japanese printed media, translators added more and more foreign settings. However, at least until the mid-1890s there remained in *hon'an* adaptations a strong tendency for character names to remain Japanese, leading to the curious mixture that occurs in Shôyô's translation: a Confederate colonel named Kogure Rishirô. Shôyô makes little of this disparity, however, and its transparency underscores how familiar the conventions of adapting Western literature had become to Meiji readers by the mid-1890s.

As a young man Tsubouchi Shôyô was an avid reader of traditional Japanese comic fiction (*gesaku*) and an aficionado of kabuki theater, and his scholastic abilities led him to study English at Japan's foremost university. During his twenties, and even prior to completing *Futagokoro,* he had embarked on his life work of translating the complete works of Shakespeare into Japanese. By the time he began his translation of *The False Friend,* Shôyô was recognized as a leader of narrative and drama reform in Japan, having written several years earlier a groundbreaking treatise on the poetics of the novel, *Shôsetsu shinzui* (The essence of the novel, 1885). He had also completed several lengthy novels that sought to embody some of his reformed poetics, as well as partial translations of Sir Walter Scott's *Bride of Lammermoor* and *The Lady of the Lake,* and Bulwer-Lytton's *Rienzi, the Last of the Roman Tribunes.* Shôyô's earliest experiments in adaptation are included among what Homma Hisao calls "enlightenment translations" because they were undertaken with the intent of improving contemporary literature through demonstrating a higher standard.[9] In his earliest works of translation and adaptation, therefore, Shôyô demonstrates his sensitivity to issues of contemporary literature and a predilection for using translations as a means of demonstrating his ideas about what literature should be.

A friend of San'yûtei Enchô, Shôyô also wrote a preface to Enchô's first transcribed novel, the ghost story *Kaidan botandôrô* (1884). In his preface Shôyô reveals some of the sharp criticisms that informed his subsequent critical treatise: "Considering the extent to which Enchô's narrative faithfully reveals the heart and soul of human feeling and evokes great sympathy within us, the shallow and inferior men of letters today, whose depiction of human feeling is superficial, whose style seems to come from the grave itself, and who do little more than try to flatter women and children, should feel great shame."[10]

With the publication of *Shôsetsu shinzui* the following year, Shôyô incorporated both traditional Japanese and Western critical perspectives into a cry for reform. While condemning adherence to traditional didacticism and idealism, Shôyô advocates the use of realism and moral neutrality. While there is little evidence to suggest that it was widely read at the time of its publication, the strident voice and critical tone of *Shôsetsu shinzui,* combined with the transformations that occurred in subsequent decades, have clearly established Shôyô as the godfather (or midwife) of modern Japanese literary reform.

Soon after the appearance of *Shôsetsu shinzui,* Shôyô began to write experimental novels that, in one way or another, sought to demonstrate some of the principles of reform he called for in his treatise. These works, in particular *Tôsei shosei katagi* (The character of modern students, 1885–86) and *Saikun* (Wife, 1889), introduced new narrative techniques Shôyô had called for in his criticism, such as flashbacks, realistic portrayal of contemporary life, intellectual dialogue, and the eschewing of melodrama.[11] For Shôyô the 1890s was a period of active translation of other works as well, including those of Zola and Thackeray, and in the early 1900s Shôyô also translated Ibsen and wrote several plays. Unfortunately his own creative works, though well-received, did not fare so well critically; over the long run, it was his translations that made him shine, particularly those of Shakespeare.

Futagokoro: Shôyô's Experimental Adaptation

Shôyô's adaptation of *The False Friend* was completed at a time when his poetics had coalesced to some degree through his theoretical writings (and their praxis in several novels), but when his theories on translation were still somewhat in flux. *Futagokoro* serves, therefore, as a window through which we may catch glimpses of Shôyô's assumptions for, and uses of, narrative translation.

It was fairly common during the mid-Meiji period for new works of fiction to appear first as serialized fascicles (as in the case of Enchô's tales in transcription) and then as bound volumes.[12] This was advantageous to the publishers, since it gave them a chance to gauge reader interest (and abort unpopular works) and did not require the same outlay of capital as a complete volume. Serialization also allowed readers to anticipate the next installment, a technique that had been used for centuries to good effect by professional storytellers, and which the fledgling Meiji newspapers found helped guarantee a steady base of subscribers.

Throughout the mid-Meiji period, one of the foremost venues for the publication of new fiction was the press, among whose numbers was the *Miyako shimbun,* a newspaper started in 1884 that played an active role in publishing new works of fiction and translations of Western literature along with its regular news items and advertisements. During its first three years in print, the *Miyako shimbun* published over two dozen serialized novels (including two by Kanagaki Robun), and in 1888 it began a concentrated run of Japanese adaptations of Western (primarily detective) novels. Among the Western authors featured in the *Miyako shimbun's* first decade were Hugh Conway, Émile Gaboriau, Wilkie Collins, Anna Katherine Green, and Fortuné du Boisgobey, who was particularly popular, having twelve adapted stories appear between 1889 and 1891.[13]

By the time, then, that Shôyô published his serialized adaptation of *The False Friend* in the *Miyako shimbun* the paper had established a reputation for carrying works of translated or adapted Western literature. Its success rested squarely on the shoulders of Kuroiwa Ruiko (1862–1920), who, as an author of detective stories, had served as the primary "translator" of Western texts. When Kuroiwa left the *Miyako shimbun* in 1892 the paper's editors were left without a source of new stories and approached Shôyô, who had provided them technical advice on earlier translations, as a temporary solution to their dilemma. The paper experimented unsuccessfully with several other author/translators over the next half year (including Fukuchi Ochi), finally settling on a former police detective who had a flare for original writing, and whose ability to compose domestic crime stories rather than relying on foreign adaptations single-handedly shifted the focus of the *Miyako shimbun* away from translations altogether.[14] This shift in emphasis from foreign to domestic stories reflects an overall change in the role of translation literature in 1890s Japan. Some of the shift may be accounted for by the growing nationalistic fervor surrounding the Sino-Japanese War (1894–95).[15]

Although the details are unclear, Shôyô apparently had made an earlier draft translation of *The False Friend* that he reworked into the serialized story *Daisagishi* (The Swindler), appearing from June through October of 1892 in the pages of the *Miyako shimbun*. In his Preface to *Futagokoro,* Shôyô gives us several clues about his source text as well as his motivations and hopes for his adaptation.[16]

The source of this story, a work called *False Friend*, was written by an American. During the summer of 1892, at the request of a certain pictorial newspaper, I completed one chapter per day in my spare time until, before I knew it, the entire work had been translated. Of course I felt that it was rather rough and needed polish, but fate appeared to dictate otherwise until this past summer, when I came across the translation once more and remembered my aborted designs. According to the original's preface, the piece played to unusually great acclaim upon the stage in America. This work is rich with elements that stir the emotions, has an interesting plot and contains many scenes that should thrill any audience. By transforming the drama into our native idiom, and fitting it to our skilled actors, it could become a new kind of realistic drama (*shinsewamono*), far superior to the hackneyed burglar or vendetta plays popular nowadays; this conviction has remained with me from the very beginning of my adaptation (*giyaku*). The first section, written in the manner of popular fiction (*kusazôshi-buri*) out of consideration for readers used to serialized stories, seeks to convey the plot of the original as closely as possible. In the second (main) section I confess to some editing and embellishment, at times writing in the style of a play book. On the Japanese stage of today historical plays (*jidaimono*) retain nothing of their former glory, and the newer domestic dramas (*sewamono*) are even more insipid; perhaps the style of this translation may serve to edify and inspire those who would seek to reform our native drama.

My original seems to have been misplaced somewhere, and so I cannot provide even the author's name, but I believe the original was a drama that someone turned into a novel. Remarkably enough, the phraseology and style of the latter retained their dramatic flair, so I have not had to overly embellish my translation. Accordingly, I have not sullied the original, albeit there are a few places where I have cut, or expanded, or added my own seasoning to the original flavor; in this indulgence I beg the reader's patience. (Harunoya Shujin, October 1896, 733–34)

Although Shôyô gives the impression in the preface that he translated *The False Friend* during the summer of 1892, his own diary reveals that the first draft of the novel took place in 1888, when he translated the English text aloud while one of his pupils, Oku Taisuke (1870–95), acted as scribe.[17] Apparently Shôyô undertook his first draft translation as a pedagogical exercise, since in his diary he also notes that it took four days, translating at a rate of 1,200 characters per hour, to complete the translation.[18] What Shôyô is referring to above as "one chapter per day" is thus his adaptation of the earlier draft translation.

As we can see, Shôyô's preface to *Futagokoro* reveals his source—albeit obliquely, since the original text went missing—and conveys in relatively strong terms both his opinion of the contemporary Japanese stage and his intention that *Futagokoro* serve as a model for its reformation. Since the Preface was written five years after the initial publication of *Futagokoro* as *Daisagishi,* it benefits from Shôyô's hindsight and is an apt and revealing expression of his artistic and critical intentions for the adaptation.

Futagokoro's Source Text: A Nineteenth-Century American Dime Novel

Shôyô mentions that his source text for *Futagokoro* "seems to have been misplaced somewhere." This fact, combined with the five-year gap between the first and second publications of *Futagokoro,* apparently erased the author's name from Shôyô's memory. This unfortunate lapse led to a case of mistaken identity that until now has led Shôyô scholars to assume that the *False Friend* noted (in English) in Shôyô's preface was a Restoration comedy written by the architect and playwright John Vanbrugh in 1702.[19] This is an odd, if easy, misidentification, since by the late 1880s Shôyô had developed a considerable interest in Shakespeare and other British playwrights. However, considering that in the Preface itself Shôyô identifies the author of *False Friend* as an American, and mentions that the novel was adapted from a play, Vanbrugh's drama does not quite fit and suggests that either Shôyô was confused or that he used some other source.

Ironically, Vanbrugh's *False Friend* bears some resemblance to *Futagokoro,* and within the context of the license sometimes exercised by *hon'an* authors, a comparison of Vanbrugh and Shôyô might lead to the conclusion that the latter intentionally changed much of *False Friend* for the sake of promoting his reformist agenda. However, any correspondence between the two seems to have more to do with the shared title, and the concomitant motifs of trust and betrayal, than anything else.

Initially, I followed the lead of Japanese scholars and began comparing Shôyô with Vanbrugh, making the assumption that Shôyô was exercising tremendous license for the sake of his poetics. However, the more I worked to compare the two the more I wondered about this, especially in light of Shôyô's command of English. After all, even within the flexible constraints of Meiji adaptation, why would a well-educated dramaturge take a Restoration domestic comedy set in Spain and rework it into a novel set in post-bellum America, Australia, and England? Moreover, Vanbrugh's text contains a key motif—entrusting a bride with a friend—that is conspicuously absent in *Futagokoro.*[20]

Accordingly, after rereading Shôyô's preface, I began to investigate nineteenth-century American popular drama as a possible source, and discovered two plays with the name *False Friend*. After a comparison of these with Shôyô's adaptation, it became clear that Shôyô's source was *not* Vanbrugh, but Edgar Fawcett's 1879 dime novel, *The False Friend,* derived from his play by the same name.[21]

Edgar Fawcett (1847–1904) emerged as a mediocre, if prolific, New York writer during the latter half of the nineteenth century. According to one biographer, Stanley R. Harrison, Fawcett was the subject of a great deal of negative critical response, owing in part to his "espousal of radical and unpopular beliefs."[22] Despite these beliefs, however, Fawcett's reputation had its high points; William Dean Howells, for example, saw Fawcett as "first . . . among all the English-writing poets of our time."[23] Another commentator, writing six years after Fawcett's death, sets his life and work in context: "Take Edgar Fawcett, for instance. Speak of him to readers below middle age now, and you will find that they know nothing of him. Thirty years ago he was a celebrity and one of the best known figures in New York, a man familiar about town as well as in literary circles, from whom came a steady flow of plays, novels and books of verse, all of which attracted attention, though opinion as to their merit conflicted and ran to extremes."[24]

The ignominy that descended upon Fawcett toward the end of his life did not escape his own reflection. In a letter to a friend written in 1889 he remarks, "I fear the muses only brought to my cradle the cast-off gifts of inferior scribblers."[25] Yet Harrison suggests that, despite his mediocrity, Fawcett stands as a "multiple man of his time, the representative man at the twilight of the century."

> He was a writer of romance during the decline of the romantic novel and a Realistic writer upon the emergence of literary Realism; he was a Naturalist whose novels were shaped by a current of deterministic thought and an agnostic in an age of skepticism, he was a critic of American capitalism during a period of consolidation of wealth, a spokesman for the impoverished at the time of industrial exploitation, and a projector of the American Dream in the finest tradition of American letters.[26]

In 1879, during one of the brighter moments in his career, Fawcett wrote a play entitled *The False Friend* that began with a prologue and then contained four subsequent acts. The play, one of five Fawcett produced during his lifetime, was performed in New York beginning in January 1880, and garnered mixed reviews. The prologue is set in the Australian outback with two down-on-their-luck gold prospectors (who resemble one another) fleeing from a band of robbers. Lucian Gleyre is an American adventurer, Cuthbert Fielding a British blueblood who left his home (and inheritance) behind fifteen years earlier to roam the world and suffers now from bush fever. Cuthbert entrusts Lucian with his personal effects and expires, and Lucian escapes into the wilderness.

Act One takes place at Fielding Manor in Derbyshire, England. Cuthbert's orphaned younger sister Edith enthusiastically greets her long-lost "brother" (Lucian assuming Cuthbert's identity), who deceives nearly everyone except Edith's suspicious guardian aunt, Lady Ogden. Lucian produces a Bible and a ring (entrusted to him by Cuthbert) to strengthen his deception. In Act Two Lucian falls in love with Edith, in jealousy casts her betrothed out of Fielding Manor, and is confronted in private by Lady Ogden, who reveals his deception by asking him to identify photographs of his mother. Before she can expose Lucian, however, lightning strikes near her and she expires. Act Three takes place a few days after the funeral. Lucian consults with a local lawyer and bailiff to make his ownership of Fielding Manor complete. Meanwhile, the real Cuthbert, now returned to health, arrives from Australia, forms an alliance with Edith's betrothed, and confronts Lucian in private. Lucian says he has the upper hand with his proof, calls for the bailiff and has Cuthbert arrested as an imposter.

In the final act Edith's betrothed frees Cuthbert on bail and the two persuade Edith to doubt her "brother's" identity. In order to expose Lucian's charade, Edith declares that her affection for him is so great that she will remain a spinster to live with Lucian. His ardor gets the better of him and he embraces her; she confesses that her love is more than filial, and asks him to tell her the truth. At her signal the bailiff, Cuthbert, and her betrothed sneak into the room. Lucian throws himself at her feet and admits his deception and his love. The bailiff arrests him and Cuthbert assumes his rightful role as Lord of the Manor.

Clearly, the melodramatic style and hyperbolic language of *The False Friend* mark it as a representative example of a maturing, yet still adolescent, American theater. Reactions to the melodrama were mixed. In an early review one critic notes, "It is worth a visit to *The False Friend* to see how much can be done by a company of experienced actors when placed at the greatest disadvantage by the piece."[27] On the other hand, the fact that the play was performed over two years later at the Boston Museum suggests that, despite its flaws, it maintained a popular appeal.[28]

Perhaps Fawcett saw in this popular reception sufficient encouragement to motivate him to adapt his play into a lengthier narrative. Six months after the first stage performance of *The False Friend,* Fawcett published a much expanded, novelized version of the play. Fawcett's adaptation, a drama rewritten by its author as a novel, represents another Western example of adaptation that comes close to the contemporary Japanese sense of *hon'an*. In this case, interestingly, both the original and the adaptation were written by the same author. I summarize the plot of the novel below.

> Lucian Gleyre, a colonel in the Confederate Army, returns home after the war to find his plantation in ruins and his father at death's door. He wanders westward, first to New Orleans, where, after suffering the humiliation of being forced to blackmail a former acquaintance, he resolves to fight society

until he "can wring from it compensation for the wrongs" he has suffered. He moves on to San Francisco, where he uses his charm to marry into the family of a wealthy speculator, only to lose both father-in-law and fortune through stock scandals. His new bride, and ensuing child, become a burden to him, so he creates a pretext for divorce (and barely survives the ensuing duel), passes guardianship of his son on to another family in the East, and heads to Mexico in search of gold. There he meets and befriends fellow miner and former mercenary Cuthbert Fielding (alias John Stanley).

After financial disappointment the two (who bear a striking resemblance to each other) sail across the Pacific to work the Australian gold fields. During the voyage Lucian learns of Cuthbert/Stanley's past: He is the sole male heir of a wealthy aristocratic family whose presence he fled from fifteen years earlier after a quarrel with his now-deceased father. Upon arrival in Australia, Lucian saves Cuthbert/Stanley from drowning, not out of love but as a cold, calculated move to win his trust, for Lucian "had never felt love . . . for any living being save himself." Once they reach the gold fields, they are moderately successful, but one evening find themselves fleeing a band of robbers. Cuthbert comes down with bush plague, and, convinced he is dying, reveals his true identity. He passes on to Lucian his diary, letters, and a Bible and a ring, with the request that Lucian return these effects to Cuthbert's sister Edith and his Aunt Catharine, who are the remaining heirs of his family's huge fortune. Lucian hastily departs, leaving Cuthbert's limp body to the robbers. He makes his way to a settler's farm, where he, too, comes down with bush plague but is nursed back to health, during which time Lucian resolves to assume Cuthbert's identity and inherit his fortune.

Once in England, Lucian manages, through a combination of resemblance, memorized diary passages, and the possession of the Bible and ring, to persuade all but the aunt that he is indeed the prodigal Cuthbert returned. He is nearly revealed by his former spouse, Nina, who has coincidentally made her way to Fielding Manor, where she teaches music, but he blackmails her into silence using knowledge of their son's whereabouts. Lucian is thus unhindered in his ambition to take over the Fielding fortune, but only temporarily. Lucian has fallen in love with Edith, but since he is pretending to be Cuthbert, he cannot act on his romantic impulses, and this predicament begins to take its toll on his caution. In a fit of jealousy he banishes Cyril Garland, Edith's betrothed, from the manor, insisting that Edith can never marry a mere soldier.

One stormy night a very suspicious Aunt Catharine visits Lucian in the library and uses photographs of relatives to trick him into betraying his charade. Lucian, who by that time has talked his way out of a number of near-discoveries, seems doomed. However, as she runs for help Aunt Catharine is knocked senseless by lightning and, before revealing Lucian's secret, expires. Once again Lucian feels that Providence has intervened on his behalf. Then Cuthbert himself suddenly appears on the scene, alive and well. The robbers had taken mercy on him and nursed him back to health. Working with Cyril, whose anger and jealousy help him see Lucian for the imposter he is, Cuthbert arranges a private meeting with Lucian and confronts him. Lucian coolly replies that he is in charge and has convinced everyone, then calls the bailiff and has Cuthbert arrested as a would-be imposter. Since Lucian possesses the documents, and Cuthbert has no proof other than his word, it appears for a time as though Cuthbert will languish in jail while Lucian controls the Fielding fortune.

However, Nina, Lucian's ex-wife, returns to Fielding Manor because she learns her son has died of scarlet fever in America and in grief and anger resolves to protect Edith from the same fate of betrayal at the hands of Lucian. While she is trying, unsuccessfully, to persuade Edith of Lucian's fraud, Lucian, upon whose nerves Cuthbert's presence begins to wear, pays a night visit to Cuthbert's jail cell to make a deal. Cyril eavesdrops as Lucian offers Cuthbert thirty thousand pounds to renounce his claim; Cyril reveals himself and, now certain of Cuthbert's identity, threatens Lucian, who laughs off the threat since both Cuthbert and Cyril stand to gain so much with their claim that they will not be believed. Cyril manages to raise bail to free Cuthbert, and through Nina's intervention a still-deceived Edith meets with Cuthbert and Cyril. After she hears Cyril's profound declamation of conviction that Lucian is an imposter, the scales fall from her eyes. Together they set a trap.

The next day, at eleven, Edith calls Lucian to the library. He is visibly distressed over Cyril's freeing Cuthbert on bail. Edith tells him that a strange change has come upon her, that she could dispense with Cyril's love. "I want no other love so long as I have yours!" Lucian, moved but despairing, says that Edith will nevertheless find someone some day and marry. "Never," she cries, "I will devote myself only to you!" Lucian, moved beyond control, kisses her passionately. Edith then says she has misgivings about their relationship, and urges Lucian to tell her the truth. (At this point Cyril, Cuthbert, and the bailiff surreptitiously enter the library.) Lucian confesses that he is not Edith's brother, but in fact is Lucian Gleyre, and that he will give up his charade if he can only have her love. Cyril and Cuthbert order the bailiff to arrest Lucian, who, when he sees Edith fall into Cyril's arms, realizes he has been deceived and all is lost.

In the ensuing trial Lucian is convicted and sentenced to twenty years of hard labor, which he foreshortens by committing suicide with a nail sharpened on a stone window ledge. Edith marries her soldier, and the novel ends with rumors that Cuthbert may very well soon wed Nina, Lucian's former wife.

Fawcett's novel was issued by the popular *Seaside Library* series, and was, both literally and generically, a dime novel.[29] Although it takes up a scant thirty pages in the newspaper-style publication, its triple-column, small-point type format is the rough equivalent of a three-hundred-page novel. Although the original drama was performed on and off for four years, and the novel itself was rewritten as a drama five years later, it was never reprinted per se, and is not considered by critics to be one of the author's better works.[30]

Yet a comparison of the play and the novel shows the differences between Fawcett the playwright and Fawcett the novelist. There are passages in the novel that come directly from the play, yet Fawcett has reworked the structure dramatically. Instead of beginning with a short Australian prologue then shifting to England for the body of the action, as in the drama, the novel opens with the defeat of the Confederacy and devotes nearly a third of the entire narrative to events leading up to Lucian's arrival at Fielding Manor. This major expansion allows Fawcett to more fully develop Lucian's lust for wealth and power, and offers a number of opportunities for him to underscore Lucian's unnatural coolness and dispassion towards others.

Fawcett also added a tremendous amount of description to the novel, and one particularly striking elaboration can be seen in comparing the endings of the two. The play concludes with Edith extracting a confession from Lucian, who is then led away by the bailiff. As he departs, he utters these foreboding lines: "Edith Fielding, one word more, perhaps the last I shall ever say. Had you really loved me, your love would have been my redemption. When in after years you recall what now I utter, may its recollection soften your spirit toward one whom the world will paint far blacker than he deserves!"[31]

The curtain falls, and the subsequent events—both the marriage of Edith and Cyril and the (foreshadowed) suicide of Lucian Gleyre—are left to the audience's imagination. The play does, however, satisfy the immediate need for justice: Lucian is finally caught in his deception, and the tension of his successful but self-serving deceit is relieved: "The purest emotion that ever filled a man's heart ruins me!"

That ruin is much more graphically detailed in Fawcett's narrative adaptation of the play. While the novel proper concludes with the handcuffs being clasped upon Lucian's wrists, Fawcett appends a conclusion to the story that describes in brief Lucian's trial, conviction, and gruesome demise:

> He heard his sentence unmoved, as he had borne himself uniformly throughout the trial. Taken back to his cell in the county jail, those who left him there at evening saw him living for the last time. A few hours later, one of the turnkeys, entering the cell with food for the prisoner, found Gleyre in a pool of his own blood, lying dead. He had opened a main artery with a nail, concealed skillfully upon his person, and afterward supposed to have been sharpened for its ghastly use on a stone ledge of the prison-window. Thus ended in suicide his faulty, daring, and ill-ordered life.[32]

Thereupon follows a description of the marriage of Edith and Cyril, and the rumor, added by a shocked blue-blooded neighbor, that Cuthbert may very well soon wed Nina, "that American lady."[33] The conclusion of Fawcett's novel thus goes well beyond the play. Whereas the ending of the drama underscores the element of justice in Lucian's downfall, and offers a note of triumph with only a hint of death ("one word more, perhaps the last I shall ever say"), the novel's ending offers its readers both tragedy (suicide) and comedy (marriage). In addition, with the impending nuptials of Lucian's ex-wife and the man he sought to displace, Fawcett's novel offers an ironic ending that provides one final, curiously satisfying proxy: Cuthbert takes Lucian's place in the marriage bed.

Fawcett thus adapts and expands his drama into a novel using strategies that mirror Japanese *hon'an* conventions. In his adaptation of his own play we find both elements of correspondence and of transmutation, with the differences suggesting Fawcett's willingness to go beyond mere narrative expansion and his keen awareness of contemporary American dramatic and novelistic standards.

The False Friend contains a number of motifs that were of contemporary interest in Meiji Japan. For example, it addresses the weaknesses of a statutory legal system by showing how documents and proof, in the wrong hands, can allow imposters to prevail. The novel also treats themes of tradition and loyalty, greed, and impoverished war veterans, and at a more subtle level national stereotypes. Melodramatic and full of theatrical conceits, *The False Friend* possessed something that caught Shôyô's eye and encouraged him to translate, and then adapt, the story.

In the context of Shôyô's other translation sources, Fawcett may be one of the most obscure writers to garner Shôyô's attention; he is certainly no Shakespeare. Yet considering the high praise Shôyô heaps upon *The False Friend* in his preface, there was something about Fawcett's work that appealed to Shôyô and resonated with his strong desires for the reform of drama. Since Shôyô mentions that the drama version "played to great acclaim," perhaps he was attracted to its apparent popularity in America, which would have given it some notability among other dime novels. Since he no longer had the text in his possession at the time he published *Futagokoro,* however, and only mentions its title in his diary, we know nothing of why or how Shôyô acquired the original. Perhaps it came from an acquaintance, or Shôyô stumbled upon it in a Western bookstore.[34] We can only surmise that, as was often the case with Meiji period adaptations, Shôyô probably did not choose his original text after carefully reading and comparing the premier examples of the genre, but rather came upon his source through the serendipity of its falling into his hands.

Looking more closely at Shôyô's text in comparison with that of Fawcett, overall the two stories retain a great deal of similarity, suggesting that Shôyô approached his task from the perspective of a literal translator. This reflects, of course, the earliest translation, done in 1888, when Shôyô recited for a scribe. This earliest draft formed the basis of his later adaptation, which tends to use an elevated style of discourse that reflects the prolixity of Fawcett's prose, and he also sticks to Fawcett's storyline quite faithfully.[35] However, throughout the narrative Shôyô exercises his license as a translator and adapter as he omits small details and expands others, adjusting elements here and there to give a subtly different weight and emphasis to his tale.

A closer look at *Futagokoro* in comparison with *The False Friend* shows not only the embellishments that Shôyô saw fit to omit or add, but also reveals interesting insights into his world, his audience, and his emerging poetics of translation. Since *Futagokoro* corresponds to its source more than either of the other two texts I have examined in this book, I note below only the major differences between *Futagokoro* and *The False Friend.*

Futagokoro's Differences

In terms of general structure, the first section of both works opens with the American Civil War and ends with Rishirô (Lucian) heading off to Derby from Melbourne. As we have seen above, the opening lines of *Futagokoro* offer more detailed description of the protagonist, and there are several other contrasts as well. For example, in *Futagokoro* the war is still raging when Rishirô deserts the fray in order to visit his father. After his father dies Rishirô's great malignant resolve to not let his heart get the better of his brains is framed in the expanded context of abandoning both duty (*giri*) and feeling *(ninjô)*. His running away from the war (absent without leave, he flees to San Francisco where "no one asks about one's past") suggests an abandonment of the former, while the death of his father causes him to eschew the latter.

While he is in San Francisco the war ends and his theretofore hidden background suddenly comes to his aid in winning Nayoko (Nina)'s hand by establishing his bona fides in light of his otherwise lowly social status. His manipulation of Nayoko and his friend Sagiori (Shackford) into providing him a basis for divorce, including a duel, runs parallel to the original, although Shôyô has added more violence to the challenge, with Rishirô doubling up his fist and giving Sagiori a bloody nose.[36] Rishirô's subsequent plan to use Katsuharu (Cuthbert) as an entrée into the British world of commerce is framed by Shôyô using a phrase straight from the modernization rhetoric of early Meiji (*risshin shusse*).

Finally, in the end of the first section Shôyô substitutes Rishirô's hiding out in a cave while the robbers steal Katsuharu's body with a desperate vine-clinging, cliff-descending wilderness escape scene. Also, where Fawcett's original leaves Rishirô recovered from his illness at the farmhouse, having "made up his mind," Shôyô takes him all the way into Melbourne, where he writes a letter to Fielding Manor, boards a steamer, and then, in an internal monologue, reveals his intentions to take over as Katsuharu and return to Australia to claim the gold he had just discovered.

The second section of both texts opens with a lyrical description of Fielding Manor just before Rishirô's arrival, with Shôyô's adaptation containing several differences that suggest Shôyô anticipating the stage production of his text. For example, after a brief descriptive beginning the first several chapters launch into passages of lengthy, melodramatic dialogue. Some of the elaborations that Fawcett added to his novel, such as the scenes where characters plan their traps for Lucian, are completely missing in Shôyô's text; he simply lets his reader watch the stratagems unfold.[37] Also, the library, where many of the pivotal confrontations take place, is a detached building in the garden rather than part of the main house; the proofs that Rishirô produces are the Bible and a *bracelet* (rather than the ring of *The False Friend*). Both of these alterations suggest changes to the original that make for easier or better staging.

Other changes include Shôyô's foreshortening a good deal of the "comic relief" subplot, making one of the characters more rough and lusty than the browbeaten gentleman of *The False Friend*. Nayoko is not a music teacher but rather Yukariko (Edith)'s maid, who feels great loyalty to her employer. Likewise, Katsuharu reveals in *Futagokoro* that he was nursed back to health by the robbers not because of a mixture of "villainy and humanity" but rather because an old companion happened to be one of the robbers and, out of loyalty, convinced them not to finish Katsuharu off. This theme of duty (*giri*) stands in solid contrast to Rishirô, who several times in Shôyô's text reiterates his resolve to abandon both his heart (*ninjô*) and loyalty (*giri*). As in *The False Friend,* Rishirô's weakness in keeping this resolve eventually betrays him as he falls in love with Yukariko, but his grisly manner of death shows a final small difference between the texts: Instead of slitting his wrists with the sharpened nail, Shôyô's Rishirô uses it to stab and slash his own throat.

As the above summary of difference suggests, *Futagokoro* in general is quite faithful to the storyline of the original, with only a few alterations, mainly for the convenience of anticipated staging. Several other omissions and additions, however, suggest Shôyô's skill in retaining correspondence while adapting the original for his Japanese readers.

One of the first alterations the reader notes in *Futagokoro* is Shôyô's use of Japanese names. Like Enchô, Shôyô gives his characters Japanese appellations to soften the foreign impact of the original. Yet unlike Enchô, only the character names are "adjusted" into Japanese; The place names remain their foreign equivalents, leading to the curious circumstance of Civil War veterans and British gentry bearing Japanese names.[38] Nothing else within the text, however, suggests that the characters are themselves Japanese; their adapted names suggest that by the 1890s Japanese readers and audiences were comfortable with such contrivances in *hon'an* texts.

Shôyô has taken great pains in his selection of similar-sounding cognates, as the following list of principal characters in the novel reveals.[39]

The False Friend	Futagokoro
Andrew the Butler	Torii Andayû
Catharine, Lady Ogden	Kazarie, Lady Kado
Chauncey, Asa	Chôshi Asahei
Chauncey, Nina	Chôshi Nayoko
Courtwell, Abercrombie	Kurondo Kurido
Fielding, Cuthbert	Hirai Katsuharu
Fielding, Edith	Hirai Yukariko
Garland, Cyril	Kariya Shizuo

The False Friend	Futagokoro
Gleyre, Lucian	Kogure Rishirô
Jacymin	Jakubei
Santley (General)	Santori Moronaga
Santley, Rebecca	Santori Rieko

Nearly all of the original names have been translated into parallel Japanese versions, and the correspondence Shôyô employs stands as a metaphor of his adaptive strategy in general: He is not seeking to literally translate the meanings of the names, but he is also not simply drawing names out of a hat. As he adapts his text he bears in mind both his audience's background and contemporary conventions as well as the characterization of the original, and works to retain a good deal of fidelity to the original while making alterations that reconfigure that original in dramatic linguistic or cultural ways.

Another example of cultural accommodation in *Futagokoro* is Shôyô's overt reference to Japanese idiomatic or ideological terms. Several times in his adaptation Shôyô adds subtle allusions to Japanese cultural references. For example, in the comic subplot, when Santori Rieko (Rebecca Santley) is trying to falsely persuade the widow Mitaya (Maitland), the subject of her father's amorous intentions, that he is mentally unstable and therefore unfit for remarriage she prefaces her remarks with "My apologies to Confucius for a child maligning a parent, but"(869).[40] Rieko, a meddling daughter, lies to protect her father; the irony of this dishonest but filial act is enhanced in Japanese with her reference to (and dismissal of) Confucian calls for filial piety.

Within the context of the same subplot, added by Fawcett for comic relief and pared down by Shôyô, we find another allusion to a Japanese cultural reference. When Rieko's suitor, Kurondo Kurido (Abercrombie Courtwell), must report to her that he has failed in his charge to prevent the marriage of her father, Shôyô adds the following description of his face:"After Kurido had failed, once again, in his attempt to conquer . . . his face took on a pale cast resembling that of Momotarô when, on the way to the Isle of Ogres, the kite stole his dumplings" (905).[41] The section of Fawcett's original that corresponds roughly to this particular scene uses in an ironic manner two Western references—one to Greek mythology and the other to a scene from Shakespeare—that would have been very unfamiliar to Shôyô's Japanese readers. Shôyô has substituted instead an allusion to the fairy tale Momotarô—the peach boy—that plays to a similar comic effect. In both of these examples, and elsewhere in his adaptation, Shôyô demonstrates sensitivity to his readers by employing cultural references that ground the tale more securely and effectively in a Japanese context.

Just as Shôyô freely reduces the comic subplot, he also does not hesitate, at times, to completely omit scenes or passages that may not serve his Japanese readers. One example takes place as Lucian/Rishirô awaits his rendezvous with Nina/Nayoko in the library. Fawcett's text has him taking out Cuthbert/Katsuharu's diary.

> He now turned to the signature of "Cuthbert Fielding," written . . . on the fly-leaf of the journal. Taking pen and paper, which were both ready at hand, he dipped the pen in a bronze ink-stand that was also near him, and wrote this signature over and over, many times. Then he compared his writing with that of the original. He seemed not altogether pleased, though perhaps this was, at the least calculation, the thousandth time that he had inscribed that same name upon paper. Tearing what was written into minute fragments, he covered another sheet as before. At length he appeared more satisfied. "Surely no expert could question this writing," he presently murmured. "Yes—I have mastered his signature perfectly. I could not tell my work from his myself, but for the difference in the colors of ink and paper."
>
> As before, he destroyed this second sheet. Then he re-closed the journal, and placed it within his pocket. After that he rose. As he did so the clock on the mantel pealed eleven chimes. It was the hour for Nina to arrive.[42]

This passage by Fawcett adds both suspense and depth to the story, not only showing Lucian's determination to make his deception complete but also revealing some of the internal tensions that haunt the counterfeit Cuthbert. Shôyô, however, completely omits the description of signature practice: "He turned to face the desk, but being in no mind to examine any of the library's tomes he instead sat himself in one of the easy chairs and was soon intently immersed in his scheming. The night deepened and at length the large clock on the facing wall began to peal, signaling the eleventh hour" (830).

Shôyô's deliberate omission of this detail, despite the scene's potential enrichment of Rishirô/Lucian as a character, is intriguing. Within the context of adaptation, and Shôyô's concern for his readers, it is possible that Shôyô felt that the strangeness of the scene would outweigh its value, since in contemporary Japan signatures were not used to authenticate written documents. In Shôyô's day legal transactions were authenticated using inscribed seals, which could be affixed by proxy in the event that the signer was not able to be there in person. Hence, forging a signature did not carry the same symbolic weight in Meiji Japan as it did in its Western context, where to forge another's signature not only opened the doors for stealing property but appropriated the right to self-representation as well. Another element that Shôyô seems to take great pains to omit is the use of English loanwords. One might expect that the contortions of adapting a novel set in the West would of necessity require a host of loanwords to describe the foreign objects and concepts that crop up in the original.[43] However, a survey of Shôyô's adaptation reveals only a handful of loanwords in nearly two hundred pages, and the majority of these come into play in the comic relief subplot section, adding a certain exotic appeal to the already exaggerated characters.[44]

In fact, Shôyô has so carefully selected indigenous Japanese vocabulary that only four nonplacename loanwords appear at all in the main storyline, and these are written using Chinese characters with English-based pronunciations glossed as *furigana* alongside. One of these words, Bible (*seisho* glossed *baiburu*), appears throughout the text, since the Bible plays an important role as one of Rishirô/Lucian's proofs. The other three loanwords occur sporadically or only once, and all three are contained in the twelfth chapter of section two, when Rieko/Rebecca confesses her infatuation with Rishirô/Lucian: heart (*jô* glossed *haato*), jealous (*shitto* glossed *jerasu*), and kiss (*seppun* glossed *kissu;* 840). The gloss, which draws attention to the phrases, itself is a playful means of giving a Japanese word multiple meanings or nuances, and Rieko/Rebecca's use of these intentionally foreign phrases is prefaced by a description of her suitor Kurondo/Abercrombie's pedantic habit of intermingling Latin and Greek phrases in his English (839).[45]

In other words, Shôyô made a conscious effort in his adaptation of Fawcett to avoid the pedantry or trendy modishness that overuse of loanwords might give his text, and uses them only to enhance his sketches of peripheral characters. This reveals his clear sensitivity to his reading audience as well as his own linguistic competence.

On a broader, archetypal level, Shôyô also brings into his adaptation elements that tie in closely with the contemporary Meiji world. For example, his adjustment of the opening chapter that places Rishirô in San Francisco as a fugitive soldier plays up the contemporary Japanese view of the frontier as a liminal space where anonymity and upward mobility are possible (as witnessed in Meiji pioneering efforts in Hokkaidô and Japanese emigration to California and Brazil). Shôyô's use of the phrase *risshin shusse* (upward mobility) to describe Rishirô's plans to use his association with Katsuharu to gain access to the British world of finance was a particularly apt metaphor, in the pre- and post–Sino-Japanese war years in which it was published, for Japan's own ambitions to enter the privileged circle of Western imperialist powers.[46]

In another instance of parallel archetypes, Fawcett's protagonist bears an uncanny resemblance to Harumi Jôsuke from Enchô's *hon'an,* in that he, too, is a disenfranchised warrior who must seek his fortune relying on his wits and poses a threat to the established social order. A shrewd, rhetorically adept figure who possesses tremendous willpower, Rishirô/Lucian not only mirrors the rhetoric of upward mobility but also embodies the greed that led to Harumi's downfall. Early on in Fawcett's text, Lucian visits a former borrower, Jacymin, for repayment of a debt, and the social order has changed so much that he must resort to blackmail. We have seen this kind of status inversion earlier in Enchô, and it reflects not only changes to the post-bellum South but also the merchant-samurai flip-flop of post–Restoration Meiji. Shôyô preserves this scenario, underscoring the humiliation Rishirô/Lucian feels at having to beg from Jakubei/Jacymin. Thus Rishirô becomes, to Shôyô's reader, a masterless samurai who eschews both *giri* and *ninjô* as he swears an oath to his new master, wealth. Ultimately lust overpowers him and he betrays his new master; in a gesture that satisfies both melodramatic and Japanese expectations, Rishirô ends his life to expiate his guilt.[47]

Fawcett's use of female characters to effect an eventual justice emerges directly from the lust and pseudo-incest motif of *The False Friend.* Despite his resolve to remain aloof in matters of the heart, Lucian falls in love with Edith, setting up a basic moral dilemma: So long as he pretends to be her brother he cannot pursue her as a woman. And as the plot thickens, Edith remaining deceived becomes increasingly essential to Lucian in maintaining both the charade and his power. On all other fronts he is able to triumph over every challenge.

Thus Edith holds the key to his undoing, yet she is herself subordinate to others, including her (false) brother, her aunt and, to a lesser extent, her fiancé. Women in both American and Japanese contemporary societies were circumscribed by dominant (primarily family) systems that offered them few independent choices. Yet Edith succeeds as a cross-cultural archetype because, despite those constraints, she manages to use the hero-villain's passion as an agent for justice. At first she exercises proper Confucian piety and, despite her passion for Cyril, yields to the demand of her prodigal "brother" that she cut off all ties with her betrothed. However, as she grows increasingly suspicious, she then yields to the combined request of Cyril and her true brother that she employ her "feminine wiles" to reveal Lucian's hoax. In an emotionally trying but triumphant demonstration of counterfeit passion, she manipulates Lucian into confessing all, and justice prevails. Despite their difference in status, Cyril and Edith marry, and the novel ends with Lord of the Manor Cuthbert ready to wed low-status Nina. Both of these unions mirrored the changing social world of Meiji Japan, and despite the fact that strong Confucian values prevailed in Shôyô's day regarding the status of women, he follows Fawcett's lead in his adaptation. Perhaps Shôyô saw a parallel of this rather revolutionary aspect of the original text in contemporary Meiji ideology (with its weak propensity towards egalitarianism); he certainly would have been personally gratified by the ending, since his own wife had once been a low-ranking geisha.

Comparing *The False Friend* with *Futagokoro,* then, we find that Shôyô retains a number of archetypes that fit the Meiji world and allow the story to "work" within a Japanese context without a great deal of alteration. He is thus able to maintain a close correspondence to the original storyline while making a number of "corrective" accommodations, including giving his characters Japanese names, adding cultural references, and omitting or reducing some important scenes. These characteristics of *Futagokoro,* along with Shôyô's minimalism in the usage of English loanwords, demonstrate that by the 1890s he had developed a style of translation that was neither literal nor wildly adaptive. Rather, he seems to have arrived at what one might call, for lack of a better English category, *hon'an* as correspondent adaptation.

Futagokoro as Visible Poetics

Andre Lefevere has noted that translators often make their choices based upon "a certain concept of what literature should be like (poetics)," and that they often adapt or rewrite works of literature to fit their own poetics.[48] As Wagner's evolving notion of what music should be like—*Zukunftsmusik*—is mirrored in his successive operas, Shôyô's own evolving sense of what translation should be like emerges in his translations. *Futagokoro* is a particularly revealing translation since he modified it three times: first, during its initial oral translation in 1888; again in 1892 when he adapted the translation as a newspaper novel; and finally in 1896 when he prepared the adaptation for publication as a monograph. Since we have samples of text from the latter two adaptations, a comparison will yield greater insight into some of Shôyô's evolving views of translation, and help us understand his changing concept of translation poetics.

After *Futagokoro*'s initial two-month newspaper run, which was well-received, Shôyô let the work lie fallow for four years before reissuing it as a single bound volume. The latter involved a few perfunctory typographical emendations.[49] By and large, however, the body of the work remained essentially unchanged except for a new title, the addition of front and back cover and internal illustrations, a preface, and a division of the main text into two subtitled sections.

Considering that the body of the 1897 text is essentially the same as that published in 1892, Shôyô's new title—*Futagokoro*—suggests not a major textual overhaul but rather his own changed perspective of the work. The *Miyako* title *Daisagishi* (The Swindler) is a straightforward description of Rishirô, a charlatan trying to usurp another man's estate. In the context of a serialized newspaper novel, such a title would be right at home with the sensationalistic stories that surrounded the literary text, and a glance at other contemporary *hon'an* narratives published in the *Miyako* reveals a list of similarly "stirring" titles, such as *Five Minutes of Terror, Tenacity, Living Hell,* and *The Dead Beauty.*[50]

Four years later, when Shôyô prepared the text for publication as a single bound volume, the context was quite different from that of newspaper serialization, and the new title reflects the more sophisticated nature of monograph publishing as well as Shôyô's own growth as a writer and translator. Instead of the prosaic "Swindler" of 1892, Shôyô selects a more poetic title, *Futagokoro.* The cover of the book represents this title with a combination of *kana* (*fu-ta*) and the Chinese character for *kokoro* ("heart," "essence," "motive," or even "psyche"), while the title page uses only *kana.* The difference between these shows us a playful depth in Shôyô's new title, for the word *futagokoro* itself contains a potential pun.

Shôyô's title at face value suggests a literal reading of "two hearts" that first points toward the essential differences between Rishirô and Katsuharu and second subtly reveals the internal struggle Rishirô faces as he falls in love with Yukariko. In addition, there is a play on words that adds an ironic dimension, since the first three syllables of the title, *futago,* can also mean "twins." By writing only in *kana* Shôyô emphasizes this reading, which underscores the physical resemblance between Rishirô and Katsuharu. The cover's use of combined *kana* and *kanji,* on the other hand, highlights the latter (*kokoro*), and the resulting focus on *kokoro* emphasizes duplicity and internal struggle, key elements of the psychological depth that Shôyô, revising in 1897, now saw in his adaptation.[51]

As was common in late Edo and Meiji fiction, the cover of *Futagokoro* contains not only the title but a colored illustration as well. The title (with Shôyô's pen name, Harunoya Shujin, tellingly listed not as translator nor adapter but rather as "author" [*cho*]) is written with a brush on a lavender block that floats above an open (English) Bible with a red Japanese inscription on the inside cover. The inscription is the Fielding family motto redone in literary Japanese that contains the phrase *iyashiki kokoro* (evil heart), echoing the *kokoro* of the title. On the front cover a yellow rose sits beside the Bible, and on the back a ruby set in a gold ring lies above the book as well.

Immediately inside the cover is the only other illustration in the book, a two-page color print depicting the conflict between Rishirô and Kado just prior to her death by lightning. The scene shows Rishirô gripping his fist and holding the lapel of his jacket in deep perplexity as Kado, cane in hand, runs away along a covered walkway. Lightning flashes forebodingly in the background, above Kado's head. The architecture of the scene is decidedly Meiji Western, with a huge potted palm dominating the center of the illustration. The opulence of the manor is emphasized visually with brocaded carpets of red and blue, marble hallway floors and balustrades, wood paneling in the library, and the bright (aniline) purple of the multi-level ceramic vase housing the palm.

Though the furnishings reflect both Japan and the West, the characters are decidedly Japanese. Kado's hair is set in a Japanese style appropriate for an octogenarian, and she wears a gray kimono and white *tabi* socks. Though Rishirô is not in kimono, but rather a jacket, tie, and slacks, his facial features are clearly Japanese and he sports a contemporary haircut reflecting the Meiji mode.

The illustrations that Shôyô has appended to his text expand the overall sense of *Futagokoro* as *hon'an*. They reflect an admixture of both cultures, and in their difference reflect an artistic adaptation of the rough, action-packed etchings found in *The False Friend* reset for a different viewing public.[52] The cover may be seen as a contemplative still life that prepares the reader for the roles the Bible, motto and ring will play within the story. The seamless contrast between block-print English and red brushed Japanese on the Bible not only mirrors the text itself, where Japanese names are used seamlessly in foreign settings, but also draws attention to the hybrid nature of adaptations and the way in which they combine the foreign and the familiar.

The internal illustration, taking its cue from the dramatic scenes found in the original, prepares the reader for the melodramatic style of the sec-

COVER OF *FUTAGOKORO* (COURTESY OF THE TSUBOUCHI SHÔYÔ
MEMORIAL MUSEUM, WASEDA UNIVERSITY).

ILLUSTRATION FROM *FUTAGOKORO* (COURTESY OF THE TSUBOUCHI SHŌYŌ MEMORIAL MUSEUM, WASEDA UNIVERSITY).

ond section. Like the cover, it also provides a visual parallel for Shōyō's use of Japanese names for his foreign characters in the text; the tale is set in England, and the characters are British and American, but their faces and furnishings are Meiji Japanese.

A Bifurcated Text: Monogatari-buri and Shinsewamono

Like the illustrations, the preface was a new addition to the 1897 republication. As we have seen, Shōyō's preface to *Futagokoro* provides several key insights into his motivations for adapting *The False Friend*. He notes, for example, its affective power ("rich with elements that stir the emotions . . . and contains many scenes that should thrill any audience") and the fact that it derives from a popular play. He also mentions towards the end of his preface that the dramatic underpinnings of the original have allowed him to translate with a minimum of embellishment. Yet, as we have seen, a comparison between source and translation reveals a number of changes, so what Shōyō may be referring to here is not the technical details of translation—certainly the *hon'an* tradition would have given him wider latitude in his definition of what constituted deviation from the original text—but rather what we may loosely define as the dramatic spirit of the original. Concerning this aspect of *The False Friend,* the preface provides us a clear view of the prescriptive aims of Shôyô's translation, and his desire to use it as a demonstration of his emerging poetics: "perhaps the style of this translation may serve to edify and inspire those who would seek to reform our native drama."

As he notes in the preface, Shôyô has taken the liberty in *Futagokoro* to divide the fifty-two-chapter work into two sections of seventeen and thirty-five chapters, respectively (the division occurring upon Rishirô's arrival at Derbyshire). The first he designates "The Commencement" (*hottan no kan*), and adds the subscription "narrative-style" (*monogatari-buri*) below this title; the second he christens "The Text" (*honbun no kan*), with the subscription "a pseudo-playbook" (*inponmagai*). This division offers readers of the book (as opposed to readers of the serialized story) an articulated indication of Shôyô's hopes for reform. The first seventeen chapters are filled with exaggerated action and description, in a narrative (*monogatari*) style that prepares the reader for the drama of the main section. The second part is firmly focused on the intrigues and complexities of social interaction, and mirrors the dramatic action of Fawcett's original.[53]

Shôyô's intentions behind the division are hinted at in his preface to *Futagokoro.* He mentions that he has endeavored to write the second part of the adaptation in the style of a playbook, and suggests that it may be seen as a new, kabukiesque drama. "By transforming the drama into our native idiom, and fitting it to our skilled actors, it could become a new kind of realistic drama (*shinsewamono*), far superior to the hackneyed burglar or vendetta plays popular nowadays" (733).

Considering that kabuki served as one model for Shôyô's later Shakespeare translations, this after-the-fact pronouncement is revealing in that we begin to view, in Shôyô's experimental *hon'an* of an American melodramatic novel, elements that are fundamental to his later translations of Elizabethan drama. These include an effort to use multiple styles of language to fit varying levels in the original (as in his use of loanwords for characterization), the use of paraphrase or free translation, and the use of culturally appropriate metaphors.[54]

As in Shôyô's earlier, original novels, where he used his creative writings to demonstrate his poetics in a pragmatic manner, he uses his adaptation of *The False Friend* to accomplish the same goal. In the case of *Futagokoro,* however, it is an adaptation rather than an original work that serves as his forum. Although by 1897 Shôyô had arrived at a level of linguistic prowess that enabled him to attempt translations that went beyond *Futagokoro's* limited experimentation, the fact that he nevertheless turned to *Futagokoro* three times between 1888 and 1897 anchors the text squarely in the center of his emerging poetics of translation.⁵⁵

This may be, on the one hand, because *The False Friend* offered him an integrated example of dramatic narrative that also provided the melodramatic and sentimental elements he saw in contemporary Japanese theater. Or it may have been the rather serendipitous fact that thematically *The False Friend* is a story *about* translation, a tale of one man assuming the place of another. As Shôyô worked to find the proper balance between correspondence and adaptation, he must certainly have found that tension fully embodied in the figure of Lucian Gleyre, a character who, like a correspondent translation, nearly succeeds in his deception but is ultimately betrayed by the inability to completely transform himself into Cuthbert Fielding. No matter how well Lucian plays the part, there is something deep within that resists complete transformation. Perhaps this is why Shôyô chose to ultimately rename his adaptation *Two Hearts*. Shôyô wishes to emphasize the impossibility of complete and correspondent replacement of identity, be that the identity of two humans or of two texts.

After 1897, Shôyô moved from *Futagokoro* to other translations and dramatic productions, but there is little doubt that the lessons he learned from *The False Friend* served him well and that he realized, more fully for having studied the story several times, that the tragic flaw of Lucian Gleyre was his inability to completely mimic the heart (*kokoro*) of another. In Shôyô's emerging poetics of translation he saw the importance of maintaining a safe distance from the impossibility of literal translation; reflecting back in 1916 on his experiences as a translator, he states that over the course of his development he "spent a very lengthy period earnestly believing that a *faithful* translation was a *verbatim* translation,"⁵⁶ only to learn, finally, that, as in *Futagokoro,* he was most comfortable with correspondent adaptation that sought to preserve the spirit of the original while recognizing the constraints of literal translation. Indeed, much of what he went through in bringing *Futagokoro* to its final form reflects in miniature the lifelong process Shôyô underwent as he reached his own reconciliation between the genius of Shakespeare and the rapidly changing world of modern Japan.

Conclusion ‿

Le temps de traductions infidèles est passé. Il se fait un retour mani-feste vers l'exactitude du sens et la littéralité. Ce qui n'était, il y a quelques années, qu'une tentative périlleuse, est devenu un besoin réfléchi de toutes les intelligences élevées. Le goût public s'est épuré en s'élargissant.

[The time of unfaithful translation is over; we have turned overtly towards literalness and exactness of meaning. What, only a few years ago, was a risky attempt has now become a well-considered need for all people of high intellect. Public taste is refined by expansion.]
    —Preface to Charles-Marie Leconte de Lisle's Iliade (1867)[1]

In announcing the end of the "time of unfaithful translation," the edi-tor of Leconte de Lisle's translation of the *Illiad* expresses a confidence that literalness has finally triumphed over license. This confidence is in part a result of the French turn towards literal translation following the example of the German Romanticists.[2] However, as we have seen, even as the era of "unfaithful translation" was winding down in France, it was only beginning in contemporary Japan, and as the three examples we have stud-ied demonstrate, adaptation was about to influence a variety of Japanese lit-erary and visual arts.

From a broad perspective, adaptations served to introduce many new narrative and visual conventions into the Japanese literary and cultural mainstream, and for at least three decades played an important role in mak-ing the Western world less strange and more familiar to a Japan that had been relatively isolated for so long. Like the earlier French translators of *Les Belles Infidèles*, Japanese translators chose adaptation in order to make obscure or difficult foreign texts accessible to the masses, and their efforts to find analogous cultural settings and circumstances reflect a great deal of insight and creativity.

Yet Japan, too, had its confident champions of literal translation. As we have seen, literal translation was the dominant expectation for commercial documents and scientific texts, and in 1887 Morita Shiken, Francophile and translator of Victor Hugo, published an essay arguing for literal translation as the standard in literature as well.[3] Throughout the remainder of the 1890s, and well into the twentieth century, translators used both literal and adaptive approaches to translation, at times to absurd effect, as in the case of a translator who even preserved the word order and punctuation of the original English text in his Japanese version.[4] However, perhaps owing to the long tradition of *hon'an* in the Japanese arts, mainstream writers of Japanese fiction, including Shôyô, Futabatei Shimei, and Mori Ôgai as well as later writers such as Tanizaki Jun'ichirô and Kawabata Yasunari, tended to argue against the style of "translationese" that develops when the drive for literalness outweighs respect for the target language.[5] In general, Japanese writers, as the gatekeepers of belletristic language, seem to have inherited from *hon'an* authors the prerogative of preserving cultural and linguistic conventions in the face of challenges from the outside. Even today the Japanese predilection for variation in translation can be seen in the plethora of modern versions of *The Tale of Genji*.[6]

In his article on interpretation and rewriting as an alternative paradigm to translation, André Lefevere notes that "we are bound by both our own ideologies and our poetics when we attempt to interpret, and this ineffable grafting to both more often than not turns us into rewriters rather than the objective interpreters we would wish ourselves to be."[7] This study has examined several examples of Western literary texts that were selected, read, and 'rewritten' by Japanese men of letters during the late nineteenth century, and although my sample has been small, I have sought to include examples that demonstrate the breadth of creative reactions and range of genres that adaptation spawned during a particularly fertile period of Japanese interaction with the West.

Any one of the three works I have examined could easily yield greater insights from any number of disciplinary perspectives. My purpose in writing this book has not been to make an exhaustive study, however, but rather to apply a variety of approaches to three very different works of adaptation in order to demonstrate how rich a neglected resource Meiji *hon'an-mono* can become for a variety of comparative disciplines. I have also sought to demonstrate that, when we study several of these adaptations simultaneously—in comparison to their sources as well as with each other—they can add a new, vibrant dimension to traditional studies that have focused on new writings, or literal translations, alone.

For example, we find by comparing Robun's 1879 text with Shôyô's 1897 adaptation new evidence of the lingering legacy of Grant in Meiji Japan, seeing, in Shôyô's emphasis of his protagonist's opposition to Grant, a kind of veiled triumph in Japan's emerging military strength during the 1890s. Likewise, a comparison of Enchô's adaptation with that of Shôyô reveals a complex archetype: The Meiji *rônin,* a disenfranchised samurai/veteran whose nascent violence and financial desperation pose a threat to the new establishment as well as to a peaceful society. Finally, as all three texts demonstrate, adaptation serves a particularly apt role in allowing authors to reveal their ideological predispositions in ways that help illuminate the period (in the case of Robun and Enchô) or the author's own poetics (in the case of Shôyô).

Further, by examining adaptations in a given tradition we can expand the canon of foreign texts that served as potential catalysts of change. In the Meiji world, the large number of *hon'anmono* texts significantly broadens the scope of inquiry into which works exercised some influence on Meiji writers, intellectuals, and the masses in general. It is, of course, wise to remember that there was a certain random element in the selection of the target texts that were subsequently adapted. We may easily speculate that, had Grant avoided Japan, or Reade's novel never made it to Fukuchi's attention, or had Fawcett never taken pains to rewrite his drama as narrative, the odds of any of these works appearing in Japanese translation then (or now) would have been slight. The element of caprice that hovers around canons everywhere is no less present in the target texts that make up the corpus of Meiji literary adaptations, and the limits of (both physical and linguistic) availability turn the canon of Meiji adaptations into something of a collective Rorschach test; as we ask ourselves why certain texts *were* selected to be adapted we begin our journey towards a more informed understanding of the Meiji Zeitgeist.

As I noted in the introduction, this study is best seen as itself being a kind of adaptation of methodologies. Like Robun, I have tried to mediate and reconcile some of the differences between translation and adaptation as I sought to examine the source texts and compare them with their Japanese incarnations. Like Enchô, I have also used this study to promote a new awareness of other ways of conducting comparative studies, hoping that some of my conclusions might spur others on to examine adaptations in all traditions with greater seriousness. Finally, like Shôyô I have also tried to use this work to demonstrate the value of seeing adaptation as a rich component of translation studies, and hope it will encourage further studies of the numerous and varied adaptations of Western (and other) literatures in Meiji Japan.

Unlike the static lens of *hon'yaku,* which in its quest for correspondence sought to transmit clearly focused information across linguistic boundaries, *hon'anmono* served Meiji authors as a mutable lens whereby they could reexamine the foreign, revising, even appropriating, the texts as familiar Japanese images. From a broader perspective, I would hope this study would invite similar analyses of the many other adaptive traditions that appear across the spectrum of human creative endeavor.

Notes ∽

Introduction

1. Richard Eder, "Beowulf and Fate Meet in a Modern Poet's Lens," *New York Times,* 22 February 2000.
2. The above translation comes from Constance Black Garnett and Ralph E. Matlaw, *The Brothers Karamazov: Backgrounds and Sources: Essays in Criticism,* Norton Critical Edition (New York: Norton, 1976), 330.
3. Paul Carus, *Karma: A Story of Buddhism* (Chicago: Open Court Publishing Company, 1894). While there is still some debate over the source of Carus' story, the fact that no such parable exists in the Japanese Buddhist canon suggests that Carus appropriated Buddhist elements and applied them to Dostoyevsky's story. See Yoshida Seiichi, "'Kumo no ito,' 'Toshi shun' ni tsuite," in *Kumo no ito, Tōshi shun* (Shinchôsha, 1968), 139–43.
4. Paul Carus, *Karma: A Story of Buddhism,* 14. Italics added for emphasis.
5. Yoshida, "'Kumo no ito,' 'Toshi shun' ni tsuite," 140. Yoshida notes that it is unclear whether Akutagawa read the English or the Japanese version of Carus' story.
6. Robert Darnton has addressed this in connection with French and German fairy tales in his book *The Great Cat Massacre and Other Episodes in French Cultural History* (New York: Basic Books, 1984). He notes that "whereas the German tales maintain a tone of terror and fantasy, the French strike a note of humor and domesticity" (22).
7. The fascination of Concord transcendentalists such as Thoreau with Eastern philosophy illustrates the more general nineteenth-century American interest in Asia. One of the most prolific and well-known reinterpreters of Japan during this period was Lafcadio Hearn (1850–1904), whose adaptations of Japanese legends and ghost stories served as a window on Japan for his English-language readers (and whose works in Japanese translation con-

tinue to be popular in Japan). Other Western interpreters of Japan and Japanese literature include William Griffis (1843–1928), James de Benneville (1864–?), and Edward Morse (1838–1925). For a study of Morse, Griffis, and Hearn in this context see Robert A. Rosenstone, *Mirror in the Shrine: American Encounters with Meiji Japan* (Cambridge, MA: Harvard University Press, 1988).

8. See, for example, Asai Ryôi's *Otogibôko* (1667), an adaptation of *Jiandeng xinhua* by Qu You (1341–1427).

9. Mario J. Valdés and Linda Hutcheon, "Rethinking Literary History—Comparatively," *ACLA Bulletin* 25, no. 2–4 (1996): 20.

Chapter I

1. Edward Young, *Conjectures on Original Composition. In a Letter to the Author of Sir Charles Grandison,* 1st ed. (London: Printed for A. Millar and R. and J. Dodsley, 1759).

2. For a thorough examination of the modes and their enumerators (complete with outlines), see Willis Barnstone, *The Poetics of Translation: History, Theory, Practice* (New Haven, Conn.: Yale University Press, 1993), Chapter 2, especially pp. 26–29.

3. "The clumsiest literal translation is a thousand times more useful than the prettiest paraphrase. . . . I want translation with copious footnotes, footnotes reaching up like skyscrapers to the top of this or that page so as to leave only the gleam of one textual line between commentary and eternity." Vladimir Nabokov, "Problems of Translation: *Onegin* in English," *Partisan Review* 22 (1955)4:496, 512.

4. "Dedication of the Aeneis" in William Paton Ker, ed., *Essays of John Dryden* (Oxford: Clarendon Press, 1900).

5. Japanese scholars often note the pragmatic appropriation of Western texts—and the transmutation thereof—for political and other early Meiji causes. See Homma Hisao, *Meiji bungaku shi,* Vol. 1 (Tôkyôdô, 1949); Muramatsu Sadataka, *Kindai Nihon bungaku: seiritsu to tenkai* (Yûbun shoin, 1969) pp. 39–47; and Hiraoka Toshio and Tôgô Katsumi, *Nihon bungakushi gaisetsu: kindai hen* (Yûseidô, 1979) pp. 11–12. For a Western perspective on Meiji translation infidelity, see Donald Keene, *Dawn to the West: Japanese Literature of the Modern Era,* Vol. 1 (New York: Holt, Rhinehart, and Winston, 1984), pp. 60, 63, 67–68.

6. For an overview of the historical uses of the term *hon'yaku,* see Sugimoto Tsutomu's *Zôtei Nihon hon'yakugoshi no kenkyû,* vol. 4 of *Sugimoto Tsutomu chosaku senshû* (Yasaka shobô, 1998), 27–30; as well as his *Nagasaki tsûji monogatari: kotoba to bunka no hon'yakusha* (Tokyo: Sôtakusha, 1990).

7. The term *hon'yaku* is used frequently to designate literal translation in

Sugita Genpaku's *Rangaku Kotohajime* (A Primer to Dutch Studies, 1815; for a modern Japanese translation with the original text, see Sugita Genpaku and Hisao Hama, *Rangaku kotohajime: fu Keiei yawa* (*Genpon gendaiyaku* vol. 54). (Higashimurayama: Kyôikusha, 1980), a memoir of the beginnings of Western studies in Japan. For a discussion of *rangaku,* see Hirakawa Sukehiro, "Japan's Turn to the West," in *The Cambridge History of Japan,* ed. Marius B. Jansen, (Cambridge and New York: Cambridge University Press, 1989), 435–48; and Marius B. Jansen, "*Rangaku* and Westernization," *Modern Asian Studies* 18, no. 4 (1984).

8. Hirakawa Sukehiro, "Japan's Turn to the West," pp. 440, 447.

9. Considering the ongoing popularity of Chinese medicine in Japan, one could argue that these *hon'an* of human physiology continue to play an important cultural role in Japan today.

10. In using *transmutation* I take my lead from George Steiner, who introduces the term in his *After Babel: Aspects of Language and Translation* (Oxford: Oxford University Press, 1975). In some respects I am also using it as does Roman Jakobsen in describing *intersemiotic* translation, "an interpretation of verbal signs by means of signs of nonverbal systems, e.g., from verbal art into music, dance, cinema, or painting." Rainer Schulte and John Biguenet, *Theories of Translation: An Anthology of Essays from Dryden to Derrida* (Chicago: University of Chicago Press, 1992), 7.

11. Some of Meiji Japan's most notable writers—and pioneers of modern narrative—also wrote *hon'anmono,* including Yamada Bimyô, Ozaki Kôyô, Mori Ôgai, Kitamura Tôkoku, Higuchi Ichiyo, Shimazaki Toson, and Ueda Bin. For detailed analyses of some of the above authors' *hon'anmono,* see Yoshitake Yoshinori, *Kindai bungaku no naka no Seiô: Kindai Nihon hon'anshi, hikaku bungaku kenkyû sôsho* (Kyôiku shuppan sentâ, 1974).

12. Georges L. Bastin, "Adaptation," in *Encyclopedia of Translation Studies,* ed. Mona Baker (London and New York: Routledge, 1997), 6.

13. Ibid. p. 5.

14. On France, see "French tradition" by Myriam Salama-Carr in *Encyclopedia of Translation Studies* (London and New York: Routledge, 1997), 411–15; on Qing adaptations see Lawrence Venuti, *The Scandals of Translation: Towards an Ethics of Difference* (London, New York: Routledge, 1998), 178–86.

15. *Ars Poetica.*

16. Myriam Salama-Carr, "French Tradition," in *Encyclopedia of Translation Studies,* ed. Mona Baker (London and New York: Routledge, 1997), 411.

17. Ibid., 416.

18. Ibid., 413. It is interesting to note that Edward Young, quoted above, and his treatise on originality exercised a certain influence on the German philosophers whose literalism served to displace the adaptive license of *Les*

Belles Infidèles. See Martin William Steinke, *Edward Young's "Conjectures on Original Composition" in England and Germany,* Vol. 28, *Americana Germanica* (New York: F. C. Stechert Co. Inc., 1917), 14–17, 39–40.

19. Venuti, *The Scandals of Translation,* 178–79.
20. Ibid., 182.
21. Ibid., 183–84.
22. See Edward Fowler, "On Naturalizing and Making Strange: Japanese Literature in Translation," *Journal of Japanese Studies* 16, no. 3 (1990): 116; and Adrian James Pinnington, "Hamlet in Japanese Dress: Two Contemporary Japanese Versions of *Hamlet,*" in *Hamlet and Japan,* ed. Yoshiko Uéno, *The Hamlet Collection; No. 2* (New York: AMS Press, 1995), 205–06. Newmark is cited in André Lefevere, *Translating Literature: Practice and Theory in a Comparative Literature Context* (New York: Modern Language Association of America, 1992), 10–11. For a brief description of Lefevere's axis, see André Lefevere, *Translation, Rewriting, and the Manipulation of Literary Fame* (London and New York: Routledge, 1992), 99–110.
23. Eugene Eoyang, "'History', 'Herstory', 'Theirstory', 'Ourstory': Gender, Genre and Cultural Bias in Accounts of East Asian Literatures," (Kyoto: International Research Center for Japanese Studies, 1998).
24. A similar theme-variation dynamic can be found in the tradition of *hommondori* (allusive variation of prose) in narrative. Traditional cross-genre examples include *hikiuta* (allusion to lyric within narrative) and *honzetsu* (allusion to Chinese poetry or *monogatari* narrative in lyric).
25. List compiled from Satô Kôki and Tomita Hitoshi, *Nihon kindai bungaku to Seiyô,* (Surugadai Shuppansha, 1984), chronology 1–2, and Yanagida Izumi, *Meiji shoki honyaku bungaku no kenkyû,* vol. 5, *Meiji bungaku kenkyû* (Shunjûsha, 1961), 463–89.
26. One particularly promising approach to comparative studies is imagology, "the typology of perceived national identity as expressed in literary texts." Joep Leerssen, "As Others See, among Others, Us: The Anglo–German Relationship in Context," in *As Others See Us: Anglo-German Perceptions,* ed. Harald Husemann (Frankfurt: Peter Lang, 1994). *Hon'anmono* are a particularly apt subject of this approach, since imagology "is not merely interested in tabulating textual typologies of various national characters as represented in literature—though that is an important enterprise. More than that, image studies wants to apply these individual typologies towards understanding the underlying structures of national imagery (e.g., the recurrent North-South distinction), and to demonstrate its *conventional* (as opposed to empirically referential) nature." Joep Leerssen, "Echoes and Images: Reflections upon Foreign Space," in *Alterity, Identity, Image: Selves and Others in Society and Scholarship,* ed. Raymond Corbey and Joep Leerssen, *Amsterdam Studies on Cultural Identity* (Amsterdam-Atlanta: Rodopi, 1991), 133.

27. Of course, Meiji writers are not alone in this predisposition, for from a broader point of view, this process of assimilation is how we all enrich and expand our lives with both material and artistic "imports."

28. Although biographical narratives were nothing new in Japan, many of the early descriptions of Western nations included lists of famous historical figures. When more detailed biographies of some of these celebrities appeared in Japan they were a natural target for translation due to the name recognition earlier descriptions of the West had cultivated among the reading public.

29. The above list is gleaned from the Diet Library Meiji materials collection, which contains a number of other adapted Western biographies as well.

30. In the case of the Bismarck adapted biography, for example, the foreword identifies the source text as "Mackenzie's translation of Hesekiel's biography of Bismarck" (George Hesekiel, Kenneth R. H. Mackenzie, and Bayard Taylor, *The Life of Bismarck, Private and Political,* trans. Kenneth R. H. Mackenzie [New York: Fords Howard and Hulbert, 1870]).

Chapter II

1. Clara A. Whitney, M. William Steele, and Ichimata Tamiko, *Clara's Diary: An American Girl in Meiji Japan,* (Tokyo and New York: Kodansha International, 1979), 257.

2. "Koko ni Kun no tokubô wo shitau no amari waga shaô rei no kyôki hansan ensho wo kaerimizu wakai no hikki wo isasaka tasukete bunka ni hitoyo wo soyuru nomi." Preface to Volume II of Kanagaki Robun, *Gurando-shi den Yamato bunshô* (Kinshôdô, 1879).

3. Ulysses S. Grant, "Letter from U.S. Grant to General E. F. Beale" (Peking: 1879).

4. For a general historical overview of Grant's stay in Japan, see Richard T. Chang, "General Grant's 1879 Visit to Japan," *Monumenta Nipponica* 24, no. 4 (1969), and Dallas Finn, "Grant in Japan," *American History Illustrated* XVI, no. 3 (1981). For other English treatments of the visit, see Julia Meech-Pekarik and Metropolitan Museum of Art, *The World of the Meiji Print: Impressions of a New Civilization* (New York: Weatherhill, 1986), 107–10.

5. Kimura Kinka, *Morita Kan'ya* (Shin taishûsha, 1943).

6. William S. McFeely, *Grant: A Biography* (New York: Norton, 1981), chapter 25, and Geoffrey Perret, *Ulysses S. Grant: Soldier & President* (New York: Random House, 1997) 432–37.

7. For example, Grant impressed the Chinese with his lack of arrogance and bias; they saw him as "a quiet and sympathetic gentleman in evening clothes smoking his cigar." (Horatio E. Wirtz, "General Ulysses S. Grant: Diplomat Extraordinaire," in *Ulysses S. Grant: Essays and Documents,* ed. David L. Wilson and John Y. Simon [Carbondale: Southern Illinois University Press,

1981], 49). Grant obliquely returned the compliment: "I must say that neither the country nor the people attract the traveler to pay them a second
visit . . . but I . . . have drawn rather a favorable view of their future from
all I have seen." Grant, "Letter from U.S. Grant to General E. F. Beale."

8. "Grant in Japan," 37.

9. John Russell Young, *Around the World with General Grant,* Vol. 2 (New York:
The American News Company, 1879), 480–81.

10. Ibid., 582–83.

11. The group made one stopover in Shizuoka, which was apparently cholera-
free.

12. Ulysses S. Grant, "Diaries of Southeast Asian Tour" (Special Collections,
Gelman Library, George Washington University, Washington D.C.) (Book
III: 3 July).

13. L. T. Remlap, ed., *General U. S. Grant's Tour Around the World* (Hartford,
Conn.: James Betts & Co., 1879), 275.

14. *Around the World with General Grant,* 563, 575.

15. See Wirtz, "General Ulysses S. Grant: Diplomat Extraordinaire."

16. Grant had personally hosted some of the leaders in Washington, D.C., seven
years earlier.

17. Only a few months before Grant's arrival in Japan (and just prior to his visit
to China) Japan had created Okinawa Prefecture out of the (disputed)
Ryûkyû Kingdom, setting Chinese diplomatic nerves on edge. For more on
Grant's role in this issue, see Chang, "General Grant's 1879 Visit to Japan,"
379–82.

18. Werner Gustav Schaumann, *Kanagaki Robun: Ein japanischer Unterhaltungsschriftsteller in der frühen Zeit der Modernisierung* (Bonn: Rheinische Friedrich-
Wilhelms-Universität Bonn, 1981), 205.

19. John A. Carpenter, *Ulysses S. Grant* (New York: Twayne Publishers, 1970),
172.

20. *Around the World with General Grant,* 477. Although a number of ambas-
sadors, and even the German crown prince, had traveled to Japan, no head
of state, retired or otherwise, had as yet made a visit.

21. In 1870 William Seward was granted a rather chilly, handshake-free audience with the Emperor. "Grant in Japan," 40.

22. Her description is from a reception for Grant held at the residence of Mori
Arinori, 28 August 1879. *Clara's Diary,* 270.

23. *Around the World with General Grant.* Several other Grant travel narratives
appeared in 1879–80, most drawing heavily on Young's account. See, for
example, L. T. Remlap, ed., *General U. S. Grant's Tour Around the World,* and
J. F. Packard, *Grant's Tour around the World: With Incidents of His Journey through
England, Ireland, Scotland, France, Spain, Germany, Austria, Italy, Belgium, Switzerland, Russia, Egypt, India, China, Japan, Etc.* (Philadelphia: H. W. Kelley, 1880).

24. *Around the World with General Grant,* 565, 532.

25. Fully one-quarter of the illustrations depict individuals at close range engaged in everyday pursuits.

26. This sense is increased by the Chinese characters displayed (backwards and somewhat stylized) on the wall behind.

27. *Around the World with General Grant,* 517–18.

28. Ibid., 587.

29. Ibid., 514.

30. Ibid., 577.

31. Ibid., 529–30.

32. Ibid., 528.

33. Ibid., 516.

34. Ibid., 583.

35. "Diaries of Southeast Asian Tour." This unpublished manuscript is located in the special collections of the Gelman Library, George Washington University.

36. The presence of the Empress suggests one of several protocol adjustments in light of the unprecedented nature of Grant's visit. Certainly the fact that Grant's wife, Julia, accompanied him to the imperial audience influenced this particular accommodation.

37. Unfortunately, Grant's Asia tour diary ends abruptly midway through the Japan trip.

38. *Around the World with General Grant,* 569–70.

39. Among the other commemorative texts is a triptych by Toyohara Kunichika entitled *Beikoku Guranto-shi go-tsûkô no san'ei* (The Splendid Procession of America's Mr. Grant) in *The World of the Meiji Print: Impressions of a New Civilization,* Plate 18.

40. For detailed biographies of Robun, see Schaumann, *Kanagaki Robun: Ein Japanischer Unterhaltungsschriftsteller in Der Frühen Zeit Der Modernisierung,* and Okitsu Kaname, *Kanagaki Robun: Bunmei kaika no gesakusha* (Yûrindô, 1993).

41. For an English study of this work, see John Pierre Mertz, "Internalizing Social Difference: Kanagaki Robun's *Shank's Mare to the Western Seas,*" in *New Directions in the Study of Meiji Japan,* eds. Helen Hardacre and Adam L. Kern, Conference on Meiji Studies and Harvard University (Leiden and New York: Brill, 1997).

42. Quoted in Nozake Sabun, "Meiji shoki no shimbun shôsetsu," *Waseda bungaku,* (March 1925), 27–28.

43. Kanagaki's aborted adaptation of Hamlet, *Seiyô Kabuki Hamuretto,* appears to have been the first attempt to introduce the plot of Hamlet in Japanese. Murakami Takeshi, "Shakespeare and *Hamlet* in Japan: A Chronological Overview," in *Hamlet and Japan,* ed. Yoshiko Uéno, *The Hamlet Collection; No. 2* (New York: AMS Press, 1995) 246. It ran in the 7, 9, and 10 September 1875, editions of the *Hiragana eiri shimbun.*

44. Other Grant biographies published around the time of his visit include Yamada Junji, *Beikoku zendaitôryô Gurando kôden* (Gakunôsha, 1879); Toyoshima Sajûrô, *Gurando-kô ryakuden* (Asahi shimbunsha, 1879); and Ôta Minoru, *Hokubeirenpô zendaitôryô Gurando-shi seisekiki* (Meimondô shuppan, 1879). Robun drew heavily on the first for the details of Grant's life.

45. The colors red and purple are particularly vibrant, owing to the use of the new German aniline dyes.

46. Robun produced *Takahashi Oden yasha monogatari,* like Grant's biography, in a very short time in reaction to a contemporary event, in this case the arrest and conviction of a young widow for slitting the throat of her money lender. She was eventually sentenced to death, and was the last person in the Meiji period to be officially executed by beheading.

47. See Schaumann, *Kanagaki Robun,* 205.

48. J. S. Motoda, "A Japanese Life of General Grant," *Century Illustrated Monthly,* July 1895, 435. Extant copies of Kanagaki's text are extremely rare; my searching has managed to locate only four to date, three of which are in archives in the U.S.

49. It is interesting to note that the Japanese transliteration of "Grant" becomes *Gurando* rather than *Guranto.* This was not, by any means, standardized in the Meiji period, and some narratives use *Guranto* while others use *Gurando.* I note that in his correspondence with Grant Iwakura Tomomi uses *Gurando,* suggesting that this may have been the preferred transliteration (possibly because *Guranto* is similar to the Japanese word *garan-to,* meaning deserted and empty, and it may have been seen as effrontery to even approach such a pun). An additional, intriguing, dimension of Grant's appropriation into Japanese is the varied use of Sino-Japanese characters, with their concomitant meanings, to represent Grant's name. Robun's choice, for example, connotes exceptionality and Westernness. Others use the same character for *ran* but vary on their choice of characters to represent the sounds *gu* and *to* (or *do*).

50. The pun I have rendered "Ap-prose-al" stems from Robun's use of the homophonic character *shô* (prize) in lieu of *shô* (passage) to make the word *bunshô* (text).

51. Each volume is composed of three sections, the covers of which line up, right to left, to form a triptych illustrating, in the case of volume I, a Civil War battlefield scene. The triptych of volume II forms a domestic scene of the Grant family in the White House, and volume III forms a row of flag-clad geisha, line dancing.

52. In the process, I admit to creating my own, admittedly prosaic, adapted translation of Robun's text.

53. In the process of transposing Western names into Japanese, sometimes small punctuation mistakes lead to large pronunciation errors. In Robun's transliteration of Copernicus, for example, the katakana syllabary for *Ko* picks up

a small horizontal line, changing it to *Yo,* and the vocalization circle of *pe* becomes two dots, changing the reading to *be.* Similar metamorphoses occur with the names Columbus and Amerigo (Vespucci) later on in the same section.

54. This African/Egyptian trip, aside from being geographically complex, did not, in fact, happen during 1879; apparently Robun was looking for a way to weave pictures of camels and pyramids into his story.

55. The night's program was a specially prepared dramatic adaptation (*hon'an*) of Grant's life written by the leading playwright of his day, Kawatake Mokuami (1816–1893). His work, *Go-sannen ôshû gunki* (Military Chronicle of the Northern War's Final Three Years), is filled with battle scenes designed to pay tribute to Grant's valor by equating him with the classical warrior, Minamoto (Hachimantarô) Yoshiie (1039–1106) (played by the preeminent actor Ichikawa Danjûrô IX).

56. Ulysses S. Grant, James Grant Wilson, and E. B. Washburne, *General Grant's Letters to a Friend, 1861–1880* (New York and Boston: T. Y. Crowell & Co., 1897), 86; Ulysses S. Grant and Jesse Grant Cramer, *Letters of Ulysses S. Grant to His Father and His Youngest Sister, 1857–78* (New York and London: G. P. Putnam's Sons, 1912), 135, 150. Grant's correspondence indicates that they intended to stay in Japan for only a few weeks, returning to the United States in July.

57. One exception to this are the works of Shakespeare, which from early on appear to have been recognized as a major part of the Western canon and were targeted for translation accordingly.

58. *The World of the Meiji Print,* 93, 112. This distinction gave them the illusion of greater permanence then, and now adds a strange (if quaint) color inequity to surviving prints.

59. Laurance P. Roberts, *A Dictionary of Japanese Artists: Painting, Sculpture, Ceramics, Prints, Lacquer* (Tokyo and New York: Weatherhill, 1976), 23.

60. Ibid., 97. He also went by the names of Baidô Hôsai, Utagawa Kunisada III, and Utagawa Kunimasa IV.

61. Ibid. In fact, Roberts calls him "an artist of no importance." His later career included depicting battle scenes from the Russo-Japanese War.

62. One can only speculate as to why Robun changed his artists mid-stream: Perhaps he wanted to give Baidô a lucky break, or maybe by the third volume subscriptions were flagging and a cheaper artist was hired.

63. Artist unknown. "Portrait of Commodore Perry," in *Kanagawa kenritsu rekishi hakubutsukan tenji kaisetsusho* (Kanagawa kenritsu rekishi hakubutsukan, 1995), 31.

64. They also demonstrate the changing Japanese attitudes towards the West between 1854 and 1879. For a study of these changes as reflected in contemporary illustrations, see Suzuki Keiko, "*Yokohama-e* and *Kaika-e* Prints: Japanese Interpretations of Self and Other from 1860 through the 1880s,"

in *New Directions in the Study of Meiji Japan,* eds. Helen Hardacre and Adam L. Kern, Conference on Meiji Studies and Harvard University (Leiden and New York: Brill, 1997).

65. *Oitsuke, oikose!*

66. An American girl, Clara Whitney, sat with the Grants during the performance and gives this enthusiastic response to the scene of geisha dancing: "What made the blood rush with a thrill through the hearts of the Americans? What in the appearance of these girls made thousands of sweet memories and patriotic thoughts arise in our minds? Ah, the old flag, the glorious Stars and Stripes! What else could produce in an American such feelings! Each girl was dressed in a robe made of the dear old Stars and Stripes, while upon their heads shone a circlet of silver stars. It made the prettiest costume imaginable. The stripes constituted the over-robe itself while one sleeve slipped off from one shoulder revealed a sleeve of stars below, their girdles were dark blue, sandals, red and white, and presently they took out fans having on one side the American and upon the other the national flag. The surprise was complete. We looked with strong emotion upon this graceful tribute to our country's flag, and felt grateful to our Japanese friends for their kindness displayed not only to General Grant but to our honored country." *Clara's Diary,* 260–61.

67. This fashion emerged from even earlier, sixteenth-century portrayals of Westerners in Nagasaki called *namban byôbu.* The illustrated screens usually have titles such as *Ryûkyûjin tojô gyôretsu zu* (Scene of the Ryûkyûan Entourage) or *Chôsen daigyôretsu ryaku zu* (Sketch of the Korean Entourage). Many of the maps and books depicting foreigners are copies of Nishikawa Joken's *Bankoku jinbutsuzu* (1720).

68. Curiously, Lincoln seems to have one of his assailants in an aikidô-style grip.

69. Private performances of the dramatic arts were the rule for the Emperor, and the Meiji theatre had only recently been elevated to reputable status, in part owing to the stature of opera in Europe.

70. As a curious coincidence, Western readers might be reminded of the death scene in *Julius Caesar.* However, Shakespeare's work was not formally translated until 1883. That is not to negate, however, the possibility of *hon'anmono* versions of *Julius Caesar* making their way into Japan by way of much earlier English-language theater performances held on the Yokohama stage for expatriates.

71. Eitaku, the illustrator for volumes II and III of the text, served as Ii Naosuke's official painter and was left masterless upon his death. It is highly possible that Eitaku, whose affiliation with Robun's workshop continued through the preparation of volume II (in which the assassination scene appears), may have had an influence on the visual composition of the scene.

72. For a discussion of *mitate* in a pre-Meiji *gesaku* context, see J. Scott Miller,

"The Hybrid Narrative of Kyôden's *Sharebon*," *Monumenta Nipponica* 43, no. 2 (1988): 141.

73. That same *gesaku* tradition contained the possibility for ironic, undermining discourse (*ugachi*) as well, which is also suggested in Robun's comparison of the Grants with Kita and Yaji earlier in his text.

74. James R. Brandon, "Kabuki and Shakespeare: Balancing Yin and Yang," *The Drama Review* 43, no. 2 (1999). See especially pages 15–16 for a discussion of *sekai* and *shukô*.

75. At the end of the Shintomiza performance, Grant presented the theater with a curtain as a token of his appreciation, a fact noted in all the public narratives. His own personal diary, however, says nothing about the event (or the gift), despite the fact that the Grants traveled to Nikkô the day following the performance, where a relatively light schedule allowed Grant to reflect back on his trip and do some general summarizing in his diary.

76. For more on the nuances of the term *wage* in nineteenth-century Japan, see Sugimoto Tsutomu, *Zôtei Nihon hon'yakugoshi no kenkyû,* vol. 4 of *Sugimoto Tsutomu chosaku senshû* (Yaasaka shobô, 1998), 27–30.

77. In point of fact, later in the text Robun does gloss the characters—as *wakai* (see epigram, above), lending further strength to the *hon'an*-as-rapprochement theory.

78. The title reads literally "The Honorable Grant's Biography in Yamato Prose/Praise." Grant's status is elevated by the use of language ("honorable"), and yet Japan is itself elevated by Robun's use of the more revered euphemism for Japan, *Yamato,* instead of the more common *Nihon* or *Nippon.* Grant—and Japan—are both honored in the title, verbally reinforcing the parity suggested by the two sets of flags.

79. For a discussion of the Freedom and People's Right's Movement, see Roger W. Bowen, *Rebellion and Democracy in Meiji Japan: A Study of Commoners in the Popular Rights Movement* (Berkeley: University of California Press, 1980), 107–25.

80. This may explain why there is no mention of the Grant-Meiji handshake in Robun's text: Readerly sentiment might very well have been offended at the idea of a leatherworker touching the Emperor.

81. Evidence of this fear emerged during Grant's tour when a rumor began to spread that cholera victims who went to the hospital would have their livers removed as talismans for Grant. See Young, *Around the World with General Grant,* 569–70.

82. It is interesting to note that, unlike Young's text, *Gurando-shi den* contains no visual rendering of the Emperor Meiji.

83. Benedict Anderson, *Imagined Communities: Reflections on the Origin and Spread of Nationalism,* (London and New York: Verso, 1991), 204–05.

84. Grant's personal diary reveals some of his own perceptions and attitudes that belie the public images offered in both transmutations.

85. "A Japanese Life of General Grant," 435.
86. Ibid.
87. Motoda, who was born in Kumamoto and became a Christian while studying at St. Paul's School in Tokyo, studied at both Kenyon College and the University of Pennsylvania, where he received a Ph.D. He was ordained after further studies at the Philadelphia Divinity School, and went on to become the first native Japanese Episcopal Bishop. "Pioneer Japanese Bishop Passes Away," *Spirit of Missions,* May 1928, p. 300.
88. "A Japanese Life of General Grant," 446. Asterisks denote footnotes in the original text.
89. Siegfried Kracauer, film historian and theoretician, did pilot studies in 1947 to measure Hollywood objectivity versus subjectivity vis-à-vis national stereotypes: "On the whole screen portrayals of foreigners are rarely true likenesses; more often than not they grow out of the urge for self-assertion rather than the thirst for knowledge, so that the resultant images reflect not so much the mentality of the other people as the state of mind of their own." "National Types as Hollywood Presents Them," in *Public Opinion Quarterly,* Spring 1949, p. 70, as quoted in Richard Falcon, "Images of Germany and the Germans in British Film and Television Fictions: A Brief Chronological Overview," in *As Others See Us: Anglo-German Perceptions,* ed. Harald Husemann (Frankfurt: P. Lang, 1994), 7–8.

Chapter III

1. George Smith, *Ten Weeks in Japan* (London: Longman, Green, Longman, and Roberts, 1861), 125.
2. W. G. Aston, *A History of Japanese Literature* (New York: D. Appleton & Co., 1899), 389.
3. Letter to Edward Marston, as quoted in Wayne Burns, *Charles Reade: A Study in Victorian Authorship* (New York: Bookman Associates, 1961), 200.
4. One of the first comprehensive studies to address the history of professional storytelling in Japan is Sano Takashi, *Kôdan gohyakunen* (Tsurushobô, 1943). In recent years other studies have appeared, among them Takeshita Kikuo, *Kinsei chihô geinô kôgyô no kenkyû* (Osaka: Seibundô, 1997); Nobuhiro Shinji and Utei Enba, *Rakugo wa ikani shite keiseisareta ka, sôsho engeki to misemono no bunkashi* (Tokyo: Heibonsha, 1986); and, in English, Morioka Heinz and Sasaki Miyoko, *Rakugo, The Popular Narrative Art of Japan* (Cambridge, Mass.: Council on East Asian Studies, Harvard University, 1990).
5. Miyoshi Masao, *Off Center: Power and Culture Relations between Japan and the United States, Convergences* (Cambridge, Mass.: Harvard University Press, 1991), 35–36.
6. See, for example, Virginia Skord, *Tales of Tears and Laughter: Short Fiction of Medieval Japan* (Honolulu: University of Hawaii Press, 1991).

7. Hiraga Gennai and Nakamura Yukihiko, *Fûrai sanjinshû, Nihon koten bungaku taikei 55* (Tokyo: Iwanami shoten, 1961). Many later comic fiction (*gesaku*) writers, such as Shikitei Samba and Jippensha Ikku, had close ties with the *yose* and/or actually performed as storytellers. *Gesaku* works also contain a number of references to storytelling.

8. A Tokyo guidebook lists 477 registered storytellers in 1876 (see Plate 99, Ogi Shinzo and Maeda Ai, ed., *Meiji Taishô zushi: Tokyo* [Tokyo: Chikuma shobo, 1978]).

9. Inouye Jukichi, *Sketches of Tokyo Life* (Yokohama: Torando, 1895), 3–4.

10. Two of the most prominent were the San'yûtei and Tachibanaya clans.

11. The installments were from twenty to forty minutes in duration. Storyteller lore contains examples of famed raconteurs whose repertoires numbered in the hundreds of epic-length stories, a few of which took several months, or even a year, to complete. Robert Adams, an anthropologist studying rural storytellers in the 1960s, confirmed that some of the master storytellers could recite over one hundred tales with great precision. Robert J. Adams, "Folktale Telling and Storytellers in Japan," *Asian Folklore Studies* 26, no. 1 (1967): 117.

12. Maeda Ai analyzes some of the fundamental differences between these subgenres in Maeda Ai, *Kindai Nihon no bungaku kûkan: rekishi kotoba jôkyô* (Tokyo: Shin'yôsha, 1983), 313–21.

13. For more on the stylistic differences between storytellers from these two urban centers, see Shogei konwakai/Osaka geinô konwakai, ed., *Kokontôzai Rakugoka jiten* (Heibonsha, 1989).

14. One such narrative, *Shiobara Tasuke ichidaiki,* developed by San'yûtei Enchô during the 1870s, describes the rags-to-riches story of a successful charcoal merchant from the provinces (San'yûtei Enchô and Wakabayashi Kanzô [with Sakai Shôzô], *Enchô sôdan Shiobara Tasuke ichidaiki* [Sokkihô kenkyûkai, 1884]). For studies of this work, see Ochi Haruo, "Mô hitori no Shiobara Tasuke," *Bungaku* 37, no. 5 (1969), and J. Scott Miller, "Early Voice Recordings of Japanese Storytelling," *Oral Tradition* 11, no. 2 (1996): 308–11.

15. In 1880, for example, *yose* audience numbers have been estimated at 2.6 million, as opposed to kabuki's 430,000 (see *Meiji Taishô zushi: Tokyo,* 57).

16. *Rakugo,* 250.

17. For more detailed treatment of the invention of *sokki,* see Fukuoka Takashi, *Nihon sokki kotohajime: Takusari Kôki no shôgai,* (Iwanami, 1978), and J. Scott Miller, "Japanese Shorthand and Sokkibon," *Monumenta Nipponica* 49, no. 4 (1994).

18. The transcribed oral tale became so popular, in fact, that it spawned a new genre of written literature, the *sokkibon* (shorthand-book) that eventually evolved into the large collections of popular literature (*taishû bungaku*) supplying many of today's large publishing firms (Hakubunkan, Kôdansha, etc.) with their initial capital.

19. It is curious to note that Enchô himself took up the pen in two of his works, *Sashimonoshi meijin Chôji* (1892; serialized 1895) and *Eikoku joô Erizabesu-den* (1885; published posthumously in 1923). Both were adaptations of Western tales that, despite the inclusion of storytelling rhetoric, were never performed on stage. For a study of the former, see Tada Michitarô, "Kaisetsu (hon'anmono)," in *San'yûtei Enchô zenshû 6: hon'anmono,* ed. Kôjima Seijirô, Ikeda Yazaburo, and Ozaki Hideki (Kadokawa shoten, 1975).

20. For more detailed studies of the changing Meiji Tokyo landscape see Edward Seidensticker, *Low City, High City: Tokyo from Edo to the Earthquake* (New York: Knopf, 1983), and James L. McClain, John M. Merriman, and Ugawa Kaoru, *Edo and Paris: Urban Life and the State in the Early Modern Era* (Ithaca, NY: Cornell University Press, 1994).

21. The so-called Freedom and People's Rights Movement involved a number of storytellers, the most famous being Kawakami Otojirô, who also experimented with political theater as a tool to move the masses. See Matsunaga Goichi, *Kawakami Otojirô: kindaigeki, hatenkô no yoake* (Tokyo: Asahi shimbunsha, 1988), 45–51; and Komiya Toyotaka, *Japanese Music and Drama in the Meiji Era,* vol. 3, *Japanese Culture in the Meiji Era* (Tokyo: Ôbunsha, 1956), 265–67.

22. Morioka Heinz and Miyoko Sasaki, "The Blue-Eyed Storyteller: Henry Black and His Rakugo Career," *Monumenta Nipponica* 38, no. 2 (1983); and *Rakugo,* 256–58.

23. The lengthy stories can be found in Volume 6 of the most recent edition of Enchô's collected works, *San'yûtei Enchô zenshû,* ed. Kôjima Seijirô, Ikeda Yazaburo, and Ozaki Hideki, 8 vols. (Kadokawa shoten, 1975). Shorter *hon'an* pieces are collected in volume 13 of an earlier edition of collected works, *San'yûtei Enchô zenshû,* ed. Kôzô Suzuki, 13 vols. (Shun'yôdô, 1926–28; reprint, 1963–64; Sekai bunkosha).

24. Hakuen used a German tale as the basis for his *kôdan* entitled *Ochirya zôshi: Doitsu kenjô* (A Wise German Daughter)(Aichidô, 1891).

25. The original editions of both works are as follows: Charles Reade, *Hard Cash. A Matter-of-Fact Romance,* 3 vols. (London: S. Low Son & Marston, 1863); and San'yûtei Enchô and Wakabayashi Kanzô, *Seiyô ninjôbanashi Eikoku Kôshi Jôji Sumisu no den* (Sokkihô kenkyûkai, 1885).

26. During the Tokugawa period, in fact, entertainers were often classified among the pariah classes.

27. Nobuhiro Shinji, "*Eikoku kôshi den* to *Hard Cash,*" *Bungaku* 47, no. 2 (1979): 61.

28. Koike Shôtarô and Fujii Shûtetsu, "Kaidai (hon'anmono)," in *San'yûtei Enchô zenshû 6: hon'anmono,* ed. Kôjima Seijirô, Ikeda Yazaburo, and Ozaki Hideki (Kadokawa shoten, 1975), 552.

29. For example, by and large Enchô retains the complex set of relationships established between the protagonists.

30. Enchô never explicitly states the sources of any of his *hon'anmono;* the closest he comes is in the introduction of *Kôshôbi* (1887), where he notes that his tale comes from "the French legend of Julia." The sources of four of his *hon'anmono* (Victorien Sardou, Guy de Maupassant, Scott, and Reade) have been traced by scholars in the intervening years, with *Hard Cash* having been identified in 1979 by Komatsu Shigeo and Nobuhiro Shinji (*"Eikoku kôshi den* to *Hard Cash,"* 53–54). The sources of two of Enchô's *hon'anmono* remain a mystery: *Kôshôbi* and *Matsu no misao bijin no ikiume* (1886).

31. Elton Edward Smith, *Charles Reade* (Boston: Twayne Publishers, 1976), 157; and *Charles Reade: A Study in Victorian Authorship,* 11.

32. Smith, *Charles Reade,* 154.

33. As quoted in ibid., 105.

34. William Dean Howells, *My Literary Passions* (New York: Harper & Brothers, 1895), 193–97.

35. *Hard Cash* is actually a sequel to an earlier Reade romance, *Love Me Little, Love Me Long* (1859), that treats the class-divided courtship and marriage of characters who appear as parents in *Hard Cash.*

36. I have taken as a basis for this summary Reade biographer Wayne Burns' precis (*Charles Reade: A Study in Victorian Authorship,* 213–15), which I have altered to emphasize aspects that compare with Enchô's adaptation.

37. Ibid., 201–04.

38. Ibid., 227–28.

39. As quoted in ibid., 226–27.

40. Ibid., 230.

41. Smith, *Charles Reade,* 123.

42. A penetrating analysis of *Eikoku kôshi* in Japanese is *"Eikoku kôshi den* to *Hard Cash."*

43. Note that Enchô even "adapts" British topography to make it conform with Japan: The journey from London to Liverpool by train, even today, averages about three hours one way, so it is the Japanese counterpart (Tokyo-Maebashi, approximately 70 kilometers) Enchô appears to be describing.

44. There is some ambiguity regarding the name *Natan Bûru* (Nathan Bull). In some later editions it has been transliterated as *Natan Bunoru,* which would suggest the English name Nathan Bunoll. However, in the original edition of *Eikoku kôshi* Liverpool (*Ribapûru*) has been transliterated as *Ribapunoru* (the katakana *no* can be confused with the glyph for double vowel in vertical writing), so the typesetter could very well have gone astray on *Bûru* as well.

45. The Japanese text gives Harumi's rank as 1200 *koku;* the rice revenue system—one *koku* equating roughly to enough rice to feed one servant for a year—was a standard of rank and status demarcation throughout the Tokugawa period.

46. 1871–72. Enchô's actual performances of *Eikoku kôshi* began in the early

1880s, and since the story actually ends around 1879, *Eikoku kôshi* has a very contemporary setting.

47. For textual analysis I am using page numbers and text from the first (1926–28) edition of Enchô's collected works (*San'yûtei Enchô zenshû*; reprinted 1963–64 by Sekai bunkosha).

48. *"Eikoku kôshi den* to *Hard Cash."*

49. This chart is a modification of one presented first by Nobuhiro, above.

50. In order to show the similarity, I am deviating here from the standard practice of placing Japanese surnames first.

51. *"Eikoku kôshi den* to *Hard Cash,"* 60.

52. See Hirakawa, Sukehiro. "Japan's Turn to the West," in *The Cambridge History of Japan,* edited by Marius B. Jansen, Cambridge; New York: Cambridge University Press, 1989, 480–87.

53. Other names suggest contemporary usage: Hamilton and George would have been relatively familiar through retellings of the American Revolution (such as that by Robun in his *Gurando-shi den*). Edward (*Edowaado* in Japanese) fits well with Edoya, and Seville could be a corruption of Savile Row (the origin, by the way, for the Japanese word for jacket, *sebiro*).

54. Nobuhiro notes that Enchô has transformed names in other *hon'anmono* as well.

55. *"Eikoku kôshi den* to *Hard Cash,"* 60.

56. Nobuhiro suggests that Fukuchi may have been attracted to the novel's focus on lunatic asylum reform owing to a contemporary event involving Viscount Sôma's sudden insanity. Ibid., 61–63.

57. Nobuhiro notes that there were only a handful of insane asylums in Japan in the 1880s; madness was still seen largely in traditional terms—an internal, family concern—and the insane were kept under house-arrest (ibid., 63). Often the mentally ill were shipped off to distant relatives in the provinces; when it came to arranged marriages, the hint of insanity was one of the most dangerous skeletons in any family closet.

58. For a more detailed description of the place of ex-samurai in the early Meiji world, see Eiko Ikegami, "Citizenship and National Identity in Early Meiji Japan, 1868–1889: A Comparative Assessment," *International Review of Social History* 40, Supplement 3 (1995): 204–09; as well as Sonoda Hidehiro, "The Decline of the Japanese Warrior Class," *Japan Review* 1 (1990).

59. *"Eikoku kôshi den* to *Hard Cash,"*, 66.

60. Ibid., 63.

61. Enchô ends this particular installment with a pun that reinforces his focus on fiscal matters:"To find out this story's bottom line you'll have to entrust me with the conclusion until next time" (580).

62. In this regard, Enchô's detailed tangents parallel those of Reade, who also includes numerous asides that educate his Victorian readers about topics as

diverse as using strychnine to kill garden moles, home remedies for various illnesses, and how to survive in London on the cheap.

63. "Kaidai (hon'anmono)," 549.

64. Nobuhiro suggests the possibility that Enchô may have received a complete translation from Fukuchi (*"Eikoku kôshi den* to *Hard Cash,"* 61), but considering Fukuchi's own access to publishers it is likely that such a monumental effort would have eventually appeared in print.

65. The relationship between Seijirô and Maki roughly parallels that of Jûjirô and Isa (as that of Edward Dodd and Jane Hardie parallels that of Julia Dodd and Alfred Hardie).

66. In an interesting correspondence with *Hard Cash,* where Hardie's son Alfred and daughter-in-law Julia care for him after he goes mad worrying about his fortune, Harumi suggests to Isa that she and Jûjirô can make offerings for his soul once he is dead (588).

67. There were strong proscriptions against *seppuku* following the Meiji Restoration.

68. Nobuhiro notes that the questions of transfer of property upon the death of a parent with no male heirs, use of stamps, and fear of complications for *seppuku* were all addressed in contemporary government statutes. *"Eikoku kôshi den* to *Hard Cash,"* 66–67.

69. *Eikoku kôshi den* contains a number of references to contemporary fashions, trends, and new events.

70. The contemporary popularity of the propagandistic political novel *(seiji shôsetsu)* may also have suggested that mode to Enchô. Two of the most popular *seiji shôsetsu,* Tôkai Sanshi's *Kajin no kigu* (Chance Meeting with a Beautiful Woman, 1885–1887) and Suehiro Tetchô's *Setchûbai* (1886), came out just after *Eikoku kôshi den.* For a contemporary critique of the genre, see Tokutomi Sohô, "Kinrai ryûkô seiji shôsetsu wo hyôsu," *Kokumin no tomo,* July 1887. For an English overview, see Horace Feldman, "The Meiji Political Novel: A Brief Survey," *The Far Eastern Quarterly* 9, no. 3 (1950).

71. The term *kanzen chôaku* (chastise evil and reward the good) dates from the seventh century, and by the Meiji period had come to signify hackneyed Confucian didacticism in narrative and drama.

72. This same sense of Confucian ideals applied to a foreign, adapted, text can be seen in a Chinese example from the early twentieth century, Lin Shu's adaptation of H. Rider Haggard's *Montezuma's Daughter* as *The Story of an English Filial Son's Revenge on the Volcano.* See Venuti, *The Scandals of Translation: Towards an Ethics of Difference,* 180.

73. Nobuhiro notes that Seijirô's ingenuity, mettle, and bravery characterize him as a typical Enchô hero. See *"Eikoku kôshi den* to *Hard Cash,"* 67.

74. When Enchô first describes Seijirô he refers to him as *otokogi* (manly); the editor of *Eikoku kôshi den* glossed the phrase with the Chinese characters

kyôki (chivalrous), underscoring Seijirô's role as a knight errant. For more on the knight errant/double in Chinese narrative, see James J. Y. Liu, *The Chinese Knight-Errant* (Chicago: University of Chicago Press, 1967); as well as Curtis P. Adkins, "The Hero in T'ang *Ch'uan-ch'i* Tales," in *Critical Essays on Chinese Fiction,* ed. Winston L. Y. Yang, and Curtis P. Adkins (Hong Kong: Chinese University Press, 1980), 24–26, 43.

75. Smith, *Charles Reade,* 155–56.

76. For an overview of the issues, see Noriko Mizuta Lippit, *Reality and Fiction in Modern Japanese Literature* (White Plains, N.Y.: M. E. Sharpe, 1980) as well as Janet A. Walker, *The Japanese Novel of the Meiji Period and the Ideal of Individualism* (Princeton, NJ: Princeton University Press, 1979).

Chapter IV

1. Tsubouchi Shôyô, *Futagokoro* (Shun'yôdô, 1897), Preface; reprinted in 1926 in Tsubouchi Shôyô, *Shôyô senshû,* 17 vols. (Shun'yôdô, 1926), supplemental volume 2, and again in 1977 as part of Tsubouchi Shôyô and Shôyô Kyôkai, *Shôyô senshû* (Daiichi shobô, 1977), supplemental volume 2. I shall refer to the page numbers of the reprinted text hereafter.

2. Stanley R. Harrison, "Through a Nineteenth-Century Looking Glass: The Letters of Edgar Fawcett," *Tulane Studies in English* 15 (1967): 124; in a letter to Hamlin Garland, 7 December 1888.

3. Tsubouchi Shôyô, "Hon'an ni tsukite," in *Shôyô senshû* (Daiichi shobô, 1977), 718.

4. Edgar Fawcett, "The False Friend," *The Seaside Library* (17 July 1880): 3.

5. *Shôyô senshû* supplemental volume 2: 735.

6. Ibid., 735–36.

7. This debate, dubbed *genbun itchi* (unification of spoken and written languages) began its written form as Mozume Takami's *Genbun itchi* (Jûichidô, 1886). For an overview of the movement, see Massimiliano Tomasi, "Quest for a New Written Language: Western Rhetoric and the *Genbun Itchi* Movement," *Monumenta Nipponica* 54, no. 3 (1999). A comprehensive study of the issues involved is contained in the works of Yamamoto Masahide, especially his *Genbun itchi no rekishi ronkô* (Ôfûsha, 1971) and *Genbun itchi no rekishi ronkô: zokuhen* (Ôfûsha, 1981).

8. For detailed and insightful English-language studies of this turbulent period see Janet A. Walker, *The Japanese Novel of the Meiji Period and the Ideal of Individualism* (Princeton, NJ: Princeton University Press, 1979); Dennis C. Washburn, *The Dilemma of the Modern in Japanese Fiction* (New Haven, Conn., and London: Yale University Press, 1995); and Peter F. Kornicki, "The Survival of Tokugawa Fiction in the Meiji Period," *Harvard Journal of Asian Studies* 40 (1980): 469–70.

9. See Homma Hisao, *Tsubouchi Shôyô* (Shôhakusha, 1959), 83–86 (reprinted in Homma Hisao and Asai Kiyoshi, *Tsubouchi Shôyô: hito to sono geijutsu* in *Kindai sakka kenkyû sûsho*, vol. 126 [Nihon tosho sentâ, 1993]).

10. San'yûtei Enchô and Wakabayashi Kanzô, *Kaidan botandôrô* (Tokyo: Tokyo haishi shuppansha, 1884); Preface.

11. See, for example, Paolo Calvetti's "Saikun di Tsubouchi Shôyô: Lingua e Stile Narrativo." *Il Giappone* 29 (1989):169–236.

12. For more on fascicle publication, see Peter F. Kornicki, "The Enmeiin Affair of 1803: The Spread of Information in the Tokugawa Period," *Harvard Journal of Asian Studies* 42 (1982): 525–26.

13. In considering the transmission of these novels, the question of the original source language in the case of the French authors remains a mystery. However, in the case of du Boisgobey, a large number of his works were translated into English in the 1880s, suggesting that they could have made their way into Japanese (as in the case of some Jules Verne novels) by way of English translation.

14. Hijikata Masami, *Miyako shimbun shi* (Nihon tosho sentâ, 1991), 534–35.

15. Shôyô's adaptation was therefore published at a time when there was a growing tendency to eschew the foreign, and this may explain why it did not appear as a bound volume until five years later.

16. A close comparison of the serialized *Miyako* text (*Daisagishi*) and the bound volume (*Futagokoro*) reveals only superficial changes. However, since there are lacunae in extant copies of the *Miyako,* and the beginning installment of *Daisagishi* is missing, we are unable to learn what Shôyô may have said in his introduction to the earlier version.

17. "Shôyô nikki," *Tsubouchi Shôyô kenkyû shiryô* 2 (1971), 98. The headline for *Daisagishi* lists the translator as Jûyondô Shujin (Oku), with Harunoya Shujin (Shôyô) as "enhancer" (*tensaku*). It was common during the Meiji period for literary mentors to attach their names to pupil's manuscripts as a means of helping them break into the publishing world, and the fact that five years later, when *Daisagishi* was republished in book form as *Futagokoro* (and Oku had tragically passed away), the cover lists Harunoya Shujin as the sole author indicates that Shôyô was, indeed, the translator and had been promoting Oku in the *Miyako* by-line.

18. "At the rate of five twelve-lined pages (each line having twenty characters) per hour we completed 100 pages in four days" (ibid.). Shôyô's aside gives us an unusual, concrete glimpse into his personal method of translation as well as his command of English (his speed translates into roughly one sentence per minute).

19. This misidentification even appears in the definitive collection of Shôyô miscellanea, *Tsubouchi Shôyô jiten* (Heibonsha, 1986), 315.

20. One benefit of my research cul-de-sac, however, has been the realization

that Vanbrugh's comedy, as with many a Restoration drama, was itself an adaptation, revealing yet again the ubiquity of adaptation as a form of translation. According to one scholar, Vanbrugh's play *False Friend* is "at once an adaptation of a Spanish play and a subtle perversion of it. Even though based on a French intermediary, it is close enough to be a free translation, and yet it incorporates changes in detail and in tone which alter the emotional impact to the point that, what in Spanish is a tragedy of divine retribution becomes in English a comedy." John Clyde Loftis, *The Spanish Plays of Neoclassical England* (New Haven, Conn.: Yale University Press, 1973), 167–68.

21. Fawcett, "The False Friend," based upon Edgar Fawcett's "The False Friend: a Drama in Four Acts and a Prologue"(manuscript in the Library of Congress, 1879).

22. Stanley R. Harrison, *Edgar Fawcett* (New York: Twayne Publishers, 1972), 16.

23. William Dean Howells, "Review of 'Fantasy and Passion'," *Atlantic Monthly* 41 (1878), 632.

24. William H. Rideing, "Edgar Fawcett," *The Bookman* 32, no. 4 (1910).

25. "Through a Nineteenth-Century Looking Glass," 126.

26. *Edgar Fawcett,* 110–11.

27. Stephen Fiske, review of *The False Friend* in *Spirit of the Times* (14 February 1880).

28. An advertisement in a March or April 1882 edition of *Boston Museum* (Boston: Lincoln, 1882) refers to it as "Edgar Fawcett's Very Successful Play."

29. *The Seaside Library* series sold at a standard price of ten cents per volume. The series, begun in 1877 by George Munro as a rival to the Beadle dime novel series that gave the genre its name, initially depended on pirated reprints of foreign novels (ironically, much like the *Miyako shimbun*). By 1880 it was publishing more original work by American authors, such as Fawcett.

30. *The False Friend* receives scant attention in the *Twayne United States Author Series* volume dedicated to Fawcett's life and works (*Edgar Fawcett*).

31. "The False Friend: a Drama in Four Acts and a Prologue," act Four.

32. "The False Friend," 32.

33. It should be noted that both the play and the novel contain a minor divertimento consisting of the gossip and humorous courtship of several highborn neighbors who intersect with the main characters from time to time and, in the drama, play the role of the chorus.

34. The fact that it was part of a prominent dime novel series increased the chances such an obscure work to make it to Shôyô's attention.

35. Again, it should be noted that there are only slight differences between *Daisagishi* and *Futagokoro*.

36. In Fawcett's original Lucian gives Shackford a quick blow on the cheek.

37. A proof of Shôyô's talent as a dramaturge is his almost uncanny ability to divine the essence of Fawcett's play despite the elaborations of the novel.

38. This suggests that by the 1890s Shôyô's readers were much more comfortable with stories set in foreign geographies than in earlier years, when *hon'anmono* were reset in Japan.

39. In order to emphasize the parallels between the names I have listed Fawcett's originals in last name–first name order, reflecting the standard practice in Japanese.

40. The Japanese reads "*Ko toshite oya no zanbôsata, Kôshi-sama niwa sumanu keredo.*" Needless to say, Fawcett's original contains no reference to Confucius.

41. The Japanese reads "*Kyô mo Kurido wa . . . seibatsu ni haigun shite, ika ni seshi ka kao aozame, onigashima e shuttatsu no tochû nite, kibidango wo tonbi ni sarawareta Momotarô no kao no aoi no.*"

42. "The False Friend," 19.

43. Loanwords are usually based upon foreign pronunciations and written in the *katakana* syllabary. Enchô could largely avoid the need for loanwords by resetting his tale in Japan.

44. These words, mostly nouns, include *katakana* versions of "knife," "stew," "stick," "lamp," and the phrase "My dear wife."

45. Chieko Ariga, "The Playful Gloss: *Rubi* in Japanese Literature," *Monumenta Nipponica* 44, no. 3.

46. And, it might be added, Lucian's fate may also have been read in the same context as a warning about the potential disaster that could befall a country trying to carry the charade too far. One subtle evidence of Shôyô's possible manipulation of his adaptation in this direction can be seen in his setting Lucian opposite Grant in the opening of the story and giving him a Japanese name to set him up in opposition to Grant/America. It is interesting to note that in 1895, during the Sino-Japanese War, the *Miyako* carried a story entitled *Nichi-Bei no kaisen* (The Opening of the U.S.-Japan War).

47. Shôyô's throat-cutting alteration allows his Lucian to die in a more traditional samurai manner.

48. "There have always been different attempts at interpretation undertaken on the basis of a certain concept of what the world should be like (ideology) as well as a certain concept of what literature should be like (poetics), and these attempts [at interpretation] . . . have accepted or rejected works of literature on the basis of the ideology and the poetics they happened to be serving but, much more often, they have adapted works of literature, 'rewritten' them until they happened to fit their own poetics, their own ideology." André Lefevere, "Why Waste Our Time on Rewrites? The Trouble with Interpretation and the Role of Rewriting in an Alternative Para-

digm," in *The Manipulation of Literature: Studies in Literary Translation*, ed. Theo Hermans (London: Croom Helm, 1985), 217.

49. A comparison between the earlier and later versions of the final chapter reveals that Shôyô has added commas in the latter (newspapers tended to avoid the relatively new—and space-consuming—use of commas), modernized some of the grammar (*miredo* becomes *mireba*), and changed some of the characters for stylistic effect. Overall, however, the texts remain identical.

50. These works were all published between 1890 and 1892 in the *Miyako shimbun*.

51. It goes without saying that both of Shôyô's titles are adaptations rather than literal translations. He could have easily rendered the words "false friend" into Japanese, but in both instances chose instead to use titles that reflect the particular publishing and theoretical contexts of his translations.

52. Although Shôyô no longer had access to his copy of *The False Friend* in 1896, the melodramatic postures found in illustrations of that text were a convention of contemporary illustrations.

53. Fawcett's novel, although not as dramatically styled as his play (in which the events prior to Derby make up a prologue only), nevertheless devotes two-thirds of its space to the action at Fielding Manor. In this regard, Shôyô's novel clearly reflects the original.

54. In an essay written in 1910, Shôyô spells out twelve "articles of translation" that summarize strategies he has derived from translating Shakespeare. Although he concludes the essay noting that these could very well change after he has completed more translations, in general the articles suggest a combination of literalist and adaptive strategies. He recommends the eclectic use of styles from kabuki, traditional narrative (*monogatari*), Noh and *kyôgen,* and even Edo period comic fiction as the Bard's own stylistic kaleidoscope requires, since, as he notes, "Shakespeare was half idealist, half realist, fifty percent Romanticist, fifty percent Naturalist." Tsubouchi Shôyô, "Saô-geki no hon'yaku ni tsuite," in *Shôyô senshû* (Shun'yôdô, 1926), vol. 5, 580.

55. Writing in 1916, Shôyô reflects on his development as a translator of Shakespeare, and notes that his first attempts at translation were merely content with giving the original a "Japanese flavor." He notes that his next stage of development happened around 1897–98, when he undertook *Macbeth,* and although he had by that time developed an appreciation for the warmth and feeling of Shakespeare he was much too intimidated, felt overly bound to the commentaries, and was so beholden to the nationalistic spirit then prevailing in literature that he restricted his translation to the high classical style, and went nowhere. His breakthrough came when he finally sought to translate for actual performance, around 1908–1909, and then when he decided to use colloquial, rather than classical, language. See Tsubouchi

Shôyô, "Saô-geki no hon'yaku ni taisuru watakushi no taido no hensen," in *Shôyô senshû,* (Shun'yôdô, 1926),vol. 5, 585–87.
56. Ibid., 588.

Conclusion

1. Homer and Charles-Marie Leconte de Lisle, *Iliade* (Paris: Librarie Alphonse Lemerre, 1867).
2. Leconte de Lisle was actually following the lead of Germans whose preference for literal translation was influenced, in part, by *Les Belle Infidèles.* Harald Kittel and Andreas Poltermann suggest that one might view the entire (Romantic) emancipation of German thought from the French as a translation issue: The will to self-identity demands the abolition of intermediaries. The sheer visibility of French adaptations made them a natural target of latent German nationalism, and so the aesthetic preference for literal translation became a political issue. If the French style was to use *adaptation,* the German will to independence would see *literal translation* as the preferred choice, both because it was anti-French and also because it represented, theoretically, a more direct, "pure" approach. See Harald Kittel and Andreas Poltermann, "German Tradition," in *Encyclopedia of Translation Studies,* ed. Mona Baker (London and New York: Routledge, 1997), 422–23.
3. As noted in Masaomi Kondo and Judy Wakabayashi, "Japanese Tradition," in ibid., ed. Mona Baker (London and New York: Routledge, 1997), 490.
4. This happened in 1913, when Iwano Hômei translated Arthur Symon's *The Symbolist Movement in Literature.* See Kawamura Jirô and Ikeuchi Osamu, *Hon'yaku no Nihongo,* vol. 15, *Nihongo no sekai* (Chûô kôronsha, 1981), 18.
5. "Japanese Tradition," 494.
6. In addition to modern translations of the classical Japanese *Genji monogatari* by authors such as Enchi Fumiko and Settôuchi Jakuchô, there are also recent adaptations in several genres, including first-person illustrated narrative, *manga* and *anime.*
7. "Why Waste Our Time on Rewrites?," 215.

Bibliography ✒

Note: All Japanese books, except as otherwise noted, were published in Tokyo.

Introduction Bibliography

Carus, Paul. *Karma: A Story of Buddhism.* Chicago: Open Court Publishing Company, 1894.

———. *Karma.* Translated by Suzuki Teitarô. Hasegawa Takejirô, 1898.

Darnton, Robert. *The Great Cat Massacre and Other Episodes in French Cultural History.* New York: Basic Books, 1984.

Dostoyevsky, Fyodor, Constance Black Garnett, and Ralph E. Matlaw. *The Brothers Karamazov: Backgrounds and Sources: Essays in Criticism.* Norton Critical Edition. New York: Norton, 1976.

Rosenstone, Robert A. *Mirror in the Shrine: American Encounters with Meiji Japan.* Cambridge, MA: Harvard University Press, 1988.

Valdés, Mario J., and Linda Hutcheon. "Rethinking Literary History—Comparatively." *ACLA Bulletin* 25, no. 2–4 (1996): 11–22.

Yoshida Seiichi. "'Kumo no ito,' 'Toshi shun' ni tsuite." In *Kumo no ito, Toshi shun.* Shinchôsha, 1968.

Chapter I

Baker, Mona. *Encyclopedia of Translation Studies.* London and New York: Routledge, 1997.

Barnstone, Willis. *The Poetics of Translation: History, Theory, Practice.* New Haven, Conn.: Yale University Press, 1993.

Bastin, Georges L. "Adaptation." In *Encyclopedia of Translation Studies.* Edited by Mona Baker. London and New York: Routledge, 1997.

Eoyang, Eugene. "'History', 'Herstory', 'Theirstory', 'Ourstory': Gender, Genre and Cultural Bias in Accounts of East Asian Literatures." Kyoto: International Research Center for Japanese Studies, 23 February 1998.

Fowler, Edward. "On Naturalizing and Making Strange: Japanese Literature in Translation." *Journal of Japanese Studies* 16, no. 3 (1990): 115–32.

Hesekiel, George, Kenneth R. H. Mackenzie, and Bayard Taylor. *The Life of Bismarck, Private and Political.* Translated by Kenneth R. H. Mackenzie. New York: Fords Howard and Hulbert, 1870.

Hiraoka Toshio, and Tôgô Katsumi. *Nihon bungakushi gaisetsu: kindai hen.* Yûseidô, 1979.

Homma Hisao. *Meiji bungaku shi.* 2 vols. Vol. 1. Tôkyôdô, 1949.

Jansen, Marius B. "*Rangaku* and Westernization." *Modern Asian Studies* 18, no. 4 (1984):541–53.

Keene, Donald. *Dawn To the West: Japanese Literature of the Modern Era.* Vol. 1. New York: Holt, Rhinehart, and Winston, 1984.

Ker, William Paton, ed. *Essays of John Dryden.* Oxford: Clarendon Press, 1900.

Leerssen, Joep. "As Others See, among Others, Us: The Anglo-German Relationship in Context." In *As Others See Us: Anglo-German Perceptions.* Edited by Harald Husemann. Frankfurt: Peter Lang, 1994.

———. "Echoes and Images: Reflections upon Foreign Space." In *Alterity, Identity, Image: Selves and Others in Society and Scholarship.* Edited by Raymond Corbey and Joep Leerssen. Amsterdam-Atlanta: Rodopi, 1991.

Lefevere, André. *Translating Literature: Practice and Theory in a Comparative Literature Context.* New York: Modern Language Association of America, 1992.

———. *Translation, Rewriting, and the Manipulation of Literary Fame.* London and New York: Routledge, 1992.

Muramatsu Sadataka. *Kindai Nihon bungaku: Seiritsu to tenkai:* Yûbun shoin, 1969.

Nabokov, Vladimir. "Problems of Translation: *Onegin* in English." *Partisan Review* 22 (1955): 496–512.

Pinnington, Adrian James. "Hamlet in Japanese Dress: Two Contemporary Japanese Versions of *Hamlet.*" In *Hamlet and Japan.* Edited by Yoshiko Uéno. New York: AMS Press, 1995.

Satô Kôki, and Hitoshi Tomita, eds. *Nihon kindai bungaku to Seiyô.* Surugadai shuppansha, 1984.

Schulte, Rainer, and John Biguenet. *Theories of Translation: An Anthology of Essays from Dryden to Derrida.* Chicago: University of Chicago Press, 1992.

Steiner, George. *After Babel: Aspects of Language and Translation.* Oxford: Oxford University Press, 1975.

Steinke, Martin William. *Edward Young's "Conjectures on Original Composition" in England and Germany.* Vol. 28, Americana Germanica. New York: F. C. Stechert Co. Inc., 1917.

Sugimoto Tsutomu. *Nagasaki tsûji monogatari: kotoba to bunka no hon'yakusha.* Tokyo: Sôtakusha, 1990.

————. *Zôtei Nihon hon'yakugoshi no kenkyû. Sugimoto Tsutomu chosaku senshû,* Vol. 4. Yasaka shobô, 1998.

Sugita Genpaku, and Hisao Hama. *Rangaku kotohajime: fu Keiei yawa. Genpon gendaiyaku vol. 54.* Higashimurayama: Kyôikusha, 1980.

Uéno, Yoshiko, ed. *Hamlet and Japan. The Hamlet Collection;* No. 2. New York: AMS Press, 1995.

Venuti, Lawrence. *The Scandals of Translation: Towards an Ethics of Difference.* London and New York: Routledge, 1998.

Yanagida Izumi. *Meiji shoki honyaku bungaku no kenkyû.* Vol. 5, *Meiji bungaku kenkyû.* Shunjûsha, 1961.

Yoshitake Yoshinori. *Kindai bungaku no naka no Seiô: Kindai Nihon hon'anshi, Hikaku bungaku kenkyû sôsho.* Kyôiku shuppan sentâ, 1974.

Young, Edward. *Conjectures on Original Composition. In a Letter to the Author of Sir Charles Grandison.* 1st ed. London: Printed for A. Millar and R. and J. Dodsley, 1759.

Chapter II

Anderson, Benedict. *Imagined Communities: Reflections on the Origin and Spread of Nationalism.* Rev. ed. London and New York: Verso, 1991.

Bowen, Roger W. *Rebellion and Democracy in Meiji Japan: A Study of Commoners in the Popular Rights Movement.* Berkeley: University of California Press, 1980.

Brandon, James R. "Kabuki and Shakespeare: Balancing Yin and Yang." *The Drama Review* 43, no. 2 (1999): 15–53.

Carpenter, John A. *Ulysses S. Grant.* New York: Twayne Publishers, 1970.

Chang, Richard T. "General Grant's 1879 Visit to Japan." *Monumenta Nipponica* 24, no. 4 (1969): 373–92.

Falcon, Richard. "Images of Germany and the Germans in British Film and Television Fictions: A Brief Chronological Overview." In *As Others See Us: Anglo-German Perceptions.* Edited by Harald Husemann. Frankfurt: Peter Lang, 1994.

Finn, Dallas. "Grant in Japan." *American History Illustrated* XVI, no. 3 (1981): 36–45.

Grant, Ulysses S. *Diaries of Southeast Asian Tour.* Special Collections. Gelman Library, George Washington University, Washington D.C.

————. "Letter from U.S. Grant to General E. F. Beale. Peking," 10 August 1879. Manuscript in the Library of Congress.

Grant, Ulysses S. and Jesse Grant Cramer. *Letters of Ulysses S. Grant to His Father and His Youngest Sister, 1857–78.* New York and London: G. P. Putnam's Sons, 1912.

Grant, Ulysses S., James Grant Wilson, and E. B. Washburne. *General Grant's Letters to a Friend, 1861–1880.* New York and Boston: T. Y. Crowell & Co., 1897.

Kanagaki Robun. *Gurando-shi den Yamato bunshô.* 3 vols. Kinshôdô, 1879.

Kimura Kinka. *Morita Kan'ya.* Shin taishûsha, 1943.

Kracauer, Siegfried. "National Types as Hollywood Presents Them." *Public Opinion Quarterly* Spring 1949:70.

McFeely, William S. *Grant: A Biography.* 1st ed. New York: Norton, 1981.

Meech-Pekarik, Julia, and Metropolitan Museum of Art. *The World of the Meiji Print: Impressions of a New Civilization.* 1st ed. New York: Weatherhill, 1986.

Mertz, John Pierre. "Internalizing Social Difference: Kanagaki Robun's *Shank's Mare to the Western Seas.*" In *New Directions in the Study of Meiji Japan.* Edited by Helen Hardacre and Adam L. Kern, Conference on Meiji Studies and Harvard University. Leiden and New York: Brill, 1997.

Miller, J. Scott. "The Hybrid Narrative of Kyôden's *Sharebon.*" *Monumenta Nipponica* 43, no. 2 (1988): 133–52.

Motoda, J. S. "A Japanese Life of General Grant." *Century Illustrated Monthly,* (July 1895):435–46.

Nozake Sabun. "Meiji shoki no shimbun shôsetsu." *Waseda bungaku* (March 1925): 27–28.

Okitsu Kaname. *Kanagaki Robun: Bunmei kaika no gesakusha.* Yûrindô, 1993.

Ôta Minoru. *Hokubeirenpô zendaitôryô Gurando-shi seisekiki.* Meimondô shuppan, 1879.

Packard, J. F. *Grant's Tour around the World: With Incidents of His Journey through England, Ireland, Scotland, France, Spain, Germany, Austria, Italy, Belgium, Switzerland, Russia, Egypt, India, China, Japan, Etc.* Philadelphia: H. W. Kelley, 1880.

Perret, Geoffrey. *Ulysses S. Grant: Soldier & President.* 1st ed. New York: Random House, 1997.

"Pioneer Japanese Bishop Passes Away." *Spirit of Missions,* May 1928, 300.

Remlap, L. T., ed. *General U. S. Grant's Tour Around the World.* Hartford, Conn.: James Betts & Co., 1879.

Roberts, Laurance P. *A Dictionary of Japanese Artists: Painting, Sculpture, Ceramics, Prints, Lacquer.* 1st ed. Tokyo and New York: Weatherhill, 1976.

Schaumann, Werner Gustav. *Kanagaki Robun: ein Japanischer Unterhaltungsschriftsteller in der frühen Zeit der Modernisierung.* Bonn: Rheinische Friedrich-Wilhelms-Universität Bonn, 1981.

Sugimoto Tsutomu. *Zôtei Nihon hon'yakugoshi no kenkyû. Sugimoto Tsutomu chosaku senshû,* Vol. 4. Yasaka shobô, 1998.

Suzuki, Keiko. "*Yokohama-E* and *Kaika-E* Prints: Japanese Interpretations of Self and Other from 1860 through the 1880s." In *New Directions in the Study of Meiji Japan.* Edited by Helen Hardacre and Adam L. Kern, Conference on Meiji Studies and Harvard University. Leiden and New York: Brill, 1997.

Takeshi, Murakami. "Shakespeare and *Hamlet* in Japan: A Chronological Overview." In *Hamlet and Japan.* Edited by Yoshiko Uéno. New York: AMS Press, 1995.

Toyoshima Sajûrô. *Gurando-kô ryakuden.* Asahi shimbunsha, 1879.

Whitney, Clara A., M. William Steele, and Tamiko Ichimata. *Clara's Diary: An American Girl in Meiji Japan.* 1st ed. Tokyo and New York: Kodansha International, 1979.

Wirtz, Horatio E. "General Ulysses S. Grant: Diplomat Extraordinaire." In *Ulysses S. Grant: Essays and Documents.* Edited by David L. Wilson and John Y. Simon. Carbondale: Southern Illinois University Press, 1981.

Yamada Junji. *Beikoku zendaitôryô Gurando kôden.* Gakunôsha, 1879.

Young, John Russell. *Around the World with General Grant.* 1st ed. Vol. 2. New York: The American News Company, 1879.

Chapter III

Adams, Robert J. "Folktale Telling and Storytellers in Japan." *Asian Folklore Studies* 26, no. 1 (1967): 99–118.

Adkins, Curtis P. "The Hero in T'ang Ch'uan-Ch'i Tales." In *Critical Essays on Chinese Fiction.* Edited by Winston L. Y. Yang and Curtis P. Adkins. Hong Kong: Chinese University Press, 1980.

Aston, W. G. *A History of Japanese Literature.* New York: D. Appleton & Co., 1899.

Burns, Wayne. *Charles Reade: A Study in Victorian Authorship.* New York: Bookman Associates, 1961.

Feldman, Horace. "The Meiji Political Novel: A Brief Survey." *The Far Eastern Quarterly* 9, no. 3 (1950): 245–55.

Fukuoka Takashi. *Nihon sokki kotohajime: Takusari Kôki no shôgai.* Iwanami, 1978.

Hiraga Gennai, and Yukihiko Nakamura. *Fûrai Sanjinshû. Nihon koten bungaku taikei* Vol. 55. Tokyo: Iwanami shoten, 1961.

Hirakawa, Sukehiro. "Japan's Turn to the West." In *The Cambridge History of Japan.* Edited by Marius B. Jansen. Cambridge and New York: Cambridge University Press, 1988.

Howells, William Dean. *My Literary Passions.* New York: Harper & Brothers, 1895.

Ikegami, Eiko. "Citizenship and National Identity in Early Meiji Japan, 1868–1889: A Comparative Assessment." *International Review of Social History* 40, Supplement 3 (1995): 185–221.

Inouye, Jukichi. *Sketches of Tokyo Life.* Yokohama: Torando, 1895.

Koike Shôtarô, and Shûtetsu Fujii. "Kaidai (hon'anmono)." In *San'yûtei Enchô zenshû 6: Hon'anmono.* Edited by Seijirô Kôjima, Ikeda Yazaburo, and Ozaki Hideki. Kadokawa shoten, 1975.

Komiya, Toyotaka. *Japanese Music and Drama in the Meiji Era.* Vol. 3, *Japanese Culture in the Meiji Era.* Tokyo: Ôbunsha, 1956.

Lippit, Noriko Mizuta. *Reality and Fiction in Modern Japanese Literature.* White Plains, NY: M. E. Sharpe, 1980.

Liu, James J. Y. *The Chinese Knight-Errant.* Chicago: University of Chicago Press, 1967.

Maeda Ai. *Kindai Nihon no bungaku kûkan: Rekishi kotoba jôkyô.* Shin'yôsha, 1983.

Matsunaga Goichi. *Kawakami Otojirô: Kindaigeki, hatenkô no yoake.* Tokyo: Asahi shinbunsha, 1988.

McClain, James L., John M. Merriman, and Kaoru Ugawa. *Edo and Paris: Urban Life and the State in the Early Modern Era.* Ithaca, NY: Cornell University Press, 1994.

Miller, J. Scott. "Early Voice Recordings of Japanese Storytelling." *Oral Tradition* 11, no. 2 (1996): 301–19.

———. "Japanese Shorthand and Sokkibon." *Monumenta Nipponica* 49, no. 4 (1994): 471–87.

Miyoshi, Masao. *Off Center: Power and Culture Relations between Japan and the United States, Convergences.* Cambridge, MA: Harvard University Press, 1991.

Morioka, Heinz, and Miyoko Sasaki. "The Blue-Eyed Storyteller: Henry Black and His Rakugo Career." *Monumenta Nipponica* 38, no. 2 (1983): 133–62.

———. *Rakugo, the Popular Narrative Art of Japan.* Cambridge, MA: Council on East Asian Studies, Harvard University, 1990.

Nobuhiro Shinji. "*Eikoku kôshi den to Hard Cash.*" *Bungaku* 47, no. 2 (1979): 52–75.

Nobuhiro Shinji, and Enba Utei. *Rakugo wa ikani shite keiseisareta ka, sôsho engeki to misemono no bunkashi.* Tokyo: Heibonsha, 1986.

Ochi Haruo. "Mô hitori no Shiobara Tasuke." *Bungaku* 37, no. 5 (1969): 48–61.

Ogi Shinzo and Maeda Ai, eds. *Meiji Taishô zushi.* Vol. 1, *Tôkyo.* Edited by Masamichi Asukai. Tokyo: Chikuma shobo, 1978.

Reade, Charles. *Hard Cash. A Matter-of-Fact Romance.* 3 vols. London: S. Low Son & Marston, 1863.

Sano Takashi. *Kôdan gohyakunen: Tsurushobô.* 1943.

San'yûtei Enchô. *San'yûtei Enchô zenshû.* Edited by Suzuki Kôzô. 13 vols. Shun'yôdô, 1926–28. Reprint, Sekai bunkosha 1963–64.

———. *San'yûtei Enchô zenshû.* Edited by Seijirô Kôjima, Ikeda Yazaburo, and Ozaki Hideki. 8 vols. Kadokawa shoten, 1975.

San'yûtei Enchô, and Wakabayashi Kanzô (with Sakai Shôzô). *Enchô sôdan Shiobara Tasuke ichidaiki.* Sokkihô kenkyûkai, 1884.

San'yûtei Enchô, and Kanzô Wakabayashi. *Seiyô ninjôbanashi Eikoku kôshi Jôji Sumisu no den.* Sokkihô kenkyûkai, 1885.

Seidensticker, Edward. *Low City, High City: Tokyo from Edo to the Earthquake.* New York: Knopf, 1983.

Shogei konwakai/Osaka geinô konwakai, eds. *Kokontôzai rakugoka jiten.* Heibonsha, 1989.

Shôrin Hakuen and Ishihara Terumichi. *Ochiriya zôshi: Doitsu kenjô.* Aichidô, 1891.

Skord, Virginia. *Tales of Tears and Laughter: Short Fiction of Medieval Japan.* Honolulu: University of Hawaii Press, 1991.

Smith, Elton Edward. *Charles Reade.* Boston: Twayne Publishers, 1976.

Smith, George. *Ten Weeks in Japan.* London: Longman, Green, Longman, and Roberts, 1861.

Sonoda, Hidehiro. "The Decline of the Japanese Warrior Class." *Japan Review* 1 (1990): 73–111.

Tada Michitarô. "Kaisetsu (hon'anmono)." In *San'yûtei Enchô zenshû 6: Hon'anmono,* edited by Seijirô Kôjima, Ikeda Yazaburo, and Ozaki Hideki. Kadokawa shoten, 1975.

Takeshita Kikuo. *Kinsei chihô geinô kôgyô no kenkyû.* Osaka: Seibundô, 1997.

Tokutomi Sohô. "Kinrai ryûkô seiji shôsetsu wo hyôsu." *Kokumin no tomo* (July 1887).

Walker, Janet A. *The Japanese Novel of the Meiji Period and the Ideal of Individualism.* Princeton, NJ: Princeton University Press, 1979.

Chapter IV

Ariga, Chieko. "The Playful Gloss: Rubi in Japanese Literature." *Monumenta Nipponica* 44, no. 3 (1989): 309–35.

Calvetti, Paolo. "Saikun di Tsubouchi Shôyô: Lingua e Stile Narrativo." *Il Giappone* 29 (1989): 169–236.

Fawcett, Edgar. "The False Friend." *The Seaside Library,* (17 July 1880):3–32.

———. "The False Friend: a Drama in Four Acts and a Prologue." 135 leaves in various foliations. Manuscript in the Library of Congress. 1879.

Fiske, Stephen. "It Is Worth a Visit." *Spirit of the Times,* (14 February 1880):38.

Harrison, Stanley R. *Edgar Fawcett.* New York: Twayne Publishers, 1972.

———. "Through a Nineteenth-Century Looking Glass: The Letters of Edgar Fawcett." *Tulane Studies in English* 15 (1967): 107–57.

Homma Hisao. *Tsubouchi Shôyô.* Shôhakusha, 1959.

Homma Hisao, and Kiyoshi Asai. *Tsubouchi Shôyô: hito to sono geijutsu.* Vol. 126, *Kindai sakka kenkyû sûsho.* Nihon tosho sentâ, 1993.

Howells, William Dean. "Review of 'Fantasy and Passion'." *Atlantic Monthly* 41 (1878):632–35.

Kornicki, Peter F. "The Enmeiin Affair of 1803: The Spread of Information in the Tokugawa Period." *Harvard Journal of Asian Studies* 42 (1982): 503–33.

———. "The Survival of Tokugawa Fiction in the Meiji Period." *Harvard Journal of Asian Studies* 40 (1980): 461–82.

Lefevere, André. "Why Waste Our Time on Rewrites? The Trouble with Interpretation and the Role of Rewriting in an Alternative Paradigm." In *The Manipulation of Literature: Studies in Literary Translation.* edited by Theo Hermans. London: Croom Helm, 1985.

Loftis, John Clyde. *The Spanish Plays of Neoclassical England.* New Haven, Conn.: Yale University Press, 1973.

Masami Hijikata. *Miyako shimbun shi.* Nihon tosho sentâ, 1991.

Mozume Takami. *Genbun itchi.* Jûichidô, 1886.

Rideing, William H. "Edgar Fawcett." *The Bookman* 32, no. 4 (1910): 436–39.

San'yûtei Enchô, and Wakabayashi Kanzô. *Kaidan botandôrô.* Tokyo: Tokyo haishi shuppansha, 1884.

Shôyô Kyôkai. *Tsubouchi Shôyô jiten.* Heibonsha, 1986.

Tomasi, Massimiliano. "Quest for a New Written Language: Western Rhetoric and the *Genbun Itchi* Movement." *Monumenta Nipponica* 54, no. 3 (1999): 333–60.

Tsubouchi Shôyô. *Futagokoro.* Shun'yôdô, 1897.

———. "Saô-geki no hon'yaku ni taisuru watakushi no taido no hensen." *Shôyô senshû,* Vol. 5. Shun'yôdô, 1926.

———. "Saô-geki no hon'yaku ni tsuite." *Shôyô senshû,* Vol. 5. Shun'yôdô, 1926.

———. "Shôyô nikki." *Tsubouchi Shôyô kenkyû shiryô* 2 (1971): 98.

———. *Shôyô senshû.* 17 vols. Shun'yôdô, 1926; reprint Daiichi shobô, 1977.

"Tuesday, April 4, 1882." *Boston Museum.* Boston, Mass.: Lincoln, 1882.

Walker, Janet A. *The Japanese Novel of the Meiji Period and the Ideal of Individualism.* Princeton, NJ: Princeton University Press, 1979.

Washburn, Dennis C. *The Dilemma of the Modern in Japanese Fiction.* New Haven, Conn. and London: Yale University Press, 1995.

Yamamoto, Masahide. *Genbun itchi no rekishi ronkô.* Ôfûsha, 1971.

———. *Genbun itchi no rekishi ronkô: zokuhen.* Ôfûsha, 1981.

Conclusion

Homer, and Charles-Marie Leconte de Lisle. *Iliade.* Paris: Librarie Alphonse Lemerre, 1867.

Kittel, Harald, and Andreas Poltermann. "German Tradition." In *Encyclopedia of Translation Studies.* Edited by Mona Baker. London and New York: Routledge, 1997.

Kondo, Masaomi, and Judy Waybayashi. "Japanese Tradition." In *Encyclopedia of Translation Studies.* Edited by Mona Baker. London and New York: Routledge, 1997.

Kawamura Jirô, and Osamu Ikeuchi. *Hon'yaku no Nihongo.* Vol. 15, *Nihongo no sekai.* Chûô kôronsha, 1981.

Index ⁊